Covert State

Murder & Espionage
Australasia 2034

Rodney Jensen

Rodney Jensen Books

CiPcatalogue record for this book is available from the National Library of Australia.

Additional License Note

First published in Australia in 2022

Rodney Jensen Books
http://www.rodneyjensenbooks.com/

**PO Box 443 Cammeray
NSW 2062 Australia**

ISBN 978-0-994-1668-1-4

CiPcatalogue record for this book is available from the National Library of Australia.

Cover illustration by **Rocking Book Covers**

Dedication to Joanne

To the memory of Joanne Winstanley (5/9/1953 – 9/3/2018) my patient wife and partner who helped and encouraged me with the first edition of this novel and many previous writings. I shall always miss her love of literature and honest appraisal of my work. She passed away before the manuscript was finalised, but still encouraged me to finish it and advised how it could be improved.

About this book

Covert State is a new edition of a previous publication which was titled End State. It forms the first volume in **The Covert Trilogy** and is followed by **Covert Messages** and **Covert Citadel**.

Covert State is set in the near future and reflects a changing world of self-drive cars, maglev city connections and the hint of alien technology, a closely guarded secret shared between Indonesia and Australia.

The central theme of the novel, the discovery of a the body of a missing high profile politician Kevin Rowe sets a scene for an unusual and complex inquiry spanning two continents.

Police procedural work remains be-devilled by sexist attitudes and embedded conservatism throughout Australia and creates a significant obstacle to the successful solving of this murder mystery. A strong willed and ambitious public servant, Kaz Ingham, has been assigned in the role to lead the inquiry and must overcome police prejudice and threats to her life by an unknown perpetrator who sets a thrilling context to the narrative and a nail biting conclusion to the story.

Rodney Jensen

PROLOGUE

It was Valentine's Day 2034, in the Mount Lofty Ranges to the east of Adelaide when two teenage brothers, Mike and Tom, were walking along a narrow fire trail, lined by tall trees and ragged scrub. In this secluded location, the air was permeated by the aromatic freshness of eucalyptus leaves, alive with the warbling of magpies, clouds of bush flies and mosquitoes. The tree canopy formed an enclosed corridor in deep shade with little relief from the oppressive heat.

The boys were exploring the trail with the help of their family dog, Rufus, a long-haired red setter with a good nose but not high IQ. They paused for a drink while Rufus sidled off into the bush, chasing after the smells and the rustling sound of a goanna leaving in a hurry.

"Rufus come 'ere," Mike shouted after him, worried that if it were a goanna, Rufus would come out second best in any fight. But the rustling stopped and there were no further sounds of any movement.

Five minutes passed.

Tom, with a water canister to his mouth, finally spotted the long-haired tail waving above the grass, as Rufus emerged through the undergrowth proudly carrying something in his muzzle. "What you got there?" he said as the dog came within grabbing distance but Rufus shied away the moment Tom tried to make him drop whatever it was. It was the start of a playful tussle as the dog refused to give up his trophy, until he finally conceded defeat when Tom pried his jaws apart and he dropped several mud-encrusted, whitened bones into the dirt at his feet.

"Do you think that's what I think it is? Come and take a look!" The sense of urgency in his brother's voice brought Mike over, wondering what the fuss was about. Tom had found a stick and was gently probing the bones. Mike watched over his shoulder, stiffening in shock as he realised what they were.

"Looks like fingers maybe," Tom said softly.

"I reckon."

"A body in there somewhere?" Tom gestured in the direction from where Rufus had emerged.

"Must be. There wouldn't just be fingers?"

Mike thought for a few moments. Being the older of the two he had always taken charge when situations called for important decisions. He was the one who was blamed when things went wrong and he'd learned to be cautious.

"Got your holo with you?" Tom shook his head. "Neither have I. We need to call the police. You wait here with Rufus. Tie him up. Leave them there," he said pointing at the bones. "Don't do anything more with them. And definitely, do *not* try and find the body by yourself. Whatever happens, I'll be back in less than an hour. We've got a crime scene here," he said, airing his superior wisdom. "The police'll be really pissed off if we stuff things up for them, and we don't want that do we?"

His brother nodded, while Mike ran back along the track.

Some days elapsed while the burial site was explored fully and the remains carefully assessed in Adelaide's Centre for Forensic Pathology. In his preliminary report to the police, South Australia's Chief Forensic Pathologist, Luigi Curillo, wrote:

'following our inspection of the burial site and surrounding bush it is estimated that the skeletal remains have been in-location for a matter of years, we think between 7.2 – 8.5 years based on an analysis of carbon traces in the soil and known bushfire events in this area during January 2027. The bones that we've recovered formed most of an adult male skeleton. In all probability the missing bones result from animal intervention.

We have successfully found matching DNA samples from selected bones, and discovered a match with a missing person listed on the National database. The deceased was Kevin Rowe, a prominent parliamentarian in NSW at the time of his reported disappearance. Our estimate of the age of the bones and burial site are consistent with the date of his disappearance. Beyond DNA matching, there is further evidence to confirm this identity having regard to physical morphology of the remains as compared with photographs we have of Rowe taken in the year before he disappeared.'

Shortly afterwards the respective state premiers of South Australia and New South Wales, Rayleigh Hudson and Eric Strong, held a secure teleconference. As premier of the host state, Hudson, much younger and more proactive than her opposite number was taking the call from Adelaide's Parliament House offices. She had been warned to be diplomatic by her colleagues. Strong, on the other hand, was a mature leader whose attitude to the 'Grape State' as he called SA derisively, was at best condescending and at worst downright unreasonable when it came to negotiating tricky matters like the Murray Darling Catchment and the lack of adequate energy linkages across state boundaries.

"It was good of you to agree to communicate at such short notice," said Hudson warmly.

Strong nodded. "Not a problem. I should however mention I have a tight schedule today and need to be back in parliament ASAP to bring this matter to the attention of the many Members and staff who knew Rowe."

Hudson showed him a map indicating where the grave was sited in relation to the Adelaide Metro. "Fuck! How did they get him there?"

"Your guess is as good as mine. All we can say is that his death cannot have been accidental. It's a complete mystery. Can you shine any light on this?"

"Not at all. But we do have a problem, which I'll come to in a moment."

"From our point of view, it's very late to be trying to find the killer. We can only do our best. Our Minister for Police is giving this top priority and we have our best detectives on the case."

At this point, Strong's attention was distracted by somebody appearing on the screen behind him.

"Just give me a moment could you? One of my staff wants to talk to me."

As Strong left the communication point, Rayleigh caught a glimpse of a man who was holding out a photograph of a young woman, but the view was cut off as Strong took him by the shoulder and nudged him out of the room, closing the door behind him. Premier Rayleigh recognised neither the man nor the woman in the photo.

It was only a few moments before Strong reappeared. He'd lost his ebullient manner and it was clear that he needed something badly. It immediately put her on guard.

"Listen Rayleigh, I realise in the past we've had our differences, but this is surely a situation where we can put all that behind us. It's in both our interests to make this a successful investigation and nothing I'm about to suggest will undermine that."

"What have you in mind? Like it or not, this is our responsibility and SAPol are putting their best resources into solving it."

"All I'm asking is for you to facilitate one high-level member of my own staff to act as a liaison officer. We don't have any idea of how Rowe's body could have landed up where it has. And the problem for us is that a crim in New South Wales is serving time for Rowe's murder based entirely on circumstantial evidence. It makes our joint investigation particularly sensitive. I can guarantee that the placement of a highly-motivated liaison officer from our side will help rather than hinder."

Hudson pondered the request for a few moments before making a cautious undertaking. "Eric I will see what can be done. I'm not ruling this out of course, but it has to be vetted by Premier's Office first. What I do ask is that you send me details of who you'd like to appoint, including their experience. We'll give it our full consideration. That okay with you?"

Rodney Jensen

"Fantastic. We'll do what we can to meet your wishes. My adviser will be back to your office before close of business with details of whom we have in mind."

Part One

Rodney Jensen

CHAPTER 1

Detective Chief Inspector Stewart Richardson of the NSW Major Crimes Branch, assigned to re-open the case from the NSW end, sat staring at his monitor already feeling himself under bombardment from a rapacious band of journalists. One story read 'Body of the missing politician Kevin Rowe has been discovered by two teenage brothers in Adelaide's Mt Lofty Ranges. This baffling discovery more than eight years after his disappearance from his home in Sydney suggests that NSW Police have a lot of explaining to do…'

He thumped his fist on the desk so hard it would have shaken the clutter onto the floor, had there been any. "Loose talk by the fucking gutter press," he fumed, not caring who overheard him. He stood and paced the room, pinching his upper left arm in a powerful grip. He could normally control the day to day that crossed his table, but this gratuitous ill-informed reporting was unbearable. It was as if he was in a public firing line with no way to dodge the bullets. His own staff he could manage with a level of calm and sternness. It was a mask he'd learnt to assume, despite his late wife's warnings, which made him seem aloof and unapproachable. But she was no longer there to advise, having met a premature end from breast cancer. His job was now everything to him, far more than his staff would ever appreciate. The gulf had widened as he grew older, but he no longer cared: *what have I got to lose?* The only thing he wanted was to get promoted out of the Parramatta office, and return to the Eastern suburbs where he had been brought up. But that wasn't going to happen any time soon, and certainly not with publicity like this.

He got up, straightened his shoulders, deciding to see what his 'Fixer' had to suggest.

As Stewart walked into the confined space of Detective Sergeant Len Mannix's office, he was overpowered by the smell of fried chips doused in vinegar and tomato sauce. His nose wrinkled in disgust at the half-finished meal on the man's desk and the dribbles of tomato sauce halfway down his shirt, stretched over a stout beer gut.

Despite his annoyance at Len's penchant for junk food and poor physical condition, he was expecting that he might be able to shed light on the situation. He knew from experience Len was an unusually good 'crap detector' and often had a pragmatic solution for the day to day obstacles that Major Crimes had to deal with, even if his methods were not always by the book.

"I'd like to wring the neck of whoever leaked this. It puts us in bloody poor light," Stewart growled.

"Don't take it to heart," Len replied, deadpan. "It may have been that one of the journos found a way to bug the teleconference. You know how the media operate with their contacts everywhere. It's well and truly out. Better face facts and deal with it."

Stewart huffed as he pulled over a chair and sat down in front of Len, trying not to gag over the half-eaten chips. "You're probably right. Finding the body in SA puts a whole new slant on our original investigation, doesn't it? Not only that, but we're now faced with two entirely different state jurisdictions. Not even sure where we stand there."

"You mean SA Premiers as well as our own?"

Stewart nodded. "Whatever happens now, it's really SA's call. I've no idea how that's going to pan out but…"

Len cut him off. "There's something else just come in on our secure connection."

"Yes? More bad news, if that's possible?"

Len fiddled with a pen he'd been making notes with. "See you weren't around, otherwise you might have been able to cut 'em off at the pass."

"Get to the point Len!"

"Jock Tarding in Premier's wants to see you about this."

"Not him again. What's it this time?"

"Throwing his weight around as usual. Tells me they're not happy about the implications. You know what? Those bastards would prefer Rowe's body'd never turned up! And now they're after blood. Just guess who's in the frame! And get this, they're blaming Scanlan's conviction on the way we handled things. As if Prosecution would give us the time of day! But what pisses them off most is the rumour flying round that our evidence was dodgy."

"What are you talking about?"

"The Terry Scanlan case, Stewart."

Stewart scowled at Len. He not only hated being in the dark but was continually irritated by Len being so familiar with him, despite his lower rank. Nor did he want to reveal certain things he did happen to know about the victim at this point, unless it proved necessary to solving his disappearance.

"When DCI Hunt was in charge?"

"Yep, the crafty bugger! I took a look at the file myself yesterday. Now Rowe's body has been found in SA, it makes the report and us a bloody laughing stock, including the forensics."

"Mistakes or concocted? What are you saying?"

Len shifted uneasily. "No way it was a mistake. Much too black and white. No other explanation. Tarding'd have to be a fool if he didn't read it same as me."

Stewart drew a deep breath and stared at Len without seeing him. "Apart from the file, what else did Tarding have to say?"

"He wants to see you now. The Premier himself will want to get his dibs in there also. They don't trust us and prefer to believe what they're reading and hearing from the fucking journalists. So be warned! They probably want your head on a platter whether or not you were here at the time."

"Okay, you'd better come with me. You can brief me on the way."

Stewart activated an AutoCab waiting outside their office in Parramatta Central and they set off. Len had punched 'NSW Premier's Office CBD' into the nav system. They settled back into their passenger bubble and accelerated eastwards into the computer-managed line of other vehicles entering the metro transit system. The nav system estimated fifteen minutes until their arrival.

Stewart didn't waste any time. "Okay, get me up to speed on this file. Can you please clarify exactly what you meant by dodgy evidence?"

Len was not looking at Stewart but was fiddling with his holo to bring up some files. It took him some moments to respond. "Well, it's only an impression. And it's a long time ago, almost ten years. That said, several things don't square up. But first, you got to understand this in context. See there was a history of bad blood between Rowe and Scanlan. Eventually, Rowe had to take out an AVO on him."

"An AVO? Why?"

"Scanlan was making threats over the holo, to his office, his home, you name it."

"Again, why?"

"It went back to bad advice he'd given Scanlan in his role as one of the advisors in the Australia Investment Bank. You know many others got their fingers burned as well. The bank had chosen Rowe because he once had his own investment business. This was all before he went into politics. He was doing so well the Australia Bank took him on as one of their preferred advisors."

"Selling their financial products?"

"That's it. Everything's going gangbusters, including Scanlan's investments. He ignored the warning signs and well and truly did his dough like a whole lot of other mum and dad investors. It cleaned him out. His property business was doing at least fifteen houses a year before the collapse. But the dill was still selling new house packages when he'd already lost everything. It was all a sham. Left many families with half-finished boxes. They complained and their case was taken up by one of those law firms that work for free, on a results basis. It meant they only got paid if they won the case. Well, they did win. Scanlan got three years for fraud and never forgave Rowe as he was the one person he could lay the blame on."

"Being angry with Rowe and a conviction for fraudulent business would hardly have been enough to persuade the Prosecutors to support a case file, particularly if there wasn't a body!"

"No, but there was a load of circumstantial evidence. Scanlan, as I read him, was a fucking loser. He started pursuing Rowe once they let him out of prison. Eventually, Rowe had to take out the AVO against all the harassment. But the real clincher was only a few days before Rowe went missing; the two were seen together in a bar. They got into an argument that turned pretty feral. According to the evidence of witnesses inside and outside the pub, Scanlan threatened to kill Rowe if he didn't cough up a large part of the money he reckoned Rowe owed him for his bad advice. That was the gist of what one witness heard, anyway. Rowe walked out of the pub with Scanlan after him. Scanlan grabbed Rowe by the shoulder, spun him around and decked him. Left him lying on the footpath with blood everywhere and walked away."

"Did Rowe report this? Did we interview Scanlan or charge him?"

"Not exactly. We brought Scanlan in for questioning because one of our uniforms was in the vicinity and could hardly ignore something that public.

Eventually we had to let him go. Rowe wouldn't press charges. He told us he felt it would put him in a bad light, and didn't want the publicity over Scanlan's bitching."

"But that all changed when Rowe was reported missing?"

"Since we all knew about the bad blood between these two, Scanlan was our first port of call. We took him into custody because he was stonewalling and refusing to give us anything. Said his prison time had taught him one thing and that was *keep stumm*. We had no choice but to let him go, there was no direct evidence he'd any contact with Rowe after this assault and before Rowe disappeared."

"And the dodgy evidence?" Stewart asked.

"Premier's intervened after we closed the books and the coroner made an open finding. The public, stirred to a frenzy by the media, wasn't happy with loose ends. They pressed Commissioner Arvill to do something and he appointed Maurice Hunt to see what we'd missed."

"Unfortunately Arvill's no longer with us either. Hunt discovered a shirt with blood on it that matched Rowe's DNA in Scanlan's builder's lockup. Scanlan swore black and blue he had no idea how it got there. But nobody would believe him. In the end, the shirt was enough to convict him of murder in the absence of a body. It now seems pretty clear that it was planted."

"Why's that?"

"The timing. It couldn't have happened the way we were claiming. We were interviewing Scanlan on the day after Rowe went missing. Not only that, we now know he was under constant watch from just after the very public punch up to several weeks after Rowe's disappearance, including all his comms tapped. None of us in the Branch, including Arvill or Hunt knew that at the time. It was organised by a separate state security unit."

"How do you know all this?"

Len tapped his nose. "I've got my contacts and I'm joining the dots, you might say. Two things spring to mind. The first was that the State and the Anti-Corruption Commission were looking for evidence to nail the police. And the other thing was that Scanlan's history of stalking and abuse would have worried other 'polies', you'd think?"

"And this didn't come out at the trial?"

"Nup. They knew Scanlan had no other contact with Rowe, and didn't bother to disclose this at the trial held a year later. Pretty shameful if you ask me. Now with this latest news who's going to believe Scanlan could've murdered Rowe, and somehow got the body over to Adelaide, for no obvious reason. The only slight possibility I suppose, is that he had help from someone else, but that's unlikely given he hadn't any cash to put out a contract. Scanlan had a record and a very short fuse. But if you ask me, that didn't make him a murderer, or someone who'd organise a murder or associate with contract crims. I haven't a clue how Rowe's shirt with blood all over it found its way into Scanlan's garage, and it's a very cold case."

Len paused for a few moments to scratch something under his collar before resuming.

"He was fitted up, no doubt about that. But I guess we're going to have to nail it before we work out how he really was killed."

Their AutoCab emerged from the tunnel into the State Office Precinct. "I'd appreciate it," Stewart said to Len, "if you'd keep all this to yourself while we're meeting with Tarding," He held up his hand as Len was about to interrupt. "Whether he knows the facts already or not, please would you just observe and listen to what he has to say. The interesting thing now is that it sounds like it's not only us who have a lot to answer for. Leave it to me to decide when and how I present this to them, okay?"

Len nodded, "As you like, Stewart."

CHAPTER 2

Stewart barely knew Tarding, but from the moment he and Len entered the room, there was a cold hostility in the air that immediately put him on his guard. Jock Tarding, the NSW Premier's key adviser, had the look of an ambitious upstart. His short cropped grey toned hair, lean build, and form fitting suit, filled the mould, embellished by the arrogance of a senior public servant on the up.

"Tell me more," Tarding demanded of Stewart, "about the police investigation leading up to the inquest, and the reason that the inquest led to Scanlan's conviction for murder based only on circumstantial evidence?"

Stewart waited until he had straightened his jacket and settled into his chair before replying. "I have to remind you that this all happened before my appointment to Major Crimes, but from an extremely quick briefing and scanning of the file it was a no-brainer. On the face of it, the evidence although circumstantial was conclusive."

"Let's not fuck around." Tarding leant back in his chair with a sneer. "I know, and I think you know too, that your predecessor's *conclusive evidence* was misleading and probably planted?"

"Very possibly. But the latest I'm hearing is that there was a high-level conspiracy to withhold critical information in the trial which would have put Scanlan in the clear. And your lot were in it up to their necks."

"Bullshit!" Tarding slammed his fist on the table as though he was about to pounce on Stewart.

"It's no bullshit," said Len quietly. "I've had access to information that wasn't available to us at the time of the trial. You and the Feds were quietly running surveillance on our high-level cases because, to put it bluntly, you didn't trust us and wanted a few heads to roll. I suppose Scanlan's innocence was a small price to pay. But there's going to be a lot of explaining to do by your lot as well, if and when this gets out."

"The fact is that your evidence was crooked. Don't try and shift the blame on us."

"It'll all come out, like it or not," continued Len, "It's bound to. There'll be more leaks. And before you start accusing us of bullshit, Mr Tarding, I think you'd better get your own facts straight."

Tarding sat back in his chair eyeing Len angrily and turned his attention to some notes on his monitor, remaining silent.

Stewart waited for him to say something more. They weren't here to disclose information to him.

When he did, his tone was noticeably less aggressive. "I'm unaware of the surveillance angle and will look into that. But the evidence produced by your office was tainted, that's obvious. No doubt you will be making your own inquiries as to how that came about. But I want to focus this morning, on the main purpose of this meeting, which is how the investigation is managed here on in."

"We've yet to work that out," said Stewart, "but we have limited jurisdiction since the body was found in SA."

"That's why you're here," Tarding cut him off. "There's already been a high-level discussion by

Premiers and they've agreed to accept a Senior NSW State Liaison Officer who'll take part in their investigations."

"Well, that sounds positive." Stewart shifted in his seat. Could Tarding be a reasonable man despite his brashness? If both sides worked together on the case it could be solved more quickly and he might get promoted out of Parramatta after all. "We're obviously as keen as you are to bring the investigation to a definite conclusion and will be happy to cooperate. There are several officers I can think of. Who would you suggest Len?"

"You've misunderstood me," Tarding butted in again. "We're organising a placement of our own. Her name's Ingham and she's one of our best and brightest managers." He pressed an icon on his desk console and spoke to the screen, "Kaz, you can come in now please."

Len's expressions moved from surprise to consternation. Stewart gestured to Len to shut up, fearing that he might come out with the explosion he was also struggling to contain. He wanted to walk out, but before he had time to act, the connecting door slid open and a woman he guessed must be Kaz Ingham, walked in. Her disarming smile was in marked contrast to the tension in the room.

Kaz was wearing designer clothes for the office emphasising her well-shaped body, obviously conditioned by regular exercise. Her brunette hair was shortly cropped with a hint of waviness. While below average height, she wore high heels making her seem tall and slender. Stewart found it difficult to read exactly what she might be thinking, but she seemed to have an air of intensity and engagement that signaled she was not to be taken lightly.

CHAPTER 3

Kaz was surprised to find the quarters occupied by Stewart's Major Crimes Branch in Parramatta so minimal. The main engine room was not much larger than a medium-sized apartment's living space. Most of the office was open plan with up to four staff positioned opposite each other in a centrally located group of work stations. Small glazed cubicles were used by Stewart and Len for their offices, leaving two other spaces for meetings or watching larger holographic displays. Otherwise, there was a lot of carpet, bare walls, a few pot-plants and a couple of ViewBoards.

The drabness of these new surroundings did little to spark her enthusiasm—*the quicker this assignment's over the better. Why am I not where I was supposed to be—in Region Armidale reviewing the new development plan's metrics—something of much greater public concern than investigating the demise of a forgotten politician?*

Stewart beckoned Kaz into his office and asked her to close the door. His body language was dismissive as he gestured for her to take a seat, though his shirt strained across such a well-toned upper body that Kaz couldn't help but notice. Despite his age, or maybe because of it, she found herself picturing what might lie beneath that shirt, and what it might look like while he worked out, or swam at the beach, or did something practical in a well-equipped workshop. He certainly radiated fitness, if not charm. The fact that he seemed totally disinterested in her also fuelled her interest. Most of her male business colleagues seemed to take notice of her looks but Stewart couldn't seem to care less about her appearance. It was refreshing. Perhaps it meant he'd pay more attention to what she was saying.

"As you can see," he said as a somewhat insincere apology, "we're not set up in here for support personnel, but—"

"That's not a concern, I'm used to flitting in and out of others' offices as a project manager." Kaz cut him off in mid-sentence.

"—I've ordered a work station for you. Meanwhile, I've asked DS Len Mannix to share his office. You'll be working closely with him on this, and from our point of view he will be in charge, although obviously it has to be a cooperative arrangement. Before getting that sorted I wanted to share a few thoughts."

Kaz inclined her head and said nothing, guessing what was coming.

"I have to be straight with you. I know nothing about you, other than your work description and most recent review of progress at State, which Tarding has been kind enough to send over. It's certainly impressive. You're obviously highly qualified in terms of your management skills. But what I don't see is any sign of experience in police inquiries. To put it bluntly, you know bugger all about police work, let alone a murder inquiry other than what you might have seen or read about in the media!"

As a high flier his attitude was something she'd encountered all her life. She took a moment to centre herself and respond suitably. "I'm sure you and Len can fill me in as we go. But to my mind, the logistics of this inquiry would be little different from Magistrates or Judges getting their heads around every new case that comes before them. It is a routine process that calls for similar skills to those that I have. I've been involved in numerous high-level projects for State and I'm confident that the issues surrounding one person going missing and subsequently being discovered murdered would have no unique logistics. In any case, as I understand it, we only have a watching brief on whatever SAPol are doing?"

"I think it's a lot more complicated than you realise. And having an unknown quantity like you imposed on me is something I could do without," Stewart retorted. "Anyway let's move on. I want you to work closely with Len, clarify your role as you see it and prepare an outline of what you'll be doing, who with, and when, by the end of this week. Now I'm going to re-introduce you to Len."

Kaz rolled her eyes behind his back and followed him into the open plan area. Len's attitude was similar to Stewart's. For a moment she wondered whether their attitude was in part just plain old fashioned sexist and would have been different if she were male. But Kaz could see it was procedure related—Len was a traditional fixer used to doing things his own way, using tried and tested steps the police had evolved over time immemorial, modified only slightly by new communications and transport technology. She found him less hostile than Stewart and the odd flash of humour made him seem more ready to accept some innovations.

"Welcome to the cave," he'd said after Stewart re-introduced them, "not much space as you can see, I'm going to have to put a line of tape along my table and we'll just have to glare at each other across it until we get things sorted."

Kaz could not help chuckling. "Perhaps we could wear dark glasses?"

She spent the morning reading the files Len had sourced before she felt she could say anything meaningful. Finally she put aside her reading and suggested they should work up a mind map on the ViewBoard.

"Go ahead, surprise me," said Len. "Mind map - bejezus!"

"I'm sure you'll see the value once it's done," said Kaz, starting to draw a series of linked circles with labels.

Len watched, reluctantly at first, but soon began to contribute thoughts of his own. Kaz graciously acknowledged his input and readily conceded where she'd overlooked something critical.

It didn't take her long before she could confidently voice thoughts on the different lines of investigation emerging. "As I see it, the prosecution of Scanlan must have either been an error or a deliberate misdirection by your predecessors. But to my mind, working out why or what went wrong should be secondary to discovering how Rowe - alive or dead - ended up in the Adelaide Hills."

"Scanlan might have something to say about that. His lawyers'll be beating a track to the Prosecutors Office, after compensation. And good luck to him. We've done him an injustice, no two ways about it. Presumably, the real killer's still out there somewhere.

Rodney Jensen

Until the bastard's nailed, no one's goin' to be happy. My take Kaz, is they're both high priority."

"I'm not going to disagree with you, but given your history with this matter, I'm suggesting that you take the lead on Scanlan and I'll focus on Rowe's real murderer. I think that will be the most efficient way to approach this and avoid stepping on each other's toes."

"Good thinking," said Len.

Kaz smiled inwardly. Maybe this project might take her into something new after all, something that would stretch her far beyond dreary Armidale. And just maybe, Len, unlike his boss, was going to let her have it all her own way.

CHAPTER 4

When Len spoke to Stewart about Kaz on the side (*'she's not just a pretty face mate, I reckon she can make her mark if you let her'*), to his credit it set Stewart thinking more carefully about Kaz's potential. Stewart had already recognised that there was more to Kaz than he'd first assumed. He could see that her superior ability to manage the information flow and focus on real priorities in the Rowe investigation could leave him to get on with other equally pressing matters. His Major Crimes Branch was ludicrously short-staffed to handle the workload and he could ill-afford to have Len spending time doing SAPol's job for them. The rationale for using Kaz more effectively was compelling. He contacted her boss in State, Jock Tarding, without further delay.

Tarding, brash as ever took the call. "No surprise to hear from you. Let me guess, you're ringing to complain she's doing her job too well, showing your lot up already!"

Stewart struggled not to rise to the bait, despising Tarding for the upstart he was. "This is actually a courtesy call. I do want to talk to you about Kaz, but it's not a complaint, quite the opposite. I just want to make sure you'll not have any objections to extending her duties beyond pure liaison to more active participation and responsibility in the Rowe investigation."

"Can't see a problem with that. What did you have in mind?"

Rodney Jensen

"I'd like to appoint her 'Special Investigator' so she can travel interstate with police powers available to her. It would give her more authority to act in our best interests. I don't know yet whether she'll need this, but it'll free up my staff and make more effective use of her time in this case."

"Fine by me. I'm sure she'll rise to the challenge. And confidentially, I think the Crow-Eaters could do with some help," Tarding responded.

"Okay we'll take it from here then," Stewart replied, not wishing to prolong the conversation.

"That all?"

"Yes that's all. I'll keep you posted," said Stewart and closed the connection. He was feeling rather satisfied with himself that he had negotiated what he saw as a win-win strategy. If Kaz responded to the challenge, it might conceivably help solve the case. If she didn't and fell flat on her face through inexperience he wouldn't particularly care. He wasted no time in giving Kaz the good news of her police promotion.

« »

Kaz had some difficulty discovering where the prosecution barrister for Scanlan's previous trial was located. Len's file indicated he occupied an office in well-known chambers in the City of Sydney but that was long out of date. It took a few calls to track him down and discover his offices were only a hundred metres away in Central Parramatta.

Jeremy Twyvern SC, had obviously made a very quick transit into the upper echelons of barristerdom, and was now located on the highest level of a very tall office tower.

As Kaz stared out of a window in the lift lobby towards the Blue Mountains in the west, she could see but not hear some of the new electric cargo planes departing from the now well-established Badgery's Creek International Airport. She recalled seeing an internal memo in Premiers, referring to liaison with Fed's Air Traffic Control and their strong objection to the height of this particular development, because it required re-routing one of the main takeoff and landing air corridors.

An urbane man, Twyvern, impeccably dressed in a tailor-made grey suit and with a full mane of dark hair, came out to greet them and lead the way to his office. It was aquarium-like, with mostly glass partitions and horizontally-slatted privacy blinds. From within, it had an impressive outlook via floor-to-ceiling windows, cleverly angled towards narrow gaps between adjacent high rise towers. In the last few decades, the centre of Parramatta had changed from low to very high rise, converting streets into canyons and people to ants, competing with self-drives for the dwindling roads.

Twyvern started without any preamble. "The message said you want to discuss Scanlan?"

Kaz nodded. "I've made a couple of calls and I gather he's now in a low-security prison."

"Have you seen him yet?" asked Twyvern.

"No, that pleasure awaits," Kaz said. "We're still going over the case file. Your name came up as prosecutor. We thought we should pay you a visit.

We've just got a few questions. Maybe you've been asking yourself the same ones?"

Twyvern absently scratched an index finger down his cheek. "I'm still not clear where you're coming from. It's been a long time. It was a straightforward case as far as I can remember, although Scanlan never showed any signs of confession, repentance or remorse. I suppose the reason you're here is because of the recent discovery of the victim's body? Could it be that Scanlan's now in the clear?" he asked with a hint of sarcasm.

"You're on the money," Kaz admitted. "We now think he's innocent. He'll have to be pardoned, compensated even. The reason for this meeting is to understand your thinking better."

Len spoke up. "Did you have any suspicions about the brief you were given, originally?"

Twyvern looked at Len curiously. "It's a bit strange that you should be asking me this. Have you forgotten that my role as prosecutor absolutely precluded my visiting such territory? Indeed, why should I be helping you now?"

"We thought that you actually might be more objective," Len threw back at him, "even generous, given that you were partly responsible for getting him banged up with a life sentence for a crime he didn't commit!"

"Hmm… well putting that outrageous suggestion aside, let me think about my perceptions at the time." Twyvern pondered a few moments. "As I remember it, there was a key piece of forensic evidence, something they found in his lockup?"

"That's right, a shirt with blood on it which matched Rowe's."

"Thank you. Yes that was the clincher. So, why the change of heart?"

"We're pretty certain that Scanlan can't have been the killer. How the shirt got into his lockup seems to point the finger at us. It isn't a good look."

"Which is why," Kaz explained, "the case has to be re-opened. I asked for this meeting in case you had any suggestions to add?"

"Well, now you come to mention it, the police witness delivering his evidence-in-chief was not a good witness. He seemed shifty to me and was unable to give any convincing explanation under cross as to how the shirt had ended up in Scanlan's lockup."

"Was there any doubt the shirt was his?" Kaz asked.

"No. Both he and his wife confirmed it. Scanlan claimed it was the shirt he'd been wearing during the punch-up he'd had with Rowe and that was why it had his blood on it. Assuming it was in the home laundry, as he claimed, I suppose it would not have been difficult for the police to pick it up while they were conducting their search at his home. But they had a different version of events. They denied the shirt had been logged in with his other possessions when he was arrested. I must say, with the benefit of hindsight, it does seem now like a stitch up. Unfortunately for Scanlan, his defence lawyer was pretty inexperienced and failed to make more of it at the time."

"Why didn't the Judge have questions of his own about this? Surely it was a key piece of evidence," Kaz asked

Rodney Jensen

"Because, my dear, he had probably already made up his mind based on three very good reasons to convict. "First-" he began ticking off on his fingers, "-was his very public grudge against Rowe, culminating in a violent confrontation in breach of an AVO that Rowe had taken out against him. Second was the discovery of Rowe's shirt by the police in his lockup; and third, that his defence made so little of the fact that there was no body." Twyvern smirked and his tone became confiding. "It was my job to prosecute, you understand, whatever personal feelings I may have had about the veracity of the evidence. If I'd been his defence brief, the outcome might have been very different. But beyond that, I have no more to say."

Len got up and walked out, ignoring Twyvern's outstretched hand. Kaz followed after him, shaking her head in disapproval. "Complete waste of space," she muttered.

« »

The low-security prison occupied extensive grounds with a fine Victorian-style mansion surrounded by a series of low profile outbuildings. The locality was on the fringe of the city where bird calls and sounds of robotic cropping machines in the distance replaced the usual background of urban noise.

This time, Kaz agreed that Len should lead the interview since he'd already met Scanlan. "This is goin' to toughen you up, so be warned," he said as they walked through security.

Kaz had been inside prisons before as part of her work for State. But Len was right—there was an atmosphere about the place heightened by conversations stopping the moment she came into view and the staring eyes of men deprived of women for too long. She felt herself the centre of attention—it put her on edge.

They found Scanlan seated in a park-like setting, away from the main buildings. He was deep in conversation with someone, his lawyer judging by the suit. Scanlan himself was a shadow of the person in the photographs that Kaz had seen on file. His hair had been reduced to grey strands, while his body scarcely filled the prison fatigues he was wearing. He stared angrily at his visitors from deeply recessed eyes. "I was wondering when we'd be seeing yous," he remarked. "Come to apologise? Go on! Surprise me."

Len addressed the lawyer. "I'm DS Len Mannix and this is Kaz Ingham, Special Investigator for NSW Premier's," he said holding out his hand. "I'm in charge of the Rowe investigation, part of which is re-opening the case that landed your client here. We're here to check Mr Scanlan's version of the events again if that's okay?"

"Derek Townsley," he responded in a measured voice, shook Len's hand, then Kaz's. "You may ask Mr Scanlan whatever you like. I'm here to advise him whether or not to make any comment. But, as you realise, the matter is subjudice and all the indications are that Mr Scanlan will be exonerated. Naturally, anything he can say which will assist him in this will be welcomed. To that extent, we are willing to cooperate. I trust that is understood?"

Rodney Jensen

Len nodded, then turned to Scanlan. "One of the main things the prosecution held against you was the blood-stained shirt they said they found in your lockup. The blood was the same as Rowe's, with 99.99% certainty of that. You didn't deny it either. Said it was your shirt and you'd been wearing it when you gave Rowe a bloody nose outside the Suttlers Arms, in Newtown. But your story was the police must have planted it in the lockup, because it was placed in your laundry basket, by your wife, when you came home after the fight?"

"If you've read the transcript," Townsley interjected, "Mr Scanlan explained this at his trial and I see no reason to revisit his version. The police claimed to have no record of the shirt being discovered in their search of his home."

Scanlan answered, despite Townsley's objection. "Yes, it was my shirt all right, the one I was wearing when I decked him. Gave him something to remember, the bastard. Had it coming to 'im. I took my shirt off when I got home. Can't remember where I put it. Didn't see it again until they showed it to me at the trial. It was pretty obvious that one of your cunts got their hands on it, and planted it in me workshop."

"Who had the keys to the lockup?" Len asked

"I can't see where this is leading," said Townsley, "the Police had a search warrant. They would have had no problem gaining entry to the lockup with a locksmith whether or not they had the keys."

"I'm just trying to help Terry, because as I read the file, the lock wasn't forced. It might help his case if we knew who had the keys?" Len replied.

"They was on me keyring, among the things they took off me when I was arrested, and never got them back," Scanlan said.

"And there's nothing else you can tell us about the shirt?" Kaz persisted.

Scanlan stared at her for long seconds as though she were an imbecile. "I told 'em at the trial and I'm telling you again. The shirt were left in my house when I was arrested. I never saw it again until the trial. Your fuckin' brethren must have picked it up—no other explanation is there!"

CHAPTER 5

Kaz entered Pittwater Glades with Len. It was a pleasantly landscaped retirement development in the upper reaches of Sydney's Pittwater. A security guard met them at the imposing entrance to check their business. He was wearing a smart uniform and carried a distinctive weapon in a special holster. It was a short block of moulded black plastic, about as big as a cling-wrap dispenser, with a snub nosed barrel projecting from the business end. Len seemed to notice it too. He remarked as he flashed his police ID, "I see you're carrying the latest Henning. We've only just taken delivery of a batch ourselves. How come a retirement place gets the special permission they require for the new nano-blasters? No disrespect, but I wouldn't have thought you'd qualify?"

"Yep, can't disagree. But the owners of this place have friends in high places, some of whom might just happen to have aging rellies or parents in here. Simple as that," he answered nonchalantly, tapping his nose.

"What was that all about—just a bit of turf war, or something I need to know?" Kaz inquired, as they wandered off in the direction the guard had pointed.

"Craps me off!" Len sounded distinctly pissed. "We just had special training in using a Henning. See it's different from conventional weapons—a lot of new tricks to learn. The feller in charge of training emphasised how restricted its use would be, virtually only the army and police have access. Now I reckon if a retirement home gets their hands on one, anyone can."

Kaz nodded, making a mental note to put her hand up for training herself.

The Manager in the reception area was waiting to talk to them as soon as they arrived. "Mr Hunt's one of our 'fortunates', still young enough to be living in a self-care residence by himself. He's right on the edge of the estate and looks out over the water's edge—nice."

He tore a glossy map off a pad and marked with a felt pen where Hunt's home was located.

A short walk later, they discovered a cluster of low-scale townhouses sited on opposite sides of a narrow cul-de-sac lane. Kaz caught a glimpse of tranquil views of Pittwater between the buildings on the downhill side of the lane. Hunt's house had a small front lawn and several young eucalypts looking like they'd recently been planted.

Once Kaz pressed the buzzer, it took the owner a long time to get his locks undone. He was a man who could have been in his early seventies, with thinning hair, and evidently experiencing some pain in his hips as he led them awkwardly into his lounge. "I've been expecting you," he said warily. Kaz, taking in his smart blazer, freshly laundered shirt, tie and navy slacks, thought him over-dressed for the occasion. *Definitely on his guard.*

They sat down around a coffee table and politely refused the offer of refreshments. Kaz wasted no time in coming to the point. "As I explained on the holo, we're opening up the Rowe case again."

"Yes," he said staring out of the window, as a pelican plunged into the water in the distance. "It came as some surprise to learn he'd been found in SA."

Rodney Jensen

I bet it did, thought Kaz. "Yes for everyone," she said. "We're still trying to work that one out. But the point is, Terry Scanlan was convicted on the basis of evidence that he cannot have been responsible for. He will shortly be exonerated and no doubt seeking compensation for the years he's been behind bars. You were in charge of the investigation and appear to have been a key witness in his prosecution. We now have to prepare ourselves for what has become increasingly obvious."

"Oh?" He turned to face them.

"The blood-stained shirt belonging to Scanlan with Rowe's matching DNA discovered in Scanlan's lockup could only have been planted. The prosecution played on the existence of the shirt in the lockup. It almost certainly confirmed Scanlan was the murderer. The only problem with that line of evidence was that the shirt had been taken by the police at the time Scanlan was arrested when they searched his house. That's what he alleges, and now we're inclined to believe that he's been telling the truth all along. The bloodstain was the result of his very public brawl with Rowe. The police claimed they had no record of his shirt when he was taken into custody where he remained until his trial, having been refused bail."

"Can you explain how the shirt he'd been wearing before he'd been taken into custody and was waiting to be laundered at his home, mysteriously turned up in his lockup? Were you responsible?"

Hunt's body went rigid. "What evidence do you have for making such an accusation? This is outrageous!"

"We now know that Rowe was murdered in South Australia. It can't have been Scanlan that did it. The evidence produced concerning the shirt must have been concocted. You were the one in charge of the inquiry. At the very least you were incredibly negligent or over-zealous in your efforts to convict Scanlan in view of his repeated protestations that the shirt was seized by the police from his house and never returned to him?"

Hunt fumbled in his breast pocket and pulled out a vapo, ignited it and breathed in the faux nicotine vapours with slightly trembling fingers. "I was not the one who discovered the shirt. That was in the evidence you must have read. I have nothing further to add. And if you require anything else I shall only talk to you again with my solicitor present."

"So be it," said Kaz. "You realise this is tantamount to an admission of guilt?"

"I've nothing further to say. Please leave immediately."

Kaz glanced at Len who nodded to her. They had reached a point of no return. They rose to their feet and stood facing him.

"Would you stand up please Mr Hunt," Len said.

Hunt got to his feet with some difficulty, gripping the back of the chair for support. Kaz momentarily felt sorry for him as Len continued. "This is a formal warning, Mr Hunt. From now on, you can regard yourself as being under house arrest. Until further notice, you must not leave this place without advising the local police of your plans. Failure to abide by this, will lead to your full arrest and a continuation of your interview at headquarters. Here's my card."

"You can't do this, not without my solicitor present. You've ambushed me!" he blustered.

Len stepped forward his fists balled like wanted to hit the elderly man.

"Listen Hunt. In other circumstances, I might have had some sympathy for you given your age and previous rank. But I'd think twice about trying to tough this one out. The cards are against you mate. I suggest you reconsider your story, and it'd better be good. Otherwise, you'll live to regret your silence. Just think what it'd be like for a man of your age and reputation to get a prison sentence for perjury. If you're straight with us, you know as well as we do, you've a far better chance of a light sentence. We'll leave you to think about that."

On their return to Parramatta, with Stewart's approval, Kaz and Len prepared a draft briefing note to the Department of Prosecutions, recommending Scanlan's conviction be quashed.

CHAPTER 6

Kaz sat in the MagRail Interstate pondering whether the police in South Australia would be any easier to deal with than Stewart or Len.

"I'm sorry Kaz," Stewart had said the previous afternoon, "but while it's a great idea that you liaise on the ground with SAPol, it's simply not possible for Len to go with you. We're critically under-staffed here, and I need him to help me sort out Scanlan. SAPol has already agreed on your role, so they will just have to accept that you're lacking in police experience. In any case, I see our input as being quite limited. We can't tell them how to do their job, beyond overview and advice that is. So, Kaz, please see this in a positive light. You've worked well with Len to date, and already made some contribution. I'd like you to do this by yourself, while he helps me sort out Scanlan. You can contact us whenever you like and we'll keep each other appraised of progress."

Len had been sitting beside her as Stewart delivered this decision and seemed taken aback. "So Kaz effectively has the same status as me now?" He sounded miffed.

Stewart had simply nodded, though he was difficult to read. While his attitude towards her had definitely softened, he still seemed aloof with a shell that was hard to penetrate. He had the aura of *a married man*, but she knew nothing of his private life, making her even more curious. She had to admit to herself she felt attracted towards his looks and character, particularly his decisive management style.

Rodney Jensen

Could there be a devious intention behind his willingness to support me, she wondered. *Perhaps he prefers to keep his own staff from the liaison role with South Australia and let me carry the can. Maybe he's half hoping that I'll fail and he'll have a good reason to get me out of his hair.*

She'd left work early, on the pretext of needing time to prepare and pack her things, but really to get out of the frosty atmosphere permeating the office.

« »

Kaz stared out of the window of the MagRail to Adelaide's Mile End terminal, until a canned voice announced its imminent arrival.

Their police can't be any worse than Stewart she thought grimly, as she pulled her lightweight case down off the rack and joined the queue of passengers at the exit door.

As she stepped onto the platform, she met a blast furnace wall of heat, conditions she'd been warned to expect despite it being late in March. A SAPol officer in uniform was waiting to meet her as she came through the exit barrier. She sighed inwardly. Although the journey had taken as little as six hours, she would have preferred to have showered and spruced herself up before confronting her next hurdle. But that was not to be, as DC Alex Webster introduced herself, and led the way to a waiting police car to make the short journey to the new SAPol Headquarters abutting Adelaide's Victoria Square.

SAPol was located in a building the heart of Adelaide, linked to a series of so-called 'investigation nodes' in the largest of Adelaide's town centres, along the 180km of urbanization up and down the coastal strip, and linked by a convenient and fast light rail system. The Adelaide HQ occupied several levels in a large floor plan, 70-storey building, mostly devoted to State Government business.

Kaz and her escort took the lift to Level 59, fast enough for her ears to pop. She couldn't help feeling impressed with the scale of the place, hoping that policing would be equally effective and enlightened. Perhaps here she wouldn't get the same bureaucratic run-around as she had in Sydney?

The receptionist led her to a nondescript doorway off a side corridor. "DCI Tania Bilson has been expecting you, please go through."

Bilson was already rising from behind her desk to greet Kaz, with a brief clasp of her hand. She was of average height and wore her brown hair neatly tied in a bun. With her tailored suit, erect stance, arms clasped stiffly behind her back, it seemed like she was about to address a larger audience. Kaz guessed that she was in her late fifties and could be in borderline retirement mode. She looked like she had the troubles of the world on her shoulders. The last thing she'd be wanting was a highly sensitive murder inquiry, media watching her every move.

She seemed to size up Kaz, and her opening lines weren't promising. "We've been expecting you Ms Ingham and I will do my best to help you. But to be candid, this situation is not one I particularly welcome."

Kaz did her best to ignore the boiling resentment she was sensing. "It's 'Kaz' please. I haven't been given a title or rank, the sort of thing I expect you're used to, and Special Investigator NSW is far too much of a mouthful." Kaz hesitated, sensing that she was burbling, and not creating much of an impression, judging by the lines of tension appearing on Bilson's forehead. "Do you have any suggestions?"

"Well you've put your finger on the key problem from our point of view," Bilson said. "The fact that you've no experience in police work makes it difficult to know what role you can play. And it's a situation which is completely out of my hands thanks to the agreement our respective Premiers imposed on us," she said.

"Funnily enough, NSWPol have similar management concerns. In fact, their reaction has been almost word for word same as yours. It's probably why they decided to send me over here to get rid of me and hope against hope I make a mess of things."

Bilson was not amused. "Well thank you for your honesty, Ms Ingham. But the question remains what am I going to do with you?"

"Funnily enough I don't seem to have any difficulty in understanding what Special Investigator with police powers actually means which, might I remind you, has been sanctioned at the highest level by your and my state governments. Under this arrangement I expect your full cooperation with my investigation. This includes a comprehensive briefing on where we're at. I want access to all your relevant files, details of the inquiries you've made, particularly the autopsy. Once I've been through that, perhaps we can re-convene tomorrow morning and assess what contribution I can make if any."

"I really don't need a lecture how you intend to conduct your investigation," said Bilson, barely able to contain her annoyance. "While you might be clear in your mind what role you are to play, it hasn't been spelt out and it's up to you to prove yourself."

"I've no intention of wasting time trying to justify myself to you, and I've had it up to *here*," Kaz said, touching a finger to her forehead, "with police assuming they are the sole repository of inquiry procedures. If you're not happy with that, then please let me know and I'll head back to NSW on the next MAG."

Bilson's frown deepened, but her response remained measured and quiet. "Believe me, it would give me the greatest pleasure to send you packing, Ms Ingham, were it not for the Premier's directive on this, which was totally against my wishes. You obviously have an extremely high opinion of yourself, but let's just see what you can come up with. I've been in this game quite a bit longer than you, but I'll try very hard to keep an open mind. Let's see some action, not words!" She paused briefly to let her thoughts sink in, before continuing.

"I'm now going to hand you over to Belinda Gotto, my DS in charge of the inquiry. She can work out where you're to sit, the equipment you'll need, if anything, and organise the information you're asking to see. But I'd allow a little extra time to go through it all, as there are some aspects you'll discover we're still investigating."

Kaz had enough sense not to press the point, wondering if she had allowed her emotions to get the better of her. "It will be your call to act as you think appropriately on whatever I come up with. You will get a full copy of my report, once I've had a chance to form an opinion about the way forward."

Bilson merely acknowledged her offer with a nod. "I'll introduce you to Gotto then," she said and gestured her to the door.

« »

Kaz warmed to Belinda Gotto, the first police staffer she'd met prepared to accept her on her merits despite her lack of police background. Gotto was below average height, with a tendency to obesity and a waddling gait. Her hair was curly and red, seemingly beyond management. For Kaz, the main redeeming feature was her sense of humour, which had seemed seriously lacking in her other police contacts. "Welcome to the land of the Crow Eaters, the Grape, and the Festival," she shook hands with Kaz jovially, "and, oh…*the heatwave*, I forgot to mention the heatwave," she added with an infectious giggle.

"Listen," she continued conspiratorially, "I've had an idea which might appeal to you, after sitting in the MagRail for hours. How about we put a bit of bush-bashing first on our program? I can show you where Rowe was discovered and that'll make the whole thing seem more real? How about that?"

"Sounds like a great idea, particularly as I've never been here before. I think I've probably read all the reports, and if there's any new stuff, it can wait I'm sure."

"Good. I've booked an ATGEV and ordered some boots and overalls for you so we can go tomorrow at 08:00 ?"

"ATGEV?"

"All-terrain ground-effects vehicle. We've got one of the latest models waiting for us downstairs. It does all the work and we've compiled a pretty comprehensive database of the terrain surrounding the site so we can go wherever you like."

"What size boots did you order?" asked Kaz.

"I saw you coming in to meet our *fearless leader* and made a guess. Anyway, you'll have a choice of sizes, don't worry about that," she replied airily.

« »

By the time they reached the site, thanks to the Adelaide Hill's microclimate, the air temperature had dropped to well below the forty degree mark. With very low humidity, Kaz found the conditions almost bearable.

Belinda led her along a narrow access track into the forest. As they got further in, the soundscape became muffled by the surrounding trees and scrub. The occasional croaking call of a crow or the abrupt shuffling sound in the undergrowth of a surprised lizard, were the only sounds to break the silence.

Without warning a number of star pickets forming a fence line could be seen leading off to the right. They were strung with strips of blue and white striped tape, bits of which were already festooned in the bushes with no evidence of clean-up. The ground was sandy at this point and bore the imprint of an army of flat-footed workmen, forming a new path traversing the hundred or so metres of bush between the track and the burial site.

"Here it is," Belinda lifted her hand, pointing at a clearing in the bush and the formation of a rough circle by the star picket cordon. Kaz was finding it difficult to focus on the scene, because the light was filtered by the tree canopy and dappled highlights moved on the ground surface, via the slight breeze aloft.

What appeared to be a shallow grave lay in the middle of a small clearing. A large mound of earth lay next to an elongated excavation and appeared to have been recently dug.

"Not much chance of finding anything new by now, is there?" Kaz remarked.

"No, you're right there, I don't think so. The trail was already cold, in any case. There's been no trace of any wheel tracks that might have been linked to the type of vehicle the killer used. Or if there wasn't a vehicle we don't have much of a clue how the body got here."

"What's your best guess then? How did the killer or killers get the body here?" Kaz asked.

"Maybe it could have been a wheelbarrow or something like that? As you can see, the grave was really shallow, and it wouldn't have taken that long to clear some undergrowth and dig down about a foot or so; no more than that. Whoever did the deed was thorough because of the way the body was covered over. There were no signs of track-marks, nothing, but over that number of years it's doubtful any track could still be detected."

Kaz pondered as she looked at the scene. She felt out of her depth. Gotto had articulated what seemed plausible explanations, but that's all they were. No hard evidence that she could see. "I don't think there's much more I can learn then. Is there anything else you wanted to show me?"

"No. I just thought it would help you understand how difficult this case is going to be for us and why we haven't made much headway yet."

"We can talk about a few things on the way back," said Kaz, "I need to know, for example what interviews you've made. How many people are living within a couple of kilometres radius of here? Have you talked to all of them?"

"We have. Produced nothing. Complete blank. But given the time this happened, it's hardly surprising is it?"

"My suggestion is that the killer could have known about this fire trail and may, therefore, have had local knowledge."

"Could be I suppose, but it wouldn't have been that difficult to find a spot like this by searching on a map base, would it?"

Kaz nodded, realising that her guess had no more likelihood than Gotto's. "Maybe we've been approaching this the wrong way. I don't think there's much prospect of finding any evidence here that will help track down the killer. It has the hallmarks of a careful disposal, as far as I can see, by someone who knew how to cover their tracks."

"I'd agree with that. A lot of effort's already gone into this area by our team and produced nothing new."

"Let's head back to the City. I've seen enough."

« »

Twenty four hours later DCI Tania Bilson re-convened with Kaz and Belinda.

Kaz didn't waste any time on tact. "I've been through everything you've given me, and to put it bluntly, I'm not seeing any progress at all in your investigations." She raised a hand to ward off Bilson's predictable response. "Now please hear me out. Forensics clearly confirms the identity of the body as belonging to our missing Minister Rowe. The environmental signs at his gravesite also support the length of time his body was buried roughly corresponding to the period he went missing. The pathology report states it's impossible to determine the cause of death and there is inconclusive evidence concerning the damage to his skull, the problem being there was no tissue, other than bones, found in the grave. Apart from those things I can see little or no progress—there's nothing in the files I can put my finger on. Am I missing something or would it be fair to say you're not progressing with this investigation, because I cannot see any real progress?"

Bilson gulped and took a breath, but didn't answer Kaz. "Gotto," she asked Belinda instead, "can we go through our inquiries?"

"The ones that aren't on file?" asked Kaz innocently.

Gotto cleared her throat and fiddled with a curl that had fallen over one eye. "Well yes, we've been eliminating the obvious, first by going through known crims who were around at the time of the murder, many of whom are now behind bars. But our fundamental problem is that we haven't uncovered any links between Rowe and any persons in this State, let alone anyone who might have had a motive to kill him. Obviously, we can't go up to anybody who's got a record of violent crime and ask them to prove where they were eight years ago!"

"Have you established how Rowe got here or why?" asked Kaz.

"No. Those are our fundamental mysteries. Assuming he was alive when he entered South Australia, the main options would have been flying, surface transport using MagRail or driving. If he came here via a self-drive or a privately owned land vehicle it would be improbable that we could track that down. We'll still try, of course. Otherwise, we've been through the airline and Mag records, but there's no record of anyone by the name of Rowe travelling for a period of up to three weeks after he disappeared. If he was in hiding in NSW and travelled later than that there's no way we can throw any light on him either."

"Did you check male passengers who could have made a return booking and were no shows on the return journey?"

"There were quite a few. We tracked down some who we could eliminate, but there are three we are still trying to locate."

"One of those could have been Rowe?" Kaz asked.

"Yes possibly. One of the most likely was using the name of 'James Howard'. He actually travelled to Adelaide the day before Rowe's wife reported him missing. We have this individual checking into a hotel in North Adelaide called 'Montenegro', on the same day as the flight, and then the trail goes cold."

"Well that sounds promising. Definitely worth investigating further. But I've got another idea DCI Bilson, particularly as it seems we might now be chasing after someone who's using a fake identity."

"Go on," said Tania.

"Might I suggest we broadcast an invitation for people in the public to come forward? If only one person saw him, that would give us a possible starting point. We've supplied you with good images of him that were taken around about the time of his disappearance."

"I think that's a good idea," said Tania Bilson, surprising Kaz with her new enthusiasm. "Belinda, we need to make a production out of this with the help of our PR unit. I think what's needed is a commercial quality Holo Vid—you know the sort of thing, persuasive voice-over, plenty of images, dramatic soundtrack, a brief outline of the circumstances surrounding his disappearance and recent discovery. PR has plenty of agencies on their books who know how to make this sort of impact. We need the widest possible community response! You can work with Kaz on this and aim to have it to air in the next couple of days if possible."

"You think that's a realistic timeframe?" It didn't sound like it to Kaz.

Bilson nodded. "Do you have a problem with it?"

Kaz shook her head. The last thing she needed was to get roped in as a de-facto film producer, but it was also important to reach the public as quickly as possible. "Happy to help, but there are a couple of things I'd like to look into further, including the pathologist in charge of the autopsy and the information you've also gleaned from the passenger lists," she said.

"Of course," Bilson said before dismissing them.

CHAPTER 7

The City Mortuary was within an old building at the end of Hindley Street on the western side of the City. The building gave no hint of its function in terms of signage and could only be identified by a street number. However, Kaz quickly discovered that there was very little connection between the external drab walls and inner space. As she came through a non-descript entrance lobby, she was jarred by the super clean, spacious and streamlined interior. The air had a chemical note, reminding her of a hospital. The lobbies were decorated with large murals depicting natural scenes in the Australian outback. Soft background music played in the waiting area, *no doubt designed to sooth the nerves of ordinary people confronting the identification of a loved one's body*, Kaz mused.

Luigi Curillo, Chief Pathologist for SA Criminal Investigations, was on the top level of the complex in one of a battery of offices lining an access gallery over the investigations floor. From there, Kaz could look down onto the work of pathologists, dissecting corpses in real time. An intercom system connected staff on both levels.

Curillo was a short man with curly brown hair, olive complexion and dark eyes that, together with his name, suggested Italian origins. A white lab coat hung from a hook behind his desk. He already had the Rowe file onscreen as Kaz was shown into his office. "I'll be with you in a moment," he said, gesturing for her to take a seat, while he continued reading something on the video in front of him. Finally, he turned his attention to her. "DCI Bilson's warned me to be circumspect and cooperative," he said with a smile. "What can I do for you?"

"In layman's terms how positive and why can you be certain the body you examined belonged to Rowe?" asked Kaz.

"Completely positive," he said without hesitation. "Our two main sources of data were Rowe's dental records and his DNA. Rowe's wife supplied some of Rowe's personal effects to the NSWPol including his toothbrush. They were handed over at the time of his original disappearance and analysed for DNA. Same for dental records. Both were positive matches with the samples we've been able to extract from the skeleton. We've also been given photographs of Rowe and the headshots clearly match the shape of the skull."

"Does his DNA match anyone else's DNA on your state records?"

Curillo, paused. "That's a very good question," he remarked finally. "But no. There's nobody else on our records who could be related to him. Which of course isn't to say there's no one in SA roaming around who is connected in some way to him and doesn't happen to be on our database."

"And the cause of death?"

"The skull did have a triangular shaped fracture in the temple, which was the most likely cause of death. It's only speculation of course, but I think it could have been the corner of say, a sharp-angled tabletop, rather than a weapon."

"You're suggesting his death might have been accidental?"

"It's possible but no way we can be certain. The fracture bears no resemblance to the damage caused by an axe or a hammer or the usual things I've come across in this line of work."

"Could he have sustained such a fracture by a simple fall?"

"I suppose so. If he was moving fast enough and lost his balance, or if he was pushed with sufficient force, that could have resulted in his injuries."

"Doesn't give us much to go on then, does it? There are no other traces which might help?"

Curillo shook his head slowly.

« »

The Montenegro Hotel was a small boutique establishment that had taken over one of the City's more prestigious heritage buildings in North Adelaide's Melbourne Street. In its heyday, Melbourne Street had been a centre for several small private art galleries, up-market restaurants and cafes. But as Kaz headed along the street, it seemed dingy and run down. A plethora of 'to let' notices, boarded up premises and footpaths badly in need of maintenance, confirmed that there was little left to appeal to the glitterati.

She finally reached her destination, a building dating from the Victorian era, showing obvious signs of wear and tear, set in formally landscaped grounds, with mature plane trees lining the once grand entrance way. Kaz walked into the high-ceilinged lobby. It had a faded yet calming atmosphere, with large rugs, period paintings mounted on white plastered walls and one or two indoor palms in large ornamental brass pots, drooping for want of attention. The Concierge's antique counter had once been a fine example of joinery built from local hardwoods but was now showing the patina of many years' use. A bellhop stood in attendance, wearing a smart uniform and pill-box cap like an extra from a 1920s film set.

"Could I speak to the manager?" she addressed a non-descript suit, stooping slightly over a display, intent on hotel business.

He glanced up with a half-smile. "Can I be of service?" he said obsequiously, "Michael Hannaford. I'm Hotel Manager. And you are?"

"Kaz Ingham, Special Investigator, currently assisting a SAPol murder inquiry."

She flashed her holo over a scanner, mounted at the front of his counter. "That should verify my credentials," she explained. "I'm hoping you may be able to help me track down a missing person. Our information suggests that he was travelling under the name of 'James Howard' some years back. He was travelling by air from Sydney to Adelaide on a date we've now verified. We have also found that this hotel recorded a guest by that name, on the SA hotel visitors' database. So I am hoping that you may be able confirm this from your own records. The person's name, as I've said, was James Howard and the date shown in the record was during the third week of June 2027."

"Good gracious. That's quite some time ago! But certainly, let me take a look. Perhaps you might care to take a seat or visit our café and wait in comfort," he indicated an arched opening in one corner of the lobby. "This might take a while, records as old as that are archived in one of our data warehouses. I will need to track down the right file location."

« »

Half an hour later, Hannaford found Kaz sitting patiently at a table engrossed in her holo. When he coughed to attract her attention, she shut it down carefully before looking his way. "Found anything?"

"Indeed I have," he said. "Actually, a 'James Howard' is in a couple of different places on our files for that period."

"Oh?"

"Yes, we do have a record of someone by that name staying here on the 24th of June, 2027. He booked a room for two nights having paid in advance. But that was actually the last this hotel ever saw of him."

A pulse of excitement caught Kaz by the throat. "He didn't check out?"

"No, apparently not. He paid, as I've said, and there were no amounts outstanding on his account. But on the day he was due to check out, our cleaning staff found his room still had all his clothes and papers unpacked. There was a suitcase, I believe, a computer and other personal effects scattered around. There's actually quite a file on this mystery man, but having skimmed through the records, there's nothing much more there to explain what happened to him."

"What does the hotel do in circumstances like that?"

"It's never happened during my management of this hotel. But I'd imagine it would have depended on how busy the hotel was at the time. According to our records, we left the room as it was for twenty four hours, which we wouldn't have done in a busier time if I'd been in charge. But he still didn't turn up. We reported this to the police and packed up all his effects. He never returned to the hotel to reclaim his luggage. We kept it in our baggage room for three weeks and finally sent it to the State Lost Property Office and never heard anything more."

"Did SAPol not have any interest in his whereabouts or belongings?"

"Didn't seem to. Nobody came forward to claim his stuff during those three weeks."

"I'd be particularly interested to see the computer?"

"State Lost Property's the place to start, but my guess is that it would be long gone. Here is a copy of our file entries and the receipt SLP gave us with their address on it. I believe they are still in the same location. Let me swipe the information for you."

She held out the holo she had been so engrossed in. He passed his own holo over hers, so that she could feel a slight vibration signifying new data had been received.

"Thank you. That's very helpful Mr Hannaford. I gather from what you're saying that this is unusual?"

"As I said, it's not occurred while I've been here, and in other hotels before that it was very uncommon. Usually *someone* comes to claim the things that have been left behind. Either there's been an accident or fatality, something like that. But in cases like these, where somebody disappears and nobody comes to reclaim the stuff." He paused, putting a finger absentmindedly against his chin. "Umm, to be honest I can't remember anything quite like that happening before."

"How long have you been at this hotel?"

"Only three years."

"Do you, by any chance, happen to know when the surveillance cameras were first installed? If there's any chance we might be able to identify him on the video when he checked in, we need to see it urgently."

"No idea. And it will take me quite some time to track that one down." He pulled out his holo to check her contact details. "I notice you have both NSW and SA contact details here, where should I send this information?"

"Send it to both links, I'm not sure how long I'll be here."

She fiddled with her own holo for a moment before putting it back in her purse, then turned to face him so that she was gaining his full attention. "Can I just say, Mr Hannaford, that your assistance in this matter is really vital to us. You may shortly be hearing an announcement in the media that we are trying to track down a NSW Cabinet Minister who went missing at the same time this mysterious gentleman was staying here. There are reasons to suppose the two were one and the same person. If we are able to corroborate the identity of your guest via any video you have on file, it would be of immense assistance to our inquiry."

"Of course, everything in our power to assist," he remarked without hesitation.

"Similarly, I believe that the NSW State Government is currently offering a significant reward for any information that would assist the police in trying to track down this man's killer. You may be aware, since it's been in the news, that this man, whose real name in all probability was Kevin Rowe, has recently been discovered murdered and buried in the Adelaide Hills. The likelihood is that the day he left here for the last time, he met his killer somewhere in Adelaide. The meeting could even have happened here in this hotel, for all we know. So you can understand why we are extremely keen to get our hands on your video," Kaz said softly. "And I'd be grateful also if you would keep what I've been telling you to yourself for now?"

"Of course, my lips are sealed." Hannaford said. His index finger had unconsciously gravitated to his cheek and began scratching it absently. "I'd also request that this hotel is not referred to in your announcements, I think it could be very bad for business."

"Strange. I'd have said the notoriety would have had the opposite effect, but I'll make sure your wishes are noted."

« »

DCI Bilson had graciously congratulated Kaz on what at first sight was a major break-through in the SA Inquiry. "You've done a great job," she said. "It's a lead which narrows our focus a lot."

Kaz suppressed the urge to ask why this, an obvious line of inquiry to her, had not been pursued earlier. But she now knew the prospects of linking Rowe with his killer from the hotel's video scanners were nil. "Unfortunately I've just learned from the Hotel Manager that their video system was installed six months after Rowe went missing, so that seems a dead end."

"What about the State Property Office?"

"All items are kept for a period of two years and then disposed of. They don't keep any records of the unclaimed items after that."

Bilson, her optimism, visibly deflated, stared at Kaz. "So, other than knowing when Rowe seems to have arrived here, we're still completely in the dark as to who Rowe came to meet and why. Maybe you and Belinda can check further into other street surveillance cameras in the vicinity of the hotel? There must be one that picks him up on the day we know he left the hotel?"

"I think that definitely is a possibility, but maybe it's something Belinda can manage without me?"

"Oh?"

"Actually, I think my time would be better spent back in NSW for now. Maybe the missing link actually lies in my state after all. I think the main chance I have there is with Rowe's family. They must know something and I'll have to follow that up in person. I'll come back if the public announcement produces something more positive here. Could you let me have a preview of your presentation before you put it to air? We may also want to broadcast it in NSW, although there may be an impact on Scanlan's appeal that could prevent our doing so. I'll let you know."

"I thought that you were going to help us produce it," Bilson remarked. She seemed disappointed.

"I have already given a suggested outline to Belinda and helped her decide who'd be best to produce it. It's not really my field in any case, and I can still liaise with you both via holo if need be."

Bilson didn't pursue the matter any further, nor assist her with travel plans. Kaz had a short meeting with DS Gotto to discuss her ideas about the follow-up work, and was gone within the hour, her bags already packed.

She was back in Sydney via MagRail in the late afternoon.

CHAPTER 8

Kaz wasted no time in scheduling a meeting together with DS Len Mannix at the family home of Lynne Rowe. The house, which was located in Wollstonecraft, was a large and intimidating edifice, without any windows facing the street. It presented an uninviting blank wall apart from the front door. "Quite a pile, you'd say?" offered Len. "Been here before. She hasn't moved since Rowe disappeared, when I had to talk to her about him going missing."

Kaz pressed an intercom panel.

A minute passed before they heard a voice asking them about their business.

"Kaz Ingham I'm attached to the NSWPol from Premier's and this is DS Len Mannix. We've come to talk to you about your late husband," she said. They both showed their warrant cards to the camera.

"I've only just had a visit from the police," came a voice. "Is this really necessary?"

"I'm afraid it is ma'am," said Len politely.

There was a long pause before they heard a click and the door opened.

Lynne was a tall woman who wore a scarf as a loose turban on her head and was clad in a baggy smock, covered in paint smears, and smelling strongly of thinners. "I'm in the middle of my entry for 'Sculpture by the Sea'," she explained. "Just doing the final clean up before having it boxed to take there in the next half an hour. It's definitely not the best time," she said, making no invitation for them to come in.

"We'll try our best not to delay you. I've read your interview files and just have a few more questions. It won't take long," said Kaz.

"So what is it this time? Let me guess, you have found something more about what happened to Kevin in Adelaide."

"Yes," Kaz said, surprised by Lynne's astuteness. "That's exactly the reason for this visit. I must apologise for the intrusion, and I've no idea how you must be feeling at this stage."

Lynne sighed and loosened up slightly. "Can you imagine having to go through all this horror yet again? The times I've lain awake at night wondering over and over why Kevin left without any explanation, just disappeared out of my life. I've spent years with a shrink helping me to deal with the uncertainty, the mess he left behind. It's taken me this long to come to terms with the realisation that I'm never going to see him again and now this! The only positive thing about the latest news is at last discovering it probably wasn't ever his intention to leave me behind." She paused to wipe the tears welling from her eyes with a piece of rag, leaving an angry smudge of paint on her cheek.

Kaz paused for several moments before gently resting a hand on her shoulder.

Len stayed standing in the background.

Lynne finally pulled herself together. "Well, you'd better come inside."

She seated Kaz and Len at a large table next to an open plan kitchen and started clattering around looking for cups and switching on the kettle. "Tea or coffee?"

"No thanks, just a glass of water."

"Same," said Len.

Lynne switched the kettle off, poured two glasses of water from a flask in the fridge and sat down beside them at the table. "Let's get this over with then."

"Mrs Rowe…"

"Please call me 'Lynne'."

"Lynne, I need to explain a couple of things to you first. We are now sure that Scanlan, the man who was stalking your husband and was convicted of his murder, is certain to be exonerated. The evidence so far is that Kevin, if I may call him that?" Lynne nodded. "It appears he went to South Australia and stayed at a hotel in Adelaide on the day he arrived. He didn't check out of the hotel and it's likely that he didn't make use of his return ticket from Adelaide back to Sydney. His remains have been discovered and his identity confirmed in Adelaide, as you've already been informed. But we have absolutely no idea what he was doing there. Can you think of any reason at all? Do you have any friends or relatives in SA he might have wanted to see? Did he give any intimation that he was heading interstate? Did…"

"No I've already been over this, years ago!" Lynne interrupted, irritated. "Until the morning he left here, there was no suggestion he had any other plans than to conduct his normal parliamentary business in his Sydney office. We have no friends or relatives in Adelaide that I'm aware of." Lynne clutched her hands before her chest.

"You're quite sure of that?"

"Absolutely certain, none!" Her right hand clutched her left so hard the whites of her knuckles were showing.

Len had got up from the table and gazed at some paintings on the wall, a series of watercolours of the immediate harbour and bushland. "These yours?" he asked, nonchalantly.

She nodded, without any particular pride. "Painting used to be my passion. Now it's sculpture, which I really must get back to, so if you don't mind..."

Kaz caught the cue. "Well we mustn't keep you. That was really all we wanted to ask. If by any chance you do remember something that you might have forgotten, even the tiniest seemingly unimportant detail, please call me. Let me have your holo for a second, I can give you my contact details."

Lynne distractedly fumbled through a bag that had been thrown onto a side table and finally produced her holo for Kaz to flash.

As Lynne put her holo back into the bag, Kaz said to her, "any information you do have on this could be critical, and at the moment we're completely in the dark as to what your late husband was doing in Adelaide. And we are also concerned that there is an unknown killer at large."

Lynne had regained her composure and seemed relieved that her interview was over. She got up without adding anything further to what she'd said. "Well, I must get back to my packing," she said, as she led the two to the door.

It closed behind them with a thud.

CHAPTER 9

"We can't put a tap on her holo *or* search her house!" Stewart fumed. The press'd have a field day, if it got out somehow. *Police insensitivity towards grieving widow.* Find some other way," he snarled. "Check her holo records if you must, but I'm not going to approve it!"

"You've got to. I'm certain she's lying. She could be in cahoots with the killer for all we know," argued Kaz.

"Get real! That's the most stupid suggestion I've ever heard. There's no evidence other than your single interview and her hesitation to answer some questions, which I'd have thought completely understandable."

"You've got no choice, I'm telling you. I've already discussed this with my boss Tarding in Premiers and he agrees. In fact he's signed the authorisation."

Stewart stared at her stunned. "How dare you go behind my back without checking with me first!"

"Because for some strange reason I've felt I'm not getting your whole-hearted support in this inquiry," Kaz replied sarcastically.

"Get out of my office! I'm taking this up with Tarding. It might be easy for you and him to play games with us, but I'm the one that carries the can. You'll have no more cooperation from me on the Rowe investigation until this is sorted."

The moment Kaz had left his office, Stewart got up and locked his door. He pulled out his holo and selected a contact.

"Hello? Who is this?"

"Lynne, it's Stewart Richardson. I've just learned that two of my officers have been to interview you. It happened without my authorisation and I'm concerned that they may have been heavy-handed?"

"That woman, Kaz Ingham, belongs to you? She's been asking all these questions, as though I'm somehow responsible for Kevin's disappearance!"

"That's probably going a bit far. But they shouldn't have interviewed you without discussing it with me first. Confidentially, Ingham needs careful handling. If I had a free hand, things might be different, but unfortunately she has the ear of the premier's top adviser. You and I must be careful with our future communications."

"What do you mean, Stewart?"

"It's quite simple. If it became more widely known that Kevin, you and I were close friends and I remained in contact with you since his disappearance, some might draw a wrong conclusion about our relationship, or more likely, pull me off the investigation on the grounds of a perceived conflict of interest."

Stewart waited to hear her response, but several seconds passed before there was a long sigh. "Stewart, that's nonsense. We *are* close friends and I'm very fond of you. But I can hold my head high and so can you. There is absolutely nothing for us to feel guilty about."

"That's true, but the sad reality is that the gutter press might believe otherwise, and the fact that we're friends must remain secret. Now, what I'm about to say is also strictly off the record."

Rodney Jensen

"Are you sure you should be telling me then, Stewart?"

"Yes, you need to understand why I'm concerned. If Ms Ingham had her way, we'd be tapping all your communications. She's actually gone over my head to get authorisation, but I have nipped it in the bud, or at least I hope I have."

"You've got to be joking!"

"Unfortunately not. But as I said, I think I've stopped that happening. From now on I just want you to be careful about what you say to anyone about Kevin's disappearance, particularly as there are some fresh developments in our inquiries. If you get any calls from the media, or anyone else for that matter, it's best to say that the matter is subjudice, and you have no comment."

Lynne sighed again. "I really think you are over-reacting Stewart. But I suppose you know more about these things than I do and have a right to be cautious, for both our sakes. I promise not to say a word to anybody."

"Thanks Lynne. I hope I won't need to bother you again about this."

« »

Kaz sat down at her desk, shell-shocked by Stewart's outburst, a side of him she hadn't seen before. The whole office had heard him too. Len walked past her workspace and dropped a slip of paper in front of her, making no eye contact. It read: *Go for a walk and let him calm down. Meet me at the Ajax Café in 20 minutes.*

« »

It was only just after opening time and the small café was devoid of any other customers. A woman was in the process of straightening out tables, as Kaz chose a table in the corner of the room, out of sight of passers-by.

Len waited until his coffee arrived to say anything, fidgeting with the menu for what seemed an interminable time before coming to the point. "Look," he said. "This is strictly between us," He put a finger on his nose. "I'm only telling you because if you don't change your ways, you'll be out of our office on your arse, whatever State's asking us to do. Wouldn't look great on your resume?"

It wasn't what Kaz wanted to hear. "What is it about you people? You know perfectly well the woman's lying and now you want me to help cover it up!"

Len kept his cool. "Listen, I know she's lying, but I don't think it's connected with Kevin Rowe. See there's something you don't know and it might cost Stewart his job if it got out."

It took a moment for Len's words to sink in. "*You're not telling me…?*"

Len nodded slowly. "He's been having an affair with the woman—"

"But I thought you meant something else—woman—what woman?"

"Lynne."

Kaz gasped. "No?"

"Yes, I'm afraid so."

"For how long?"

He shrugged. "About a year after Rowe went missing, I reckon."

"Was he somehow connected with Rowe himself, while he was still alive?"

"They once belonged to the same club in town, went to school together too. Rowe probably helped him get promoted—he *is* much younger than most other DCIs."

Kaz stared at her coffee for a moment, allowing the information to sink in. "But Mrs Rowe? How do you know that?"

"Accidentally, as it happens. I was called to a case nearby. It was a few years ago when I was working in North Sydney Command, same time as Stewart, well before we moved here. He had a distinctive car, chosen it himself. Unmarked of course, but distinctive. It was a dark purple-blue Falcon and there were very few of them around in that particular colour. I was on night shift. It was very early in the morning as I drove past the Rowe place. Her house was on our watch list, so I knew it right enough. I spotted his car parked right outside her house. It was his number plate for sure. He'd been careless—instead of parking it in a side street, there it was in full view. I was gob-smacked. That time of night, there could only be one conclusion."

Kaz was silent, stunned.

"Since then," Len continued. "I've been wary about anything to do with her. Any need for follow up, questioning, any reports connected with her—I leave 'em alone. But you in your wisdom have gone and trampled all over it now."

"I suppose they became close after Rowe disappeared, given Stewart's friendship with her husband?"

"That's my guess. Being a detective it wasn't difficult for me to make a couple of background checks and satisfy myself that there was no other explanation. That was when I found out that the boss and Rowe had been at the same school together. Then everything fell into place."

Kaz thought through the possibilities. "Do you think he's in the frame? He wanted Rowe out of the way? He would have had a motive, wouldn't he?"

"I can understand you're thinking that, but no, not possible, I've checked. He was away on a Police Conference in Canberra at the time Rowe went missing."

"So where does this leave us?"

Len scratched his jaw absently and took a sip of his cappuccino before answering. "When you asked Lynne about any Adelaide connection, that's when I knew there was something more she wasn't saying. But the thing I can't get my head around, is the possibility of her being responsible for her husband's murder. She's stood by him through thick and thin, including the time things went pear-shaped for him with the financial meltdown. She wasn't lying about her loss. Genuine enough, if I'm any judge of character," he continued. "But—and there's a big 'but'—normally, searching the place and following up her holo records and such would be an obvious line, and I'm sure the boss would've approved it, if nothing else to eliminate her from the frame. But he's involved with the woman—he can't see straight. Who would, given the mess he's put himself in? So if I was you, I'd be wary right now. When you go back to the office you're best off apologising and letting sleeping dogs lie until you can come up with some real evidence and not guesswork."

"Okay. That sounds like good advice, thanks for being open with me about this. Coffee's on me."

Len smiled. "Don't worry about that. You can buy me a drink on Friday instead."

"Oh? What's the occasion?"

"It's my fiftieth as a matter of fact. I've invited everyone in the office, plus some other mates to help me celebrate at the Palace Arms. It's not far from here. We've got a private room booked. Stewart's coming by the way, so it might give you a chance to get back in his good books."

« »

Kaz found Len's party on an upper floor at the Palace Arms, where everyone could meet and talk freely. Len spotted her as she came in, wandered over and shouted in her ear. "Put your purse away. There's a tab at the bar. Have what you like."

"I've brought you a little something," Kaz shouted over the din and handed him a small package.

"You shouldn't have, but that's sweet of you. I won't open it now, if that's all right. I'll put it on the chair here with the other things. Now let's get you a drink. What would you like?"

"Vodka cruiser, lemon lime, please." Kaz followed Len to the bar and waited until he'd handed her the drink.

"Mmm. That hit the spot," she remarked sipping slowly. "Is Stewart here? I haven't seen him," she asked in as casual a way as possible. The quicker they got back into friendly territory the better.

"Er yeah, I think so," he said vaguely. "Look, there—he's on the stage. You've got to give the man some credit!"

Kaz followed Len's pointing finger and noticed Stewart in the far corner of the room bravely harmonising with a 3-D virtual lead singer. Kaz recognised the performer as 'Hudson Michael', still in his mid '20s, he originated from humble beginnings in Parramatta, claimed to have written the hit song 'Revesby Rita', and was a finalist in the Whammy Global Song Contest.

"Let's take a closer look!" she pulled Len by the sleeve.

"No, you go," he said. "I wouldn't want to hamper the boss's style."

Kaz couldn't resist the opportunity to take a closer look at the new 'Yoki' system, claimed to have spawned quite a few famous names, including Hudson's, from the privacy of their own home systems.

Stewart was really getting into the song too, swaying to the pounding beat and singing enthusiastically, even when his voice had to hit a few high notes. As she looked more closely, she realised, compared with Karaoke, Yoki provided a far more sophisticated aid to performance. It not only had the usual song sheet to follow but there was also a background singer, cleverly programmed using artificial intelligence to fill in when a try-hard like Stewart stumbled with his song lines.

It made his performance convincing enough to satisfy his mates, who erupted with loud applause at Stewart's final warbling words

> "…And Rita lay, crying and dying,
>
> In the arms of Revesby's black heart."

"Well done, Stewart!" Kaz said to him, clapping and laughing.

Stewart seemed taken aback by her enthusiastic attention. "I didn't see you Kaz, thanks!" Obviously having drunk a few, he stumbled closer.

"I didn't know you could sing like that. It sounded great—but don't give up your day job!" she added softly, determined to make him feel more relaxed and at ease with her.

He laughed in spite of himself. "You and Mr Tarding can relax. I won't be putting it as a speciality in my work experience!"

"Can I get you a drink sir? It looks like your glass is empty."

"It's 'Stewart', no need for formality here. Yes I would like a drink. A schooner of the local draft will do fine."

CHAPTER 10

Kaz spent the weekend with Stewart on her mind. She tried to distract herself by booking a session down at the special gun range and training facility. Len's remark at Pittwater Glades had piqued her interest in the latest gun technology, but there wasn't an immediate slot available. So she walked to the gym, did her standard work-out and walked back home, took a shower and felt a bit more relaxed.

But it wasn't long before she found herself putting things away out of habit, trying to neaten the mess in her house. An overriding sense of wanting to get out of her four walls returned. She decided to take a look at the newly re-built technology museum, sited on the river in central Parramatta. It had just re-opened with some fanfare, after its ground level, along with some of the most fascinating old tech systems on display, had been seriously damaged by major flooding five years earlier.

Try as she might, her mind wasn't on any of the displays. It kept wandering back to Stewart, as she distractedly listened to the holographic reconstruction of a 200 year old working beam pump, in a re-imagined copper mine in Burra, in South Australia's 1850s. As she watched the restored hissing behemoth slowly going through its paces, Len's party came back to her. There she'd seen a different, more relaxed side to Stewart.

After she brought him a drink, they'd spoken more about the Yoki system, the latest Whammy Global Song Contest, discovering they'd wanted the same contestant to win last year. Then they'd talked about their favourite television shows (a case where they were most at odds), their favourite places overseas and others on their bucket lists, where they grew up and where they hoped to retire. They had more in common than she'd expected, and, under any other circumstances, she might have considered a relationship with him, particularly when he had his defences down and stopped treating her as a mere underling.

Len's revelation that Stewart had been having an affair with Lynne, though, got her thinking about him in a different way. What else was he hiding?

She let Len's advice sit for nearly a week, until she felt she could no longer let the issue of Lynne, a key witness in her investigation, continue unresolved. Then, at the end of her normal shift, she tapped on Stewart's door. He beckoned her in and she sat down at his desk.

"Sir, I'm sure you have your reasons for not wanting me to put Lynne under the microscope, and I'm sorry that I upset you last week. But there's something I want to ask you. To be honest, I got the feeling that there's more to this than you're telling me. And I have to know. So I'll ask—have you somehow been connected with Kevin Rowe or Lynne Rowe in the past? Your opposition to my bugging suggestion seemed like there was more to it? Am I right?"

Stewart cleared his throat fiddled with his papers and then looked Kaz straight in the eyes. "Firstly, when we are by ourselves, you can call me 'Stewart'. But secondly, it sounds like someone's been talking to you about me?"

Kaz was taken aback. It was as though he had helped her to relax her guard, while sliding a knife into her. She paused wondering what on earth to say. "Possibly, but it was in confidence."

"Aha!" he said with a wry grin of satisfaction. "Okay, I suppose I must consider myself sprung! So I'm going to be straight with you then. Yes, I was friends with Kevin in the past before he disappeared and, in all honesty, he helped me get my promotion to this office. My wife and I used to know the two of them socially and we sometimes dined together. My late wife was a close friend of Lynne's. And after she died, there were one or two occasions when I stayed over at Lynne's house because she needed company and I'd had too much to drink, as you do sometimes! But completely innocent, nothing happened, hand on heart, conscience clear."

"I didn't know you had a wife?"

"It's not the type of thing you mention in the pub. And it was quite a long time ago now. She was diagnosed with breast cancer and died within twelve months. I haven't remarried. No one's measured up to her and my life revolves around my job these days. So that's why I get angry when you talk about bugging Lynne, because I know she's a very honourable woman and if there were some things she was unwilling to talk about with you or Len, I'm quite confident there was a good reason for it. I think the best thing would be for you to come straight out with it and ask her yourself."

Rodney Jensen

"Thank you for being so candid about this Stewart, I feel now that it's my turn to apologise. I've put you in an awkward position and I'm sorry for that. And I will definitely follow up your suggestion when another opportunity presents itself."

She paused and drew a breath. "Now this might seem a little presumptuous of me, but my boss Jock Tarding has just given me some tickets for the next performance of Mozart's 'Don Giovanni' at the Opera House, which he couldn't use because he and his wife will be overseas. It's next Friday night. Do you like classical music or opera? Could I tempt you to join me, as an apology?"

Stewart raised his eyebrows and smiled. "Well let me think. I must say, apart from the odd birthday, I avoid fraternising with my staff, male or female; but I do happen to love opera. As a matter of fact, I've noticed there's a curious association in some classic detective novels between their main players and a love of opera music."

Kaz laughed. "You're not that different from the rest of us surely?" she said, risking an even greater familiarity than she'd dared before.

Stewart could not help laughing despite his normal reserve. "Bugger it! I'll make an exception for you and thank you very much for the offer."

« »

During the following week, Kaz felt she might have mistimed her invitation to Stewart and given him too long to reconsider and was surprised how much it meant to her that he'd agreed to come. She left work early on the night of the performance, on some pretext or other and spent an afternoon at her hairdresser, before going through every dress in her wardrobe and making sure that her makeup was elegant but not overstated.

They had arranged to meet in the Opera House Bar and Kaz's AutoCab was held up by traffic. It was only five minutes to opening when she swept into the bar to discover Stewart chatting with someone she didn't recognise. She was about to tap him on the shoulder to catch his attention when he looked up, with an expression of surprise as he saw her. "Kaz, you look fantastic. I hardly recognised you."

Kaz sensed that he was slightly embarrassed by the interest his friend was showing at her sudden appearance, judging by the way he was staring at her. *Did this person know Stewart's late wife?*

Kaz could barely resist nudging Stewart, as he stood there awkwardly, seemingly lost for words. She suddenly guessed he had forgotten his friend's name. "I'm Kaz by the way, DCI Richardson's gofer. He lets me out occasionally," she said holding out her hand.

"George," he said, introducing himself. "I'm just another copper who loves opera."

The bell started ringing and people were already drifting away from the bar. "We'd better move. I was beginning to worry," said Stewart to Kaz, before turning back to his friend. "Maybe catch you after the performance, George?"

The other nodded, a quizzical expression on his face.

« »

Kaz never did get to find out more about George, who was forgotten by the time they came out into the foyer after the conclusion of the opera to an ecstatic audience.

Kaz was feeling relaxed and uninhibited by their work relationship. "That really moved me, there's nothing like a quality live performance to tap into your feelings, is there?"

"Wonderful, completely wonderful. It's a very long time since I've enjoyed an evening so much." Stewart's voice tailed off, a sense of awkwardness returning. Kaz could guess what might be going through his mind and felt it was time to take the initiative.

"It *was* amazing. I must remember to send some flowers with a thank you note to Jock and his wife when they come back from their travels. But listen, we can't just go home to the real world, straightaway, can we?" she asked. "Do you feel up for a stroll?"

Stewart's face brightened. "Why don't we wander down to Macquarie Place and find somewhere for a drink or supper?"

They found a bar called "The Crossing" in Bridge Street and settled in a corner where they both ordered coffees.

"So, Kaz, if I may call you that?"

"Of course," she smiled.

"I'm intrigued about your invitation. Really you had no need to share such a fantastic performance as an apology. But how come you didn't invite a friend? A boyfriend, perhaps?"

"Boyfriend? No, don't even get me started on my boyfriends."

"You have more than one?"

She chuckled. "No, I don't have *any* at present—every time I find someone I like, they can't handle the job I have, what that entails—the late hours, the phone calls, all that. They want me to be available irrespective of what I've got on. But it's usually the case that I'm busy at work and can't just drop everything to fit in with them. Well, you know how it is."

"I do." He sighed. "My late wife, God bless her soul, found it hard too. But she understood."

There was something in his voice that made Kaz want to weep. "She was a rare find?"

"She was. It wasn't easy to pick up the pieces she left behind."

"And have you now, picked up your pieces?"

"I have."

"Still, it will take you all the luck in the world to find another woman like her."

"Maybe not all the luck." He smiled at her, his eye contact suggestive, almost flirtatious.

Kaz felt her cheeks flush and looked away. *Be careful,* a persistent voice inside her head was warning. *Keep this professional. This man could easily break your heart.* "It's getting late," she murmured, once she'd found her voice.

"Well, I suppose we both need our beauty sleep. I'll get the bill."

"Not sure where you live, but can I escort you home?" Stewart said as they emerged from the bar and arrived at the edge of the footpath. There were still several people standing around waiting for AutoCab pick-ups.

Kaz felt flattered and amused by his unexpectedly gracious offer. "No I couldn't let you do that. I'm sure it's right out of your way?"

"Well, I live in King's Cross—what about you?"

"Surry Hills close to Crown Street."

"There you are then! No distance at all. Let's go!"

« »

Stewart helped her in to the next available AutoCab and within no time they were whisked across the CBD to Kaz's street. Stewart set the AutoCab on hold, took her by her arm and walked her to her front entrance.

Kaz wondered whether to ask him in but decided that might seem a bit forward. "Thank you for seeing me home. I very much enjoyed the evening, and I hope we can do it again?"

He gave her a gentle peck on her cheek and squeezed her arm. "Thank you Kaz, I've really enjoyed your company too, and I'm intending to organise something similar very soon."

"Good night, Stewart." With that she opened the door and let herself into her apartment, feeling a frisson of regret, but judging that a softly-softly approach was the better way to go.

CHAPTER 11

Kaz was in the gym, in the basement of the NSW Premiers Office. She had a set routine to keep her muscles in good shape, particularly her tummy, which she'd always taken pride in being flat. She was in the middle of an old-fashioned exercise known as 'the plank', where she would hold her body in a static position, as though she was doing a press up. She would lie face down on the floor, her body stretched flat and rigid as a plank, supported only by her forearms, elbows and her toes. She had built up her strength, so that she could hold this position for well over two minutes. She'd learned to progressively extend her limit by emptying her mind of day-to-day distractions, while ignoring her quivering and protesting abdominal muscles.

Without warning, in the middle of her reverie, the image of Stewart Richardson's face and body swam into view beneath her. He seemed to be lying there on her mat, with a smile on his face, relaxed and ready to embrace her in his arms. He was naked and his trim body was taut. His chest had a forest of curly black hair; his mouth was close enough to kiss. Her pelvis was just brushing his penis. Her body was shaking and she could feel herself growing wet. He seemed so near, yet so far. She finally gave up and subsided to the mat with a groan.

She clambered shakily to her feet and reached for a towel, colouring red and hoping that nobody who might have been watching her performance could read her thoughts.

Rodney Jensen

Kaz had been back at the State Government offices for several days, since her work on the Rowe case had come to a standstill. New South Wales had its own high priorities and she had temporarily forgotten about Rowe. The trail had gone cold, and police on both sides of the border were no nearer to finding any leads on Rowe's killer. Despite SAPol issuing a highly professional announcement, the responses had been muted across all the media. It was hardly surprising that the discovery of the body of a missing cabinet minister of a NSW government nearly ten years before had done little to arouse interest in South Australia, particularly as the Festival of Culture, an annual event with a proud history, was seizing all the attention at that time.

And there were more personal reasons for taking a break from the Parramatta office—Stewart had shown signs of awkwardness around her, making it increasingly difficult to concentrate while waiting for new leads in the inquiry. When Tarding invited her to come back for a while to help out on the Armidale project which had been left in abeyance and was now becoming critical, she seized the opportunity, albeit with an equally difficult challenge to deal with: Jock Tarding.

But her respite was short-lived. Tarding surprised her one morning as she was reviewing some financial projections. "SAPol want you back," he said, coming into her office, "to listen in on an interview. They're saying it's important, could be the breakthrough we're looking for. You'd better pack your bags. You're booked on the afternoon MAG. The interview's tomorrow morning, I'm told."

Kaz saved what she'd been reviewing and rose to her feet. "I'm on my way."

« »

Kaz shook the man's hand which felt moist and noticed he had difficulty looking her in the eye. "Adams," he introduced himself. He was middle aged, with grey wavy hair, a creased face and steel-rimmed spectacles. There was awkwardness about the way he carried himself, nearly knocking over a potted plant as he came further into the room. He was carrying a travel-weary brown leather briefcase, looking even older than him, hugging it under one arm like it contained the crown jewels.

She introduced him to Gotto, then invited him to take a seat. To Gotto and Kaz's surprise, Bilson had previously asked her to lead the interview. She agreed, provided that Gotto would be doing more than simply listening in.

"Shall we begin?" Kaz asked him.

He nodded, fixated on Kaz to the extent that no other person existed in the room, then started the interview himself without warning and without being asked, expecting Kaz to know what the context was and what he was talking about.

"It was him on the plane. Same face for sure. Sat next to each other. Told him about my work. He wasn't interested in the job they were offering me in Adelaide. Though I shouldn't have been talking about it—you know, thought I could, disinterested party wouldn't matter, like he could advise me whether to accept, seemed smart enough."

"What made you think him smart…?" Kaz tried to interrupt his flow.

"He was smart, no doubt about it," he brushed off the question. "When we touched down he was out of his seat and off. Not a goodbye, nothing, no offer of help to get my bag out of the locker, he was in the aisle and off he went, the prick. Well I followed, got to the luggage hall, and there he was, right in front of me again, but he didn't notice. He had a holdall on the carousel, he grabbed it and was off. I thought it was the last I'd see of him, but coming out of the airport to join the queue for the AutoCabs, there he was again, not in the queue, just waiting outside the exit door. Then someone came up to him and they shook hands. They both looked like they'd not met before, appeared awkward. Didn't seem like the sort of person I'd have expected him to be meeting. Didn't see him again after that. The other one had an AutoCab waiting for them. They got in and were off."

"What made you think the person he met was not one you'd have expected?" Kaz asked.

"Good question, good question, good question," he muttered obsessively. "Difficult, can't remember now. It was a strong feeling I had, very strong. Maybe it was that the other man wasn't wearing business clothes like him."

"How did this man he met look then?"

"He was younger, much younger, I'd say. He didn't seem happy at all. Neither of them did, that was clear. The passenger I sat next to on the plane was definitely not keen on getting into the AutoCab with him. It was difficult to guess why, but the young man practically had to push him in."

"You seem to remember a lot about someone you'd only met briefly," Kaz said.

"I remember things. Always do. Details you wouldn't imagine. I see patterns sometimes. Nobody understands it. I can't explain. It's just the way I am."

Kaz showed him a photograph of Rowe taken ten years earlier. It was similar to the one that had been used in the public announcement. "Is that the person you were sitting next to, then?"

Adams hardly glanced at the image. "Positive, no, doubt about it."

"And why has it taken you so long to come forward and tell us this? When Rowe first went missing nearly ten years ago, there were similar photographs like this in the paper asking for help to find his whereabouts? Didn't you see them then?" Gotto asked angrily.

"No, of course not. I wouldn't have, would I? I was overseas. Had the interview in Adelaide. Left the next day, 'cos they told me I hadn't been successful. No point in hanging around in Adelaide, or Sydney for that matter. Back to Timor base camp where I've been working on an oil and gas rig. That's why we got talking."

"You mean Rowe?" Kaz asked. Adams nodded impatiently.

"Mentioned he knew Indonesia himself. Embassy or something, I think. But he wasn't interested in me after that."

"Can you tell me more about the young man he met? What did he look like? You say you can remember details we can't begin to understand. Do you think you could draw this man with the help of one of our Identi-kit programs?"

"Suppose so. I'm an engineer, not an artist of course, but there was one thing that struck me most and I do remember that?"

"Go on?"

"It was like they were complete strangers, the way they acted: awkward, uncomfortable unfriendly. But the look of them both could've been father and son. Not only their faces, but gestures. That's why I remember. I don't know why, but I felt sorry for the young man. It's like he wanted something and wasn't getting it."

"Remarkable," said Gotto as an aside to Kaz while absently pulling at her hair in a gesture of frustration. "His memories are too good to be true, bordering on completely unbelievable." Then adding to Adams, "I can't help feeling that either you know a lot more than you're telling us, or you're the sort of person who loves being important in your normally empty life. You've made the whole of this lot up. That's it isn't it? You never were on that plane, were you?"

Gotto's annoyance blew over Adams' head totally unnoticed. "That's easily proved. I kept my flight details, I always did for tax reasons. You can even see my seat number and check the passenger who was sitting next to me."

"We already think we know what flight Rowe was on and the seat he was occupying. Have you by any chance got those details with you? Your boarding pass, perhaps?"

Adams fumbled in his briefcase and pulled out a folder of papers. Sorted through them and triumphantly waved a dog-eared pass in their faces. "Check that out," he said triumphantly.

Kaz took one look at the pass, and sat back in her chair with a curious expression on her face. She leaned forward finally. "Interview terminated," she said switching off the recording machine.

"Thank you very much for your help with this, Mr Adams. It appears that you have verified your meeting with Rowe and we now have to ask you to help our artist develop a likeness of this person Rowe met. I can't stress how important this information is, and how grateful we both are that you have come forward. I trust that you will not have been offended by my colleague," she said turning to Gotto warningly, "but you must understand that we have already received numerous crank calls, for want of a better word, and we naturally have to be sceptical of the things people tell us. Come with me and I'll introduce you to our expert facial recognition artist, a whizz with the software, I'm told. You may think yourself no artist, but believe me, he can turn you into one!"

"I'll do what I can," Adams muttered and walked out of the room without saying anything more to either of them.

<< >>

The attempt to develop any meaningful portrait from Adams proved fruitless. "It's been too long," explained

Rodney Jensen

Gerry Schmidt, the SAPol face artist. "And I don't think Adams was ever near enough to our target to get a close look at his face. He said that it was his overall bearing, height and gestures that made him think they could be related. We tried a few ideas, but the moment they started going from outline to something more definitive he backed off immediately saying it just wasn't working."

"Well where do we go from here? Kaz asked. "It's so frustrating being so near to tracking this fellow down. He must have been involved in Rowe's disappearance. I'm certain of it."

"I do have one idea for you. It's also a longshot but maybe worth a try," said Schmidt. "How about going through the airport's surveillance footage and see if there's any record of the meeting that took place? I'd imagine that pick up area would have been on camera, don't you think?"

"I'll get on it," said Gotto. "Good idea, I'm sure you're right. I know they scan all the public areas, I've noticed them myself. Airport Security will know how far back they keep their recordings."

« »

Kaz called Stewart with some trepidation. She'd hardly spoken to him in the office since their opera evening. But letting him know directly what was happening with the inquiry would help relieve an itch that wouldn't go away.

Does he really like me, or is he going to stifle any feelings he might have because he's not ready for another relationship, let alone with someone in his own office?

She picked up her holo, keeping it in *voice only* mode. "Sir, I just thought I'd like to keep you in the loop with what I'm up to here in Adelaide. We've found a definite contact with someone who sat beside Rowe on the plane to Adelaide, the day his wife last saw him."

"Kaz please, it's 'Stewart' when we're not being overheard. It's really nice to hear your voice. And it looks like you are making real headway with the case. I've already seen the report of interview."

"Yes, I was quite excited and thought that we might be onto a real suspect. But now we haven't had any luck identifying who it was Rowe met when he landed, it seems like we're back to square one."

"That's nearly always the way, Kaz. You've just got to keep at it. When you get back I want you to take the initiative in tracking the killer down, even more than you have already. We'll have a joint session with SA and plan our next moves together."

"Fine," said Kaz. "I'm intending to follow up with Rowe's wife Lynne again. This Adelaide connection cannot be something she's completely unaware of, you'd think?"

The line went quiet again.

"You still there, Stewart?"

"Yes, we'll need to tread very warily with that one. There's been absolutely no question of her involvement of any kind in his disappearance. You'll have to check with me first about what you're intending to ask her, given the sensitivities."

"Okay Stewart, I have been intending to discuss it with you, which is partly the reason for this call."

"Let's wait until you get back and can involve Len as well…"

There was another long pause. "Stewart?"

Kaz felt her pulse rise, wondering what he was about to say. "Kaz I wanted to tell you how much I enjoyed being with you the other evening."

"Yes, I enjoyed getting to know you a little better too. It was good that we seem to have a lot in common apart from our tastes in popular vid broadcasts," she responded, wanting to lighten things up.

"I think you're a most unusual person. And I haven't felt so together in a very long time. I think without even trying particularly, you've made a real impression on me."

"I feel the same Stewart, but at the same time we should be careful if we wanted to take this further. You know how people can talk. We could both lose our jobs if we are indiscreet about our feelings."

"Yes, it goes without saying that while we're in the office, or in public for that matter, we'll have to treat each other exactly as we always have, how should I say…"

"With cold professionalism."

"Exactly. Couldn't have expressed it better myself." Then he went quiet again.

"You still there, Stewart?"

"Yes, I'm just thinking about all this. The implications…"

"Are you sure that you're ready for *us*? I can understand if you say 'no'."

"It's just difficult to take in what is happening to me. It's like we've crossed a line. And once it's been crossed there's no turning back, is there?"

"Relax, Stewart, we're not talking about marriage here—just a few more dates perhaps? Then we'll see how we feel. The expression 'Life is not a dress rehearsal' might sound like a platitude, but it applies to both of us doesn't it? I do understand the ground rules we have to operate under, but let's not allow them to make things so impossible that we don't even give *us* a chance."

"Okay, Kaz. I'll continue what I was going to say." Stewart's voice had regained its composure, as though he'd made his mind up. "There's a play coming up soon in a theatre not far from the office—the Riverside West. Would you like to come and see it with me?" I can give you the details when you get back from South Australia.

It was Kaz's turn to catch her breath and centre herself. "Stewart, I'd love to.' She paused, thinking what to say next. "In all honesty, I wouldn't really care what it was you were inviting me to see. But you understand that don't you?"

"Yes, I feel the same, although uncharacteristically nervous!"

Kaz laughed. "For someone who routinely confronts murderers and various other difficult professional obstacles, I'm not sure whether I should take that as a compliment!"

"Point taken. I hope the rest of your trip works out for you and look forward to catching up when you're back in the office. Take care, Kaz, I'm thinking of you."

Kaz closed the connection and stared into space, deep in thought.

CHAPTER 12

Kaz was back in Sydney the following morning, explaining to Len where the investigation had got to at the South Australian end. "While the Adelaide Flight Centre produced video recordings from several cameras of passenger movements, no luck" she told him disappointed. "We were able to work out the time Rowe and Adams arrived at Adelaide pretty accurately from Adams' boarding pass. I thought we were really onto him when I found video of him picking up his suitcase in the luggage hall. I was ninety-nine percent certain it was Rowe. There was also a second camera located over the AutoCab rank which showed Rowe less than five minutes later meeting someone else. But the man had his back to the camera the whole time. The footage was virtually useless for identification purposes, except for the clothes he was wearing, which were not exceptional in any way."

"What about the vehicle they got into?" Len asked.

"It was an AutoCab without any interior surveillance. In their wisdom, the South Australian State Government had recently banned surveillance cameras in taxis and AutoCabs on the basis that it's a 'breach of privacy'. So we're almost back to where we started, as far as this mystery man's concerned."

"So what do we have?" asked Len.

"The only thing we have now definitely proved is that Rowe travelled to Adelaide that morning. What's more, the date and time he checked into the Montenegro correspond pretty closely to the time the plane landed, allowing for him to collect his luggage, meet his contact and make the short trip into North Adelaide where the hotel's located. Mystery man could have dropped him there or gone in with him and then resumed a journey into the Adelaide Hills together with Rowe. Unfortunately, we've nothing to prove what happened once the two of them left the airport other than Rowe's check-in record at the hotel. It's as though his contact didn't want us to find him."

"I don't suppose he did," said Len. "Funny that!"

"Anyway, now that I'm back, I want to catch up with Mrs Rowe again, confront her with evidence of this meeting that occurred in Adelaide. Could it be a relative of Rowe's? Was Adams correct about that or was he dreaming. His inability to recall any details of the man for SAPol's identity artist, makes me wonder how much weight we should be putting on that suggestion."

"If she doesn't know about it, I reckon it'll scare the pants off her. If she does know, and for whatever reason doesn't want to talk about it, she's likely to stonewall. The only way to get around that is to avoid meeting in her house. Got to talk to her on neutral territory. Catch her when she's least expecting us—a place where she might prefer to give us enough to get rid of us and avoid being embarrassed in public."

Kaz nodded at this sage advice, before she remembered something. "What about 'Sculpture by the Sea'? She told us she had an entry for it. At the opening she'll be there for sure, after all that hard work." Kaz said.

"Brilliant, but when's the opening?"

They had a race to discover the date on their holos. Kaz won. "Shit it's on now! Let's go! We might still catch her."

« »

'Sculpture by the Sea 2035' was in full swing. Crowds of onlookers from far and wide had come to make their pilgrimage to view the world's most contemporary and original sculptures. The event, which had started in Sydney in the late nineties, now provided an extended presentation of sculpture in three dimensions, real and simulated, along the cliff top track between Bondi and Bronte. The official opening set the scene for special award-winning works, including the coveted SCULSEA Award for best entry—an award that would place the successful artist on the world map if they weren't already there.

The opening event was always held in the late afternoon rather than evening to avoid anyone who'd indulged in too much booze or other drugs from blundering over the cliffs. The setting, easily as impressive as the entries, was nevertheless perilous in places, with only a low safety fence separating incautious viewers from a one-way drop to the ocean fifty metres below.

Kaz and Len arrived just as the awards were being announced, within a large marquee crowded to capacity by artists, interested public and the media. The major prize was won by a local First Nation's sculptor, whose work fused traditional Country motifs with themes linked to contemporary local development pressures. It was all contained within a complicated walk-through installation and displayed to the audience as a series of holographic images, projected onto a centrally located dais.

"Looks more of a political statement than a work of art," Len remarked.

"It succeeded in getting the judges attention though, didn't it?" said Kaz.

At the conclusion of the ceremony, Kaz and Len found themselves propelled out of the marquee by the bevy of people talking excitedly and heading for the separate entertainment areas. One was for 'special guests' where champagne and canapés were delivered by a bevy of smartly dressed waiters.

"I haven't caught sight of Lynne yet," said Kaz.

"I don't think there's much chance we're going to catch her, whether she's here or not. Far too many people and some of them already headed off home I reckon," said Len gloomily.

"Let's check inside the marquee again. She may be hobnobbing with someone suitably prestigious," said Kaz with a trace of cynicism.

Len finally spotted her. "You've nailed it—there she is. She's talking to the judges."

"Naturally! Let's go and embarrass her shall we?"

"You've got a nasty streak, you know that? You can do the talking," said Len.

They sidled up behind Lynne and waited to catch her attention as soon as she'd finished her chat with one of the judges, who'd seemed only politely interested in what Lynne was telling him. Kaz tapped her on her shoulder.

Lynne turned away from the judge. It took her a moment to place her interrogators.

"Sorry to bother you again," Kaz said, "but there's been some fresh evidence which is really important. We need to ask you about it. Won't take a moment."

Her eyes narrowed to angry slits. "How dare you hound me like this? Do you realise how inappropriate it is?" she hissed in a low voice.

"It's important, otherwise we would not be here. Let's find a quiet place."

They walked together to a spot close to the service tent, from which normal guests were barred. Len flashed his police ID and they were admitted without any fuss.

"Well, what is it?" Lynne snapped. "This information that's so important you would ruin my chance of being recognised for *my* work for once?"

"Someone came forward," Kaz explained, "someone who saw your husband on the day you last saw him. He was sitting next to Kevin on a plane to Adelaide. The date corresponds to the time you reported him missing. Our contact recalled Kevin saying he'd worked in Indonesia once—he thought the Embassy was mentioned. He also said that he saw Kevin meet a young man in Adelaide who looked as if he could have been his son. We don't think this was entirely fanciful, because our informant was able to verify his own and your husband's flight details. Do you have anything to say?"

Lynne looked stunned, thinking what to say. "Yes, the first part's true, he did work in Indonesia, I think as military attaché at the Embassy or something like that.

Rodney Jensen

It was quite a bit before my time. But someone looking like his son and living in Adelaide! Christ! News to me. Where's this going to end?"

"You're quite sure about that? You're completely unaware of this Adelaide connection?" Len asked. "I hope you realise that withholding relevant information in a murder case is a serious offence?"

Lynne paused and drew a deep breath. "Well there is one thing I remembered which might help. I don't think I've told you…" she faltered.

"We must know everything!" Kaz urged.

"It was years ago, quite early in our marriage. Kevin did a lot of his work at home in his study. Quite by chance, one morning he'd left the door of his office ajar and I overhead him talking to someone, and it got heated. He was so angry. I could just hear enough to be certain it was a young man, by the sound of his voice, but not what he was saying. When I asked Kevin about it, he was annoyed that I should be 'listening in on his conversations', as he put it. But he wouldn't say what it was about, just explaining that it was one of his constituents, and then rushing off on the pretext that he had an urgent parliamentary matter to deal with."

Lynne paused for a second, taking a breath. "That should have been the end of it but I did something I do not make a practice of and I'm not proud of."

"You checked who it was?" asked Kaz.

"Yes I did a callback and this youngish sounding man answered. The number was in South Australia. I knew Kevin must have been lying to me, he seemed unusually de-railed by that call, and the man's tone had a familiarity, like he knew him very well, I'm quite certain of that. But it was early in my marriage. We both had our pasts which we'd agreed to leave in the past. So I left it there as it really wasn't my business."

"Did you keep a record of the call-back number?"

She shook her head. "No I already felt I had gone behind his back. I'd done enough and if he didn't wish to discuss it with me that was his choice."

"You never asked Kevin anything else about this? That seems strange."

"He was a very private man. I thought it might open up a can of worms. Now this latest revelation proves it. I really don't want to hear anymore!"

"We can understand that this must be upsetting for you. It's not great to learn that someone this close to you has been concealing something as important as this. But the reality is that we all have our secrets, and—"

"Yes—well thank you for your thoughts," she butted in before Kaz could finish. "I've told you all I know now. I never met the man who made the call. It's the first I've heard about this man in Adelaide. Whoever it was, he must have had a strong hold on Kevin for him to make that flight without telling me. You'll have to draw your own conclusions. Please don't bother me again in public like this. If it happens again, I'll be making a formal complaint."

"Thank you for your cooperation Lynne," Kaz responded diplomatically. "We can understand why this must be upsetting. But I'm afraid that there may well be follow up. The only thing I can promise is that now we understand what and why you've been holding things back, we will only check with you further if it's absolutely necessary."

CHAPTER 13

The Commonwealth Archives was based in a repository in Canberra, housing paper documents dating back to Australian Federation, a century and a half before. Kaz's application to view Australian Embassy Records from Jakarta for the years 2000-2006 required her to make a visit in person to the main office and negotiate patiently.

"Most of the records for that period are sealed and will remain sealed until 2050 for very good diplomatic reasons," James Manning, Senior Archivist explained. "Australia had a delicate relationship with Indonesia at that time because of the East Timor conflict. At one point we were extremely close to a complete breakdown in diplomatic relations. And since those times relations have always been awkward at best, despite what you might be led to believe by the media. So if you're working on the assumption that Kevin Rowe was a military attaché to the Embassy in Jakarta, anything to do with him on file would almost certainly remain classified."

"But I'm a senior state government employee and therefor bound by the Official Secrets Act," Kaz protested.

"That will help a bit, but you would still have to have Commonwealth Security Clearance and even then, any files you might request would have to be vetted by one of our own staff. Any sensitive content would be redacted before you'd be able to see it. From what you've told me, it would take a considerable time to sieve through such sources and we're short-staffed as it is. What I suggest is you put a series of questions to us in writing, and we will endeavour to answer them. No guarantees of course."

"What about the contact details or whereabouts of the ambassador during that period?"

"Yes, I think I can find that out for you easily enough," said Manning. He made a quick search of the database before handing Kaz a slip of paper. "There were two, but neither of them is still alive, I'm afraid."

"Could you look up the Heads of HR or PR then?"

Manning was shaking his head. "I doubt very much whether our records on this database would have that level of detail. Most of the documents holding specific information like that would also have been archived long ago."

"And sealed?" Kaz huffed, frustrated.

"Yes I'm afraid so," said Manning. "Listen, Ms Ingham, I know I must be sounding discouraging, but I think your best bet would be to try to find someone in the Foreign Office who might have had their earlier career in Indonesia or know someone who did. You could also check the media including the ABC and organisations such as Reuters and Jakarta Post. They might be able to suggest high-level local journalists or correspondents who would have had contact with Embassy people at that time."

Kaz brightened at his suggestions. "Anyone in particular you can suggest?"

"Roy Hartley in the Foreign Office would definitely be old enough to recollect that period, I think. But please don't tell him I told you that!" He said with a smile. "As to the media, you'll have to make your own inquiries there. Actually, could I say that the information you're seeking might even be better investigated in Indonesia itself. Expats usually do not stay there forever, but there are some who've married Indonesians and do choose to remain there. Also, a lot of expat retirees, I happen to know, live in Bali for example. There's a very good chance you could find somebody there with the information."

Kaz had by now stopped listening, because Manning's suggestions were becoming less practicable by the second, and she doubted that NSW Premiers Office would sanction a trip to Bali on such a flimsy pretext. She thanked Manning politely for his suggestions and left his office still undecided whether or not to bother with the Foreign Office contact he'd mentioned.

« »

A week later Kaz was back at NSW Premier's again while various inquiries were gestating. Against her better judgment she had met Roy Hartley, an aging bureaucrat with a far-away look in his eye. He became more animated when Kaz explained the reason for her visit.

"Ah yes Jakarta, wonderful place, makes life here seem so humdrum! But it's not going to be easy for me to recall any specific information that long ago, you realise."

"What connection did you have with the Embassy in Jakarta?" Kaz asked, hoping to jolt his memory.

Rodney Jensen

"It was just after 2000 and not the easiest time to be liaising with Indonesia and advising on Foreign policy. The turmoil over East Timor put our friendships under great pressure and at one stage there were threats by the Indonesian Government to expel some of our top people. Our Prime Minister of the time, John Howard, had much to answer for with his extremely limited understanding of the dynamics. This coupled with the inexperience of Indonesia's new President Habibie in calling a referendum on East Timor's sovereignty was a recipe for disaster. We all thought that both he and Howard must have been very poorly briefed, but it's all a long time ago, and I'm just trying to remember the name of a chap who was their head of public communications. I need to check my diaries and I'll come back to you."

« »

It was a week before Kaz heard anything more from Hartley. She'd already written him off as yet another dead end. His call came out of the blue while she was deep in an unrelated state government policy issue, and it took her a moment to register who it was and what he was talking about.

"Roy Hartley. I must apologise for taking so long over this, but there's been a personal crisis in my family to deal with. I've been on leave for several days," he said, without reference to their previous discussion, assuming she'd remember him.

"Anyway, I've finally unearthed my diaries. The name of the man I was referring to, the head of public communications, is Joseph Last. I've also discovered via my contacts that he retired ten years ago and is now living with his wife in Port Macquarie. Here are the details," he pointed to an embedded text message on the holo-screen.

"I suppose that you haven't come across anything about Kevin Rowe, the military attaché?" asked Kaz.

"There were one or two references to him in my diaries as well, but nothing substantive. I think he was one of the Embassy's shadowy figures."

"You mean he was a spook?"

"Yes, I think so. But Last may recall more about him."

"But is there anything more specific that made you think that was what he was?"

"Not really. It was the fact he was never around and never ever discussed what he was up to. If one ever asked him a question he would give a vague answer or change the subject."

"Thank you very much I do appreciate this," said Kaz and closed the contact, impatient to follow up the lead he'd given her.

CHAPTER 14

As if the forces of random circumstance were conspiring to obstruct Kaz's pursuit of information, she met yet another setback in her call to Port Macquarie. "Joe's off on a fishing trip with his mates at the moment," Cheryl Last explained. "I'm not expecting him back until the end of the week. But I'll give him your message. I'm not sure when he'll contact you because he prefers to leave his holo off most of the time on jaunts like this."

It was therefore a surprise when she received a call from Last later that day.

"Cheryl said you wanted to discuss something about my time in Jakarta?"

"She told me you were on a fishing trip?"

"That's right I was. But one of our party had an accident and we had to get him into hospital. So here I am. What was it you're after?"

"Kevin Rowe, do you remember him?"

There was a very long pause. "Kevin Rowe… it's funny after never hearing anything about the bastard for decades then I heard recently they'd found his body. I suppose that's why you're calling?"

Kaz ignored his question. "Can you explain the nature of your relationship with him when you were both working together at the Australian Embassy?"

"Well he was supposed to be the military attaché, reporting directly to Andrew Marsden the ambassador. But as a matter of fact I did get to know him quite well, socially you might say."

"Mr Last, there's actually quite a lot I need to talk to you about and I'd rather do this face to face. Can we arrange to meet tomorrow morning?"

"Must be very important, but why not!" he sounded amused.

"It is, extremely important, but I'd rather we didn't discuss it right now and will you please keep this conversation to yourself."

"You've really piqued my curiosity, and brought back memories. It was a very different world from what I was used to and one had to be one's toes!"

Stupid old fool Kaz thought.

"Of course! No worries. You have my address, why don't you come over here around mid-morning if that suits?"

"Fine, thank you. I'll catch the early service."

« »

Joseph Last came to the door and introduced himself to Kaz. He was elderly, walking with a slight limp, and wearing a peaked hat, a worn sweater, slacks and running shoes. He had penetrating eyes which never seemed still and a conspiratorial habit of talking in slightly hushed tones. "I've been at the gym, doctor's orders," he explained, proffering a hand. "Come in and have a drink." There was an already open bottle on the table as she sat down. "What can I get you?"

"I'd love a glass of water, thanks."

Joseph poked around in a fridge under the breakfast bar, pulled out a bottle and began rummaging in an overhead cupboard for a glass.

"Just the bottle's fine," said Kaz, who by this time could hardly control her excitement. She launched into a brief background on the purpose of her visit, hoping at last to get his full attention.

"Well I must say I'm intrigued to know how your investigation is going," he said as he sat down on a sofa next to her, beside a low table.

"Since finding his body in the Adelaide Hills, there have been more questions than answers. It now looks like the Indonesian part of his early career could be relevant to our investigation," Kaz replied.

Joseph responded as if this was no surprise. "Yes I did hear about Rowe in the news when his disappearance was first announced. And since your call, I've taken the opportunity of reading the recent online media feeds. Then I realised that there must be some connection between your visit and the fact he's finally been found, murdered? Was he murdered?" Kaz nodded. "And what would that have to do with his time in Indonesia?" he asked quizzically.

"I was hoping that you might be able to help me there, anything you've got on him that might be relevant to our inquiry."

"I need to understand the context first. I still don't quite understand the relevance of Indonesia to this?"

Kaz didn't much like her interviewee turning her question back on her, but she decided that she had to offer him at least something new, something he couldn't have found out about online. "What I'm about to tell you is not for anyone else's ears, because it's highly speculative at this stage. We think that there's some possibility he has an unidentified son living in South Australia. According to the description we've been able to compile, this man's age would correspond approximately to a birthdate around the time Rowe was living in Jakarta. Do you know anything about this? Could he have been responsible for an illegitimate child while he was working there? Any thoughts?"

"Hmm," Joseph rumbled awkwardly. "Yes I did mention on the holo that Rowe and I and met socially on several occasions outside the office. One night in particular, I remember he invited one of the girls from the Embassy office, who was clearly more than just a friend. In fact he told me confidentially that he and she were engaged. I happened to mention this to the ambassador, assuming he would know and had given him special dispensation since it was contrary to regulations. Anyway, I'm afraid I put my foot in it and the ambassador went ballistic, especially as the girl in question was his PA. He hauled both of them in to explain, and they both strenuously denied any such relationship. It put me in an extremely embarrassing position, and I had no option but to resign and return to Australia. I never saw Rowe again. As you can imagine I felt quite bitter about the whole experience."

"And you confirm that you have had no contact with him after you left Indonesia?"

"Yes as I said, I never saw the man again and never particularly wanted to for that matter."

"The woman who was the ambassador's PA, what was her name?"

"Hmm, it's been a long time and my memory's not what it used to be. It might come to me and I'll let you know if you give me your contact details. "Is there anything else?"

"Well assuming it wasn't the PA, were you aware of anyone else he was having a serious relationship with?"

"Now you're asking! Let me think…I'm not sure I met anyone else."

"Perhaps someone said something, then?"

"Yes, there were rumours, and that's all, but I heard some of the staff mentioning that Rowe had been consorting with an Indonesian woman, someone who'd actually been invited to one of our parties, I think it was the Christmas one."

"Why would this woman have been invited to an Embassy party?"

"Good question. The reason was that she was related, I believe, to a general in the Indonesian Army. She also had a senior position with the Department of History and Culture, or whatever it was called."

"Can you remember the name of the general or his female relative?"

"Now you've really got me. I've no idea. Most of my diaries and stuff I kept at the time have been chucked out years ago when we down-sized to live here."

"Do you think this PA might remember?"

"It's come to me. Her name was Julie something or other, name of a British town, quite unusual…Bristol! That was it, Julie Bristol. I think she came from Adelaide too. Maybe you could track her down there. She might well know because she would have been responsible for the guest lists of such functions. Before her time at the Embassy, she'd been one of the senior staff in another Australian Government department, I think, and had her fingers in many pies. She was particularly concerned that too few Indonesians seemed to appreciate their own history and heritage sites, she once told me." Joseph paused to sip his beer. He seemed to be relishing the interview.

"Someone else we've spoken to thinks Rowe was a spy?"

"Well I can't confirm or deny that. From time to time there were snippets of things he said which definitely made me suspicious. As well as that, there were unexplained movements he made, all over the country—Kalimantan one time, Timor-Leste another, as well as Aceh in northern Sumatra. He was always on some trip or another. Those are the only ones I can recall right now of the ones he mentioned but he kept stumm most of the time. Always changed the subject when I asked him what he was up to."

"What do you *think* he was up to then?"

"Your guess is as good as mine. But I was pretty certain he was gathering vital intelligence. In that respect he wasn't alone. Everyone in the Embassy realised how delicate our situation was over East Timor, for example. We were even bombed on one occasion—but that was terrorists now I come to think of it, and probably unconnected, but nevertheless made us pretty paranoid!"

"Did it make you want to leave?"

"No, of course not! It was like living on 'speed'. But getting back to East Timor, no one in the government seemed to understand who was in the driver's seat once the East Timorese voted for independence. In particular we were worried how the Indonesia Government might turn their anger on the INTERFET Forces and specifically on us."

"What did Rowe think?"

"Rowe spoke to me about these issues in general terms frequently, and I could see that his appreciation was far superior to anyone else's—sometimes he let slip something that he could have only learned from someone in high places like the TNI."

"TNI?"

"Tentara Nasional Indonesia - the Indonesian military forces."

"If he talked to you about such things, are you quite sure he didn't mention aspects of the espionage you suspected him of?"

"Absolutely sure. I think he put the two parts of his life into entirely different compartments. One had personal implications, even if they put his career at risk. The other was of national significance and for him to divulge state secrets would have been unthinkable. It wouldn't simply have been a matter of losing his job but possibly getting banged up in an Indonesian jail for the rest of his life!"

"So can you please confirm when this woman Julie Bristol left the Embassy and where she went?"

"Hmm…the exact date this all happened I'd have to look up but it was around about 2003 I think because I left shortly before she was due to go. Where she went I'm unsure. But I did overhear some of the office staff whispering about her next to the coffee room the day her plans got out, and the word 'Elizabeth' which is in Adelaide, I believe was mentioned. They shut up the moment they realised that I was in earshot, no idea why."

Maybe they didn't trust you, Kaz thought.

CHAPTER 15

Kaz spent the next few days in the SAPol headquarters tracking down the whereabouts of Julie Bristol. She finally came across the name with the address: Nefertiti Retirement Village, Salisbury. She contacted the village immediately to be advised, "Yes she's one of our 'young' residents, living in one of our self-care apartments. Would you like to speak to her?"

"Yes, please put me through."

Once connected, the person on the other end preferred not to use video, but the voice was of a mature lady with a precise way of talking. "Julie speaking. Who is this?"

"My name's Kaz Ingham, I'm calling from SAPol, where I'm working as an investigator."

"Oh you mean police! I can't get my head around these acronyms. They seem to change by the moment."

"You're not wrong," Kaz replied patiently. "The reason for my call is that I am following up information into the recent discovery of someone I believe you knew in Indonesia, Kevin Rowe."

There was a long pause. "Yes I knew Kevin," her voice sounded agitated. "He was our military attaché in the Embassy and we did become quite friendly, but he died didn't he?"

"Yes, I regret to say he did Julie, if I may call you that?"

"Of course, dear."

"I would really like to talk to you in person about this, as they are matters of importance and you are one of the few people I've been able to track down who knew Kevin during his time in Indonesia.

Julie's voice sounded doubtful. "I'm not sure. It's been a long time and I'm wondering if anything I know or can remember will help you very much."

Kaz ignored her reluctance. "Would it be convenient if I met you at your apartment tomorrow morning?"

"Just to put my mind at rest, can you send me your contact details on police letterhead so that I can verify that you are who you say you are?"

"Yes of course!"

"Well…then, it must be important, so of course I'll do what I can to help. But could you make it around mid-morning, say eleven o'clock, to give me time to find anything that might help to jog my memory."

« »

The retirement housing estate was built in a secluded part of Adelaide's northern suburb of Salisbury. Julie's apartment formed one of a small group, sited around a cul-de-sac accessway and backing onto a pocket of natural bushland. Each of the dwellings had small front gardens and neat pathways to individual entrances.

Julie was on her knees in the front garden, absorbed in pulling weeds out of the lawn judging by the pile beside her. She was wearing a floppy straw hat to ward off the heat of the sun, which was hot despite it being autumn. Kaz could see the perspiration breaking out in patches under her armpits.

"Ms Bristol, it's Kaz Ingham. We spoke yesterday."

Rodney Jensen

The woman started slightly at the unexpected voice. "Oh! It's eleven o'clock already? I'm sorry that you should catch me like this, but do come in. I'll put the air conditioning on to make us more comfortable."

Julie led Kaz into a large lounge area, sat her down on a comfy settee and offered her something to drink.

"Just a glass of water will be fine thanks," said Kaz, and waited interminable minutes for Julie to change out of her gardening clothes, put the kettle on and return with a tray of tea things and a cake, which looked specially baked for the occasion.

"You shouldn't have gone to so much trouble," protested Kaz.

"It's nothing, dear. I don't get visitors here so often, and I'm looking forward to talking about the old days in Jakarta." Julie settled herself into her armchair and looked inquiringly at Kaz, as if sizing her up with alert eyes. "So what is it that you would like to know about Kevin Rowe?"

Kaz had assumed there might be a certain innocence about the lady, but quickly realised she hadn't lost her mental acuity. Rather than directly answering her question, she preferred to broach the details of his recent discovery more gently.

"Julie I'm not sure whether you're aware of the fact but Kevin Rowe disappeared quite a few years ago in Sydney. It was a mystery and he wasn't found at the time. Anyway, quite by chance, his body was discovered earlier this year in the hills behind Mt Lofty and we are still trying to find out what happened to him, and why."

Julie surprised her with her immediate response. "Yes, I did hear about his disappearance some years ago. It was before I moved here, and I was working at the local library and saw the papers every day. I must say I felt very shocked when I read the report, because it seemed like he must've been mixed up in something very peculiar."

"How did you get to know him in the Embassy?"

"Oh that was quite simple. I was Ambassador Marsden's personal assistant and had many dealings with Kevin. He often had meetings with the ambassador to discuss his briefing reports. I read most of the documents he sent in and highlighted the important bits as part of my job."

"Do you recall another person, 'James Last', who was the press secretary in your time? He said that he knew you and also knew Kevin pretty well?"

"Last... Yes it's coming back to me. He was a person I learnt to be wary of. He was a rumour-monger and had a way of sidling up to girls when they were by themselves and making sleazy advances, that is if he felt there was some prospect of getting his way."

"Last told us that Rowe might have had a relationship with an Indonesian woman. Can you remember anything about that?"

"Gosh now you're asking!" She paused to reflect, at last becoming more animated. "But as it happens I do remember something! I was at a Christmas party, which I had a lot to do with the planning of in fact. It was shortly after Kevin had arrived in Jakarta, and I helped to introduce him to a few of the guests. Anyway one of the people we'd invited was a TNI general,

Rodney Jensen

Bhudi Wistranto. He was well up on our guest list because of his importance in the military and had connections with all sorts of highly placed people, the ones we wanted to be on familiar terms with. He was delighted to be asked and via his own PA asked whether his niece could come along too. Of course we said 'yes'. I think that he was keen on getting her out of her shell. When I eventually met her, she was gracious with me, but shy of her English. She had a senior government post herself, probably because of her uncle's connections. That's how things worked there, you know?"

Kaz was growing a bit impatient. "And did Rowe meet this woman?"

"Yes, one couldn't help noticing. It seemed like she and Kevin were deep in conversation as soon as they'd been introduced. Maybe Kevin's real target was Wistranto, for his potential as source of information, or maybe it was more than that and he actually was really attracted to the girl. He certainly was very attentive and I watched as the three of them left the party towards the end of the evening."

"You've got a good memory."

"Well, yes, but also Wistranto was so much larger than life, with a laugh you could hear across the room. By contrast, his niece seemed rather shy, the opposite of her uncle. Her uncle seemed to want Kevin to get to know her. He certainly wasn't discouraging, as a real father might well have been. It occurred to me that both he and Kevin saw some benefit in getting to know each other better, and the girl probably could not see it."

"But that's as much as I can remember. Kevin never talked to me about her again and of course there could well have been many other Indonesian women that Kevin would have known during his time at the Embassy."

"Thank you Julie, that's been very helpful. Do you remember where this niece worked?"

"Yes I think it was in a government department that looked after education and culture. You should be able to find her because I think she was using her uncle's surname."

"Another thing I want to ask you about is how much you knew about what Rowe was doing while he was in Jakarta?"

Julie paused to sip some tea. A faraway look had come into her eyes. Kaz could not help feeling that, although a little older than him, she had once had more than a passing interest in Kevin Rowe.

"Well that was the thing you see?" Julie continued. "He was supposed to be the military attaché, but of course it wasn't his real position at all. As far as I could make out, his job was to dig up whatever information he could about the activities of the Indonesian Government, including the stand-off between East Timor and Jakarta at the time. But more than that, he would never say and none of the reports he gave the ambassador even hinted at his real role in what could *only* be described as espionage."

"The reports—did you see them?"

"Of course!" she said with a derisive *hmph*. "Worthless! They were full of common knowledge, the stuff that anyone could read in the papers. It seemed obvious to me that he was just going through the motions for the ambassador's benefit."

"According to AuSecurity, Kevin resigned on grounds of ill-health quite suddenly. Did you know anything about that?"

"Yes, he left at about the same time I did. We promised each other that we would stay in touch back in Australia, but the fact was I was living here in Elizabeth, working in a library and he was based in Sydney, so sadly, we never met again after our time together in Jakarta. I was very shocked when I read about his disappearance and now his body being found which appears to confirm he was murdered. If I might be so bold, your interest in his time in Indonesia suggests to me that you think the two things might somehow be connected?"

It was Kaz's turn to be put on the back foot by her question. "That's insightful Julie. I am beginning to understand why you held such a senior position in the Embassy. All I can say is that what you have told me today will be a great help in checking possibilities which have been raised by some of our other contacts. One of these is quite strange and just speculation at this stage."

"Something to do with that woman no doubt?"

"I can't really confirm that. Obviously, we're very keen to find out how Kevin was killed and why his body was disposed of in South Australia. That's about as much as I can tell you."

"Yes I can quite see that, it all sounds most peculiar, particularly the Indonesian connection?"

It was as though Julie had turned the interview around. Kaz paused as she realised she had been doing too much of the talking. "It's one of quite a few lines of inquiry we're looking into, that's all. Now is there anything else you can think of before I leave you in peace?"

"Talking about Kevin has brought a few things back and there is something I can tell you, which at the time I thought was pretty remarkable given the context of how it happened."

"Please go on," Kaz urged.

"Well once Kevin left the Embassy, his replacement turned up shortly afterwards. I can't think of the name at the moment, it doesn't really matter. We organised a special welcoming function to which a few select Indonesian officials were invited, including General Bhudi Wistranto. Now, to really understand this, you would have had to know Bhudi. He was always jovial, up front and charming in his way. But on this particular occasion, there was obviously something seriously troubling him, and I had the distinct sense it had to do with us, I mean Australia. It was peculiar, because by that time, good relations had been restored between our countries, I thought. There was nothing I was aware of that might have been a concern about us from Indonesia's perspective, nothing to make him look angry, anyway."

"Was that all?"

"No! I haven't quite finished. It was when I introduced the new military attaché to him that he made this extraordinary remark, one which almost stopped the conversation around me. It was extremely embarrassing and lacking in diplomacy."

"What was it he said?" Kaz asked with growing interest.

"Well he said to the attaché, 'I hope you better man than last one'. I think he meant it to sound as a joke, but I could tell that he meant every word of it. We all laughed and changed the subject. You know how these things go. Nobody was brave enough to ask him to explain what exactly he meant. But it was completely out of character. I've always remembered the exchange. This conversation brought it back. Kevin must have done something pretty bad to have rubbed him up the wrong way like that."

Kaz felt a surge of excitement. "Maybe it was connected with his espionage work?"

"Could have been that I suppose. But I felt at the time it was more of a personal offence."

"Something to do with his niece perhaps?"

"Yes that could have explained it."

"Julie, I can't thank you enough. I must get out of your hair now. But if you think of anything else, you know where to contact me."

CHAPTER 16

Kaz, Stewart and Len were standing around the office's Interactive Display Panel ('IDP'). Each was wearing geeky looking neural interface goggles which registered a series of reactions, including items of particular interest or potential interest and possible investigation paths. A summary report and chart was then available for review to assist the direction of future investigations.

"Now let's try to summarise what we know, and where there's strong evidence before we get into supposition and speculation," Stewart remarked.

Kaz tried to suppress her reluctance to let him take over despite his position. "Okay. Here are the certainties," she said, beginning to scribble points on the board as she was talking. "One, we are now certain that Rowe travelled from Sydney under an assumed name to Adelaide by plane two days before he was registered as missing by his wife." She paused to let that sink in. Nobody said anything. "Two, we know he checked into the Montenegro Hotel in Melbourne Street North Adelaide, later that same day." There was still no contribution from the others. "Three, we know he left the hotel without checking out or taking luggage within the period he'd booked, which according to the hotel was for two days."

"Four, we know that Rowe had a return air ticket and the return journey was not made on the booked date. That, of course does not prove he didn't leave the state some other way."

"Five, we know that Rowe met his death approximately eight years ago, according to the forensic evidence, and in all likelihood it occurred somewhere near the burial site, or at the very least in South Australia."

"Okay. That last one is really in the supposition category, isn't it?" remarked Stewart. "What else have we got reasonable but uncertain evidence for?"

"The biggest and most vital ones are the two suppositions that the person he met in Adelaide on the day he flew there, was firstly related to him, and secondly, connected to his death," said Kaz. "This is based on the evidence from Adams who reported seeing him meet such a person at the airport, and claimed he could see some sort of family resemblance. Unfortunately we are yet to have any visual evidence on record to back that up."

"Anything more?" asked Stewart.

"Yes, one of the contacts we've spoken to, James Last, was a workmate of Rowe's during the time he was working for the Australian Embassy in Jakarta during the early 2000s. He suggested that Rowe had formed a relationship with a highly placed Indonesian woman. That has now been partially corroborated in my latest interview with a woman who was the ambassador's PA at the time. Could Rowe have got her pregnant and she had a son, and was this the person Adams saw Rowe meeting outside Adelaide Airport?" She paused to allow that to sink in. "You can imagine how well that would have gone down if it had been discovered by the Embassy at the time. We don't know the circumstances, but my guess is that she would have had to declare her situation before it became obvious and while she still had some bargaining chips up her sleeve."

"What do you mean?" asked Len.

"Again this is all speculative, but maybe her affair with Rowe was not what it seemed and Rowe somehow was forced to leave before the reason got out."

"Sounds like you've already formed a pretty negative opinion of Kevin Rowe?" Stewart observed drily.

"It's guesswork, and we badly need corroboration from other people who were in the Embassy while all this was going on. Joseph Last, the former Press Secretary put me onto the ambassador's PA, Julie Bristol. I met her in my most recent trip to South Australia. Other than knowing that Rowe had met this Indonesian woman, she was unable to confirm anything further."

"So if I can summarise the situation," suggested Stewart. "We're still pretty much in the dark as to why or how Rowe was killed and who did it. Our best guess about there being a son is still tenuous but should be our main line of inquiry from now on. Is everyone agreed on that?"

"I think it's really the only thing we've got at the moment," said Kaz quietly, feeling deflated by Stewart's pragmatic assessment. "I've booked a flight to Indonesia, because I'm pretty sure it's the only place we're going to get to the bottom of this."

Rodney Jensen

While Kaz was speaking, Stewart's PA came into the office and whispered something in his ear. "Hang on everyone, I have to get this. Back in a minute."

A full forty minutes had elapsed before he came back into the office looking hangdog. "There's been a development," he said. "Kaz, you'd better cancel your travel plans. This investigation has been put on hold, and I'm not sure what the outcome will be right now."

xxx"Who's put it on hold?" Kaz demanded.

"It's on the highest authority both I and my opposite number in SA report to. Somehow we've managed to get up the nose of AuSecurity, and unfortunately their powers concerning National Security transcend State rights. Until we get the green light, I regret to say we're in limbo."

« »

As Stewart and Kaz were leaving the office, about to head their separate ways, Stewart stopped and turned. "You doing anything tonight? I've got tickets for the play I told you about, at the Riverside West."

"Ah yes, I remember. I have been looking forward to it. What's the play about?"

"All I know is it's contemporary, revisiting a classic of the 20th Century. They're having a week of short plays by Parramatta's CULT-X students. You know the place, it encourages local cultural projects. I'm not expecting too much, but it's just walking distance from here."

"Of course, I'd love to come. It wouldn't matter what's on offer. It's the company that really matters."

She smiled up at him and turned to make sure they weren't being watched before kissing him softly on his cheek."

« »

There was muted chatter from the audience at the play's conclusion. "Oh dear," remarked Kaz, "that was an ordeal. I thought it was going to be bad from Scene One onwards."

"I don't think you're alone," said Stewart pointing out how few of the audience had survived to the final curtain. "I was ready to walk out myself, with all those cheap shots at our soldiers."

"Yes I thought it was snotty and elitist and not well thought through. I suppose it's the sort of thing you expect from students. It takes a long time for anyone to become a good playwright, if ever."

"That's being charitable," mused Stewart. "I thought I had some talent at writing way back, when I was at Uni, but quickly realised I didn't. It's one reason I turned to police work."

"But I just didn't like that play, and it wasn't just the crap acting! Whoever wrote 'The One Day Revisited' obviously had no understanding of the events or the motivations of the main characters of the original play. It's an icon of the 20th century and should have been left in peace!"

"You can't expect students who were born well over half a century after World War 2 to understand enough of what went on to carry that off successfully. Give them a break!" Kaz laughed as did Stewart.

Rodney Jensen

They walked along the Parramatta River Walkway, arm in arm, enjoying each other's company. Kaz had not expected Stewart's attitude would have changed so much towards her, after his previous uncertainty. He now seemed so relaxed and familiar. "So what now?" he asked casually.

"Why don't we have supper near my place in Surry Hills. There's continuous services there in most venues, so we can eat as late as you want. And it's convenient for both of us," Kaz replied.

« »

They had emptied two bottles of wine and ploughed their way through generous helpings of pasta at 'La Bites', before realising they'd outstayed their welcome. Apart from themselves, all other customers had left, and staff were stacking up chairs and making other pointed hints it was time for them to pay the bill and leave.

They walked arm in arm contentedly along the footpath in the direction of Kaz's house. Kaz was slightly tipsy and sensed that Stewart well and truly had his guard down for once.

"This time, I hope you won't say 'no' if I invite you in?"

"No, I won't. And thank you for persisting with me," he said, surprising her with his change of tune.

As he put his arm around her, Kaz snuggled into his shoulder. They stopped on her doorstep, while she fumbled for her keys. She was trembling inwardly. *He seems so different now from the person I first met.* They almost fell through the door together, as Stewart tripped on a doormat that had its edge curled up. Kaz caught him, grabbed him by the head and kissed him on his cheek, then full on his mouth.

She felt his hands roaming around her buttocks and pressing her into him. He was growing rock hard against her. She slammed the door shut behind them, undid his belt and opened his fly. She felt inside and teased him. He groaned and began peeling off Kaz's top and undoing her bra without fumbling. He started sucking her taut nipples and then exploring below her breasts and over her tummy. She shivered in ecstasy. "Let's go to bed, it's far more comfortable there," she said huskily.

Kaz led the way into her small bedroom and threw back the covers of her double bed. She embraced Stewart again and pulled him down so that they could face each other side by side. He continued kissing her, working his tongue all over her body finally darting it into her. She groaned in unbearable pent-up hunger. "Slowly! Take your time, Stewart, we've got all night," she whispered in his ear.

CHAPTER 17

At Last! Kaz terminated her call with a receptionist at AuSecurity, relieved to be getting somewhere. It had taken a considerable time to fill out the extensive questionnaire required to gain security clearance via a secure holo-link. AuSecurity had required wide ranging personal information, including details of her parents, siblings and other relatives, her education, and her work experience. At the end of the questions, she was required to provide contact details of all her known immediate family members still alive, plus three referees who could confirm their longstanding acquaintance with her. She also had to complete a confidentiality agreement.

With that, Kaz had to wait for a further three days before she finally received an email advising her that an officer called Marcus Searle would now be willing to discuss the case with her.

She wasted no time in catching an AutoCab set to follow the CabLink data the PR person had sent through her holo. The Cab took her via back streets, close to Central Terminus into a narrow lane, and stopped outside a low rise concrete tower block, flanked by much older terraces. The block itself had a sinister unwelcoming feel, marked by featureless rough cast concrete external walls and small dark glazed windows. She glanced up to the roof and noticed a forest of communications antennae and dishes, including surveillance cameras pointing directly at where she was standing. She resisted the temptation to wave. The main entrance was low-key, with an unsigned door and a standard entry scanner mounted beside it. The scanner sensed Kaz's universal identity chip, and the door opened automatically. She proceeded to Level 4, where she found a man waiting to meet her. He looked like he wasn't long out of university.

He was casually dressed in a t-shirt, jeans and trainers. He had bleached white hair, was clean shaven and wore frameless glasses. He looked closely at Kaz and compared her with 3-D images on a holo-tablet he was carrying. Finally, he nodded and smiled slightly. "We might as well go and have a coffee in the plaza down the lane, if that suits?"

"After all the clearances, aren't you worried that someone in your office might be watching us?" asked Kaz, dead-pan.

"No, we do have to follow protocols," he replied seriously, "but we never had any concerns about your background or anything else. What you've been through is simply a formality that we all have to accept. Anyway, I think you'd agree a coffee shop's more conducive to a relaxed discussion wouldn't you."

"Yes, I suppose so."

« »

Marcus waited until the coffee had been served before beginning to talk quietly about her inquiry.

At long last! thought Kaz.

"How much do you really know about Kevin Rowe?" he asked.

"Not as much as we'd like. We know about his schooling and his subsequent officer training at

Duntroon. We know he was appointed military attaché to the Australian Embassy in Jakarta where he was in place for about three years before returning to Australia in 2003. We know little or nothing about what he did there, nor what he did in Australia prior to getting married to Lynne Rowe in 2005. After that we know a lot more from information that's publicly available and from his wife Lynne who has been able to fill us in with his business dealings and entry into politics."

"I'm here," she continued, "because I need to understand his role in Indonesia more, what he got up to there and immediately after that. We think his activities there might be connected with his disappearance—it's a period of five years in his life which is almost a complete blank. One of our contacts who knew him in the Jakarta Embassy, was the Press Secretary at the time, 'James Last' was his name. He was convinced he was a spy. That would explain why we know so little about what he got up to in Jakarta. Was he spying for you? Is there a connection between something that happened to him in those blank years and the reason you have suspended our inquiry on us?"

"How interesting!" His narrowed eyes smiled slightly at her. "You are obviously right about the spy role. You wouldn't be sitting here with me otherwise. But some of the information we have on Rowe's file is so sensitive, that even I'm not allowed to know. There's one specific thing he reported while he was in Indonesia, it's been marked to be kept sealed until 2050."

"You've got to be kidding!"

"No, I don't joke about things like this."

"You must have something on file explaining the reasons for putting a lid on our inquiry then?"

"It's actually not at all unusual to discourage inquiries by other government agencies that could lead to classified information getting leaked. There is a memorandum from Foreign Affairs raising this possibility, concerned that you are trying to track down Rowe's contacts in Jakarta, and that you have a theory that Rowe may have had a son. The latter I understand is based on a sighting by one of your contacts?"

"That's correct. We now know that Rowe met a young man not long after his wife last saw him. The sighting was in Adelaide from an informant who'd sat next to him on a flight from Sydney to Adelaide and happened to see him being met by a man he said bore a family resemblance. But we have no visual recordings of this encounter. Do you have anything on file that would help us confirm it?"

"That he has a relative in Adelaide? No, I think it's highly unlikely. And there's nothing on file about it. However there is a note that the circumstances under which he left Jakarta were unclear. He claimed to have contracted tuberculosis while there, but subsequent independent examinations back in Australia provided no corroboration for that."

"Could the real reason have been he wanted to escape responsibility for some girl he'd got pregnant?"

"Again I doubt that. As a highly trained agent I would have expected he would have avoided any such close relationships and taken suitable precautions if he did. As I've said, there's no evidence in the file of that being the case."

"So what part of the file has been redacted?"

"I can only see that he went on a mission to somewhere in Indonesia in early 2003 and returned as little as three days later. Anything else he reported about that excursion is subject to a 'red' seal and there would be little or no chance of you finding out what he got up to, or what was so important to Australia's security for such a long-term classification. My own guess is that it might have had something to do with East Timor, but that is only a guess and there's no evidence at all to support that either."

"But why then would AuSecurity have slapped this discontinuance order on us? I still can't see the relevance to our inquiries." Kaz sipped her coffee and watched him squirm over the rim of her cup.

"We simply don't want Rowe's history turned over by other arms of government, particularly a state government with a different political allegiance to those of our masters," he remarked pointedly. "The more people who start to delve into his background, the greater the possibility that they might come across the highly classified stuff. That's the reason I think."

"Is there anything more on the file that you *can* tell me?"

"Very little I'm afraid. Even though you've been granted security clearance, there are some things that must remain on file and cannot be divulged, particularly to outsiders."

"Such as?"

"The identity of his handler in Indonesia would be one of the main ones."

"Is there anything else, such as the people he knew at the Embassy apart from James Last. Anyone we can speak to about him who might be able to help?"

Marcus had pulled a vapo, one of the latest models, and inhaled deeply. It blew nicotine-scented steam over Kaz as he exhaled.

"As I've already explained, there is nothing further on file I can divulge and no hint of this supposed relative. And let's face it, your own evidence for this is tenuous. The reality is that the information you're chasing about Rowe is now decades old. It's a well and truly cold case, isn't it? If you went to Indonesia there would be few people alive able to help you. To be honest with you Kaz, I really think you're wasting your time on this."

"Can we meet again if I do come up with anything?"

"Absolutely, I would have requested it anyway. There's hardly any meat on the skeleton at the moment and it would be good to fill in the gaps if possible. I have to admit to being curious about what Rowe got up to wherever it was he went, but it could cost me my job if I spent time trying to find out."

"What about the discontinuance order now? Is it still in force?"

"Okay that was the main thing I meant to discuss with you. Since you've passed our security vetting, we've decided to authorise continuance of your inquiries into Rowe by you personally, on condition that anything you uncover is shared with us.

Depending on the nature of such information, we will reserve the right to suppress it from any further investigation. Is that clear?"

"Not sure about that. It puts me in a difficult position with my colleagues in State and also the police hierarchy, the ones I deal with on a day to day basis."

"Oh that's okay," Marcus replied airily. "We've made these conditions clear to all staff you report to and it's been agreed. Quite frankly, we have the legislative power to do whatever we like in such matters. We've put you in a highly privileged position of trust, which we hope you'll respect."

"I don't suppose my bosses are going to love me when I invoke our version of the Fifth Amendment every time they're looking for answers!"

"I don't suppose they will. But if I'm any judge of character, Ms Ingham, I'd say you wouldn't give a damn!"

Kaz laughed, warming to Marcus. "I think you might just be right."

Part Two

Rodney Jensen

CHAPTER 18

2001

Lieutenant Kevin Rowe was at a point in his life when things were finally going right. He crossed his legs on the office chair in his study, as he had done every day for the past two weeks, scratched his chin, then ran a hand over curly, short-cropped hair before locking fingers behind his head and leaning back to gaze at the noisy Currawong birds calling from the trees in his back garden. It reminded him of the trees that flanked the assault course at Duntroon where he'd done his officer-training. If there was one thing that training had taught him, it was to relax when he had the chance. Before long he would have confirmation of his future role in the Army, and be off on a new adventure. This time in Canberra might be his last chance for a while to choose just to watch leaves blowing in the breeze.

The soft putting of a postie's bike delivery interrupted his musing, becoming louder as it approached his mailbox and he could hear the lid slamming. He wasn't expecting anything and put off taking a look at what was most likely to be advertising literature. He finally came to the end of the whodunit he'd been reading and lazily eased himself out of the chair, pulling the waistband of his jeans over a belly he knew needed serious attention. He then sauntered outside to pick up a parcel and tear off the wrapping. It was annoying to discover he was right—the moment the paper was peeled away, he found a brightly printed card with an embedded audio chip and speaker. It played a tinny sounding jingle, extolling the virtues of a really *cool* summer holiday in Hobart, '*the only place to escape your city burnout.*'

"Thanks," he muttered, irritably thinking of ways that he could blast the company that had somehow got his name on their marketing list. Thanks to his military discipline, it was just a tempting fantasy. Instead, he thought it was high time to be getting his orders. He closed the flyscreen door, tapped the computer in his study, and checked the latest downloads. He felt a pulse of excitement as he ran his eye down the list, seeing a message from the Australian Department of Defence. He clicked it open and read a curt email marked 'High Priority':

Please confirm to this office, your availability to attend meeting tomorrow (Wednesday) at 1100 hrs to meet with the undersigned. Robert Kitchener.

Kevin had been hoping to receive a straightforward set of orders for his new posting rather than a cryptic summons like this. He didn't know Kitchener, and assumed he was a civilian, since no rank was given, nor any other information.

It was a confusing and unexpected turn of events.

« »

As Kevin entered the Defence complex the next day, he felt a sense of foreboding that he was about to encounter a turning point in his life. The Duntroon friendships and experiences he'd relished were now all in the past. Yesterday's cryptic message heralded the start of a new future. The uncertainty of what he would be facing left him with mixed emotions.

He was very familiar with the drab offices of Australia's main military headquarters, located on the shores of Lake Burley Griffin, but he still had to ask directions at the main Reception Desk to locate Kitchener. He had never before visited the specific offices he'd been summoned to, since they were located in some mysterious underground level. Neither he, nor any of his former trainee friends, had any idea what went on there.

He found himself in a small reception lobby, where a clerical assistant in civilian clothes told him he was expected and ushered him into an office down a short corridor. He found two people in the room, seated around a table, one of whom he knew, a Captain Marshall who had been in charge of his military training, and another man he didn't recognise, but assumed must be Robert Kitchener.

The man was middle-aged, with well-trimmed grey hair and a neatly cut beard. He was dressed as a civilian in a business suit, with white shirt, gold cufflinks and a club tie. As he got up to shake hands, Kevin felt sure he had a military background by his erect bearing. He also had an aura of authority, looked serious and quietly confident, bordering on intimidating.

"Kitchener," the man introduced himself. "It's a pleasure to meet you Kevin. I must congratulate you on your excellent training record. I'm grateful to Captain Marshall for arranging this meeting, but I understand we have to excuse him now, as he has something more pressing to deal with."

Marshall nodded, and without saying anything further, left the room. Kevin had the distinct feeling that the meeting had been deliberately arranged in such a way that it would be for his ears only.

Kitchener without warning then continued in fluent Indonesian. "Lieutenant Rowe, I need to know how well you speak Bahasa. It is critical for me to assess your language ability first. Can you tell me a bit more about yourself, including why you studied Bahasa and what your plans are now you've completed your officer training?"

Kevin, initially taken aback, had to focus on Kitchener's words before delivering a suitable response. He began slowly after some moments, in Bahasa as requested. "I was lucky to attend a selective high school in Sydney that offered Indonesian language classes," he said. "At the age of fourteen, having already started to learn Indonesian, I was fortunate to be given the opportunity of visiting Kupang in West Timor to help practice my spoken Indonesian. It was organised as a school excursion by our Bahasa Indonesia teacher. I've been interested in the language and culture of the Indonesian people ever since."

"Not bad," said Kitchener, returning to English. "I understood you well enough, but you need to work on your Australian sounding vowels and intonation a bit more. That's something we can help you with."

"We?" Kevin also reverted to English.

"Yes we. I'll come to that in a minute. But before we continue this interview I need you to sign this declaration. It states that anything I tell you from now on is strictly classified. Your signature confirms you are aware of the Australian Security Act and the sanctions it provides for any breaches of said Act. In a nutshell what this means is that you cannot discuss anything you are about to hear with anyone other than me, unless the person involved can prove to you they have similar security clearances. Failure to obey that piece of legislation will in all probability put you in a high-security prison. Understood?" He slid a form across the table and handed him a pen to sign it. "I might add that you've already been vetted and you would not be having this interview with me otherwise."

Kevin signed the form and handed it back. "How does this relate to my military training and knowledge of Bahasa?"

"Good and to the point," Kitchener nodded. "As you may have gathered, I work for Australian Security, and we maintain a close liaison with Defence and possible candidates for intelligence roles."

"You want me to become a spy? That's not what I've been trained for!"

"Very few of our agents have. That can be fixed with our special training courses. But to answer your question, you have the profile of the sort of people we look for, including your language ability. Your role would be gathering intelligence in Indonesia and it would be essential to have a very good grasp of Bahasa. I am now satisfied on that score. How well you would cope with the rigorous training you'd receive only time will tell, although your record at Duntroon gives us confidence that you will succeed."

"Can you tell me anything about what I'd actually be doing?"

Kitchener stared back at him, taking his time to respond. "I can't say much until you've done your training and been inducted. All I will say is that your official status would be military attaché for the Australian Embassy in Jakarta. The rest will depend on what's happening there and what proves important for our greater understanding of Indonesian foreign policy."

Kevin was about to say something, but Kitchener put up a hand to cut him off.

"No more for now. Please consider this verbal offer carefully. It is well paid, although our vetting suggests money would not influence your decision. What we do think would appeal to you is that the work you'd be doing will be of immense importance to our relationship with Indonesia. The intelligence you'd be compiling could play a pivotal role in our diplomatic relations."

Kitchener paused again, as if he was unsure how to put the next point. "I'm also assuming you understand that your decision is not to be taken lightly. There is little glamour attached to this work, and in some circumstances your operation could put you in life-threatening situations, often ones where we'd be powerless to help you."

"Yes, I understand that. I will think about this very seriously as it would impact not only me but my family," Kevin answered.

"Understood. Please let me know one way or the other by six pm this evening. Use the same email address as the meeting request you received. If we don't hear from you we'll assume you're not interested. Either way, I must remind you of the document you have signed, and as far as the rest of the world is concerned, this conversation never happened. Okay?"

Kevin shook hands and left the office feeling a mixture of excitement and trepidation.

He'd already made up his mind what he was going to do.

« »

A full six months passed before Kevin received his final briefing from Robert Kitchener. Kevin found him in the same office in the basement of the Department of Defence studying a manila folder of papers.

He looked less intimidating this time, and shook Kevin's hand warmly. "It's an impressive start," he said. "These reports suggest you have the potential to greatly assist building our intelligence capability wherever you are sent. As I explained at your induction, our intention has been that you should serve as military attaché to the Embassy in Jakarta. That of course is merely a title, one that enables everyone to feel comfortable with you, both inside and outside the Embassy."

"Actually I was hoping you would explain my role in more detail. My training has never really pinpointed what I'm going to be doing or how for that matter," Kevin said.

"Your key focus will be for you to get to know high ranking members of Indonesia's military, and to become familiar with some of the politicians and their advisers if possible. There are lots of things we need to find out about. Primarily we want to understand how well the two countries can co-exist in the future. It appears to us that right now there's a very uneasy truce, which could easily be fractured. The worst case scenario could be further flare-ups between us over East Timor."

He went over to a map pinned on a corkboard behind him and stabbed a finger on a line which was highlighted with a red felt pen. It ran from east to west in the seas between Timor and the northern coast of Australia. "This is one of our biggest intelligence priorities, the 'Timor Gap' as it's known."

"That line," he said, drawing his finger along its length, "holds the key to Timor's future and to our own economy to a lesser degree. The line divides immense gas and oil fields which we somehow have to agree to share. That's the position of the line for now, but it could move north or south depending on future negotiations."

"Obviously," he continued, "those in charge of Timor's fledgling economy will be pushing as hard as they can to move the line closer to Australia. We, on the other hand, want it to stay pretty much as it is. The resources buried deep under the sea there are enormous, with the potential to make both countries wealthy. But it's the balance that's critical and we need to know much more about Timor's thinking and how far we can push a better deal for Australia in negotiations."

"I see. Will there be more briefing notes on this? Do we have any existing sources in East Timor?"

"Regrettably few. Unfortunately, one of our key Timorese sources was sprung quite recently. His outing has understandably created a lot of bad blood between us, and they will be redoubling their efforts to prevent anyone replacing him. I will let you take a look at the file before you go, and we can talk about it in further detail down the track."

"What role will the ambassador play?"

"Very little, we hope," Kitchener's tone was dismissive. "The man's about to retire and he isn't willing or able to be involved in any form of espionage that could impair his future. That wouldn't be our wish in any case." He paused to reflect still staring at the map.

"Beyond the obvious in terms of your movements, he will not know about, nor have any responsibility for your operations. You will be completely independent of the Embassy and not subject to his authority. You will have your own bank account. You will be free to make whatever transport movements you need and build up your list of contacts including running suitable agents if opportunities present themselves. The priority, as you would imagine, is to identify someone to replace the agent we've just lost in East Timor."

He paused again as Kevin was taking this in. "Which brings me to a practical matter and hopefully one that will help avert similar stuff-ups in the future. Generally, we'd prefer to have all our communications on what you're up to face to face with a go-between we trust, and definitely not transmitted via the embassy system."

Kevin frowned in confusion. "Surely I will need to have an ongoing line of communication?"

"Yes you will, but not via Embassy-encrypted signals. We've learnt at our cost over the years that they can't be relied on. There will always be someone, somewhere, who can break them. Similarly we can never be entirely confident that all our Embassy staff are trustworthy. To keep our secrets safe you will be contacted by an agent of ours. Once you're in place, he will make contact and you will be able to check his identity by his code name—we'll give you this before your deployment."

"So you're ready to leave?"

"Absolutely," said Kevin, nodded and stood up. "I'm looking forward to some real action, at last."

CHAPTER 19

The Embassy's HR Group had secured a floor in the nearby Australian-owned Hotel Connaught for the annual Christmas bash. Everyone from the Embassy was invited with their partners, and special invitations had been sent out to high ranking officials in government and the armed forces. There were also guests from Australian companies, particularly the ones importing significant quantities of Australian products to Indonesia. The bar was decked out with Australian vintage wines and an assortment of Australian brewed beers. A chef and three assistants were busy barbequing meals that would suit the Indonesian palate, as well as meeting halal requirements.

As Kevin Rowe walked in, wearing a smart batik shirt and loose cotton slacks, the walls were reverberating to evocative songs like LeAnn Rimes' 'Can't Fight the Moonlight' and Nikki Webster's 'Strawberry Kisses'. He was balancing a cold Australian white wine in one hand and a fusion spicy beef shish kebab in the other while working the room. Everyone had been given name cards and he made a point of personally welcoming any Indonesian guests, including a group of high-level officials from the offices of Indonesia's first female President, Marna Widaya.

President Widaya was surrounded by a retinue of her own staff, mostly beautifully dressed women who were talking discreetly among themselves. Two or three high ranking officers in full military regalia were also standing at the back of the room chatting in low voices.

Rodney Jensen

Kevin was drawn to this group as one of them, a large man in a splendid uniform and wearing many medals on his chest, seemed particularly merry. His laugh was infectious and all his group seemed to be sharing something hilarious. Kevin was curious and could not resist trying out his Bahasa to find out what was amusing them so much. As he reached the man who had started it all, he realised from his name card that he was a very senior officer in the Indonesian military forces, the 'TNI'.

The General noticed him and introduced himself. "My name is 'Bhudi', I compliment you on this great party and big welcome. Maybe you wondering why we all laughing?" he said speaking English well but with a strong accent and typical Indonesian sentence structure. Kevin nodded.

"I say to my friends, my niece used to love this music. She played it all the time at home loud. Now grown up and peace at last! My friends who have teenagers all say same! They love noise!" His laughter was infectious, and Kevin grinned back. Bhudi took another sip of his cold drink. "You know we like you Aussies and your ways. You make parties like this...how do I say...?"

"Informal, fun, not so serious?" Kevin suggested.

"Yes, all that of course. Bondi Beach and football for you. Troublesome politicians and many hungry, angry people here. Maybe you think we take life too seriously. No fun." He paused for a moment searching the nearby crowd, before lighting on someone close by. "Come I like to introduce you to my niece, Marayan. She working for Kemdikbud, you know? It our office for education, our history, things like that. She love it! I know she want to talk to you about Australia." He took Kevin by the arm and guided him towards a group of Indonesian women chatting together nearby.

"Marayan," he said, "I like you to meet my new friend. He speak good Bahasa and he talk about Australia. Maybe he get you visa?" he laughed.

"Oh Uncle, please!" She looked distinctly uncomfortable. A tall woman by Indonesian standards, her face was finely featured with large, almond-shaped brown eyes and minimal makeup. She wore her hair in a modest bun and was dressed in a traditional *kabaya* over a form-hugging ankle length skirt. Both the top and skirt were tailored in fine Indonesian silk. She was balanced on very high heels, yet moved gracefully across to Kevin. Her shoes brought her eyes almost level with Kevin's, and his pulse quickened as he smelt a faint waft of her exotic perfume.

"You like to visit Australia, Ibu…?" Kevin started, not sure how he should be addressing her so using the formal Indonesian title equivalent to Ma'am.

"Please call me Marayan," she said, softly shaking his hand. "Must not listen to my uncle! But what he say this time—true. I like Australian TV very much. But I have not travelled there. Just TV. I want to see koalas, I want to talk to—umm yes—Aborigines—we learn at school they trade with Indonesia long time ago before you take their country. You know this? Maybe you help me meet please?"

Kevin was momentarily stumped. "Not so many Aboriginal staff in our Embassy now, but if you come to Australia I promise that I can introduce you to some, including a few who work in our Government and others who live in the outback, work in tourism and can show visitors around. They are very proud of their history and can explain which places are important to them, and sacred. I'm sure you'd find that interesting."

"I do." She smiled.

« »

Quite apart from Marayan's potential for supplying intelligence unwittingly, Kevin felt strongly attracted to her. She had an exotic aura that made him want to meet her again in more private surroundings. Before she left for the evening he asked if she could join him for lunch sometime soon and could she suggest a place they might both like. He sweetened the invitation by promising to tell her more about Australia, "provided you do the same for me about Indonesia."

"Thank you, yes I like that," she responded, but then had a second thought. "But maybe I bring my friend from work. She speak better English and want to know about Australia too."

While Kevin spoke fluent Bahasa, he was happy to help her practice her English. He also understood the common need for 'chaperones' in Indonesia. Added to this, there was the potential for another contact, so Kevin was more than happy to go along with the extra company.

One week later they met at an upmarket café in Kota, a place Marayan had suggested. It was located on the edge of one of the large squares in the northern part of the city.

"It called Fatahilla Square," said Marayan, "Fatahilla very famous general we learn about at school. He threw out Portuguese before the Dutch come here. I know this place very well because that one of our main museums here." She pointed out the large obviously traditional European styled building opposite them. Even Kevin, no expert in traditional architecture, could see it looked like it belonged in an historic square somewhere in Europe.

"They government offices long time ago, built by the Dutch," she said. "Oh this 'Annisa'," she remembered at last to introduce her friend standing next to her. Kevin had already looked her over and thought she was no competition to Marayan, being neither tall nor slim. In any case, her head was covered by a headscarf, and her eyes were hidden behind dark glasses making it difficult to read her expression, although her lips were curved in a smile.

They entered the café and were immediately transported into the Colonial era, helped by a recent makeover. The walls and plush carpet looked new and freshly renovated. The room had been re-modelled in the art-deco style of the Dutch colonials in the 1930s. They ascended a wide staircase with an elegant mahogany handrail, to the first floor. Here the walls were decorated with black and white poster-sized images from the pre-war era in Jakarta. A smart maître-d' ushered them over to a large table on the balcony.

Once they had ordered drinks, Kevin started the conversation with a question he already knew the answer to. "Does President Widaya have much to do with your office?"

"Oh no!" Annisa piped up. "She not interested. As you say, 'she have much bigger fish to fry'. She spend most of her time meeting her close friends and working out what sound best on TV and in the papers." They all laughed.

"Sounds like politicians the world over," Kevin remarked. 'Survival comes first. We in Australia never expect much to change from one government to the next, despite what they tell us. But seriously, though, what is her position on East Timor? Will there be more cooperation in the future, do you think, between your countries?"

Marayan gave a warning glance to her friend and spoke first this time. "It not good to talk about these things. Most of us in Indonesia very angry with Timor-Leste. Why they want their own country? Habibie a fool. Wrong to allow them leave Indonesia."

Annisa, nodded seriously. "She right, most of us think this. But Australia not? We cannot understand this. Why you care about Timor-Leste? None of Australia's business!"

"Annisa," Marayan's voice sounded louder than it should, and Kevin thought she would have kicked her friend under the table, if it hadn't been such a large one.

"It's perfectly okay!" Kevin laughed at her obvious discomfort. "Not a problem. One thing I've learned in life is that I can trust people who are willing to speak their mind—like you do Annisa. But maybe we'd better change the subject." He picked up an elaborate menu which everyone had so far ignored. "Anything you'd recommend here?"

Kevin decided not to guide the conversation back to East Timor again, and instead, save it for later. As they were leaving the café and Annisa had excused herself to visit the Ladies', Marayan said to Kevin. "I hope you not mind my friend. She not diplomatic. That why she not in higher job in my office!"

"Of course, it's OK. In Australia we like to discuss topical issues that are in the news and many times we don't agree. So I'm not offended, I hope we can do this again and you could help me improve my Bahasa while I help you with your English. Would you like to be my guest at an Embassy concert next week?"

"Of course, I like that. I must go now, here come Annisa. Thank you for lunch Kevin. I enjoy it very much."

As she swept off with Annisa at her side, Kevin watched her parting back pensively. He felt excited that she'd accepted his invitation so readily. But he also began to have misgivings about her family, and more specifically how her Uncle Bhudi might feel about her linking up with a Westerner. But she radiated a powerful attraction that was hard to resist. His rational side was warning him in no way to consider getting involved, especially given his clandestine role, one which she could never know about. But on this occasion, it was his reckless side that had the upper hand and was telling the annoying voice of logic *go take a hike.*

CHAPTER 20

Sometime after Kevin's lunch with Marayan, he was seated at the bar of San Francisco Hideaway, a popular watering hole for expat journalists. Kevin was happy to share gossip unrelated to security matters and found the people he met there helped to keep him in touch with the buzz, including interesting stories doing the rounds that hadn't been printed.

Kevin, just as he'd finished talking with a news reporter who was about to leave, noticed out of the corner of his eye someone standing close by but didn't recognise him. The man ambled over. His hair was limp and mousy coloured and he wore thick-lensed glasses making his deeply recessed eyes seem unusually small. He was dressed in a loose jacket with frayed cuffs and baggy trousers that looked like they could do with a wash. Kevin thought he could detect a slightly Germanic accent as he spoke. "The name's Hadley," he said, holding out a hand. "I'm with Indonesian News (as far as everyone here's concerned)" he added quietly. "The folks back home have asked me to keep an eye on you," he continued, revealing who he really was. "If you've anything of interest to pass on at any time I'll explain where you can leave it securely."

"Do you think it's safe to talk here?" Kevin muttered under his breath.

"Probably not, but it's a good picking up place. If you see me in here at any time and catch my eye, just make an excuse and leave five minutes later. I'll be down the street a couple of hundred metres and we can talk privately if necessary. As a matter of fact, I do have something I'd like to discuss with you, so if you're not planning on meeting anyone else this evening, I'll see you in five minutes, okay?"

Kevin nodded.

As they sauntered down the street together, Kevin said, "Before I continue, I need to have your verbal password?"

"The banana season," Hadley said.

"Okay, what have you got for me?"

"Just some procedural stuff. If at any time we need to meet, send me an email to Hadley@INEWS.com with 'MEETING' in the subject line and we can begin our meeting at the Frisco the same evening around 8.00pm. Alternatively, if I need to see you, I'll leave a rolled up copy of Indonesian News in the mailbox where you're staying, and we can go through this same routine at the Frisco as well. That understood?"

"Sure," said Kevin.

Hadley had nothing further to say and wandered off by himself, while Kevin turned and hailed a taxi passing in the opposite direction.

As he sat in the back seat, Kevin felt bemused over his first encounter with another agent. He felt compelled to trust him given he knew the password AuSecurity had given him to confirm identity. It seemed almost unnecessary cloak and dagger procedure, the sort of intelligence he was gathering was little more than common knowledge. However he decided there and then, for his own preservation, to be very wary of anything he passed on to Hadley until he

had proved his worth and reliability, particularly if it
was high-level intelligence.

CHAPTER 21

Kevin's taxi, with its air-con at full blast, fought its way through the endless traffic jams of Central Jakarta. It was a good hour after leaving the Australian Embassy before Kevin reached his next appointment in the leafy upmarket precinct of Menteng.

General Bhudi Wistranto had given Kevin his name card at the Embassy party and Kevin lost no opportunity to request an audience. Bhudi's PA called back on the day of his call to say that her boss had invited him to a sundowner the coming Friday afternoon at his home.

Kevin was dropped off at the head of a leafy street because all traffic was barred at the entrance by a boom gate. The street lay eerily empty of cars or passers-by, since there were special security guards monitoring movements at each end. Kevin had to show his passport just to be allowed through, his name checked off against a guest list. It seemed truly remarkable that the military had the power to close an entire residential street in favour of this general. *He must be powerful*, thought Kevin.

The address he sought contained a large, three-storey house, situated well back from a lush and well maintained front garden. It had tall palms, neatly mown lawns and thick tropical greenery. The front entrance to the house was attended by a servant in a dazzling white uniform, who showed him deferentially through to the rear. The buzzing of conversation and the clinking of champagne glasses, sounded over the dulcet strains of 'Summertime', creating a surreal atmosphere. The singer was a young man with a husky nightclub voice, clad in traditional batik clothing, and for backing, he was surrounded by a small and slick jazz ensemble. The effect was heightened by the sound of water trickling into a large pool, the central feature of which was a sculptured nymph clad in flowing robes and surrounded by gorgeous lotus flowers.

General Wistranto spotted Kevin arriving and shook his hand vigorously. He was the centre of attention in a group of some thirty people. "Come meet my friend, Sam Harjanto. Sam this is Lieutenant Kevin. I tell you about him."

Sam, Kevin guessed, was also a military man, who seemed affected by the champagne, judging by his slight slurring of words. "Bhudi say I must be nice to you because you from Australia and you are Army too."

Kevin sensed an undertone behind the humour and responded carefully. "I've been told to be nice too, by my superiors, so here I am, let's be friends," Kevin laughed. *Damned East Timor*, he was thinking, *there's still deep resentment and it's hardly surprising given the resources it took for us to head the so-called INTERFET peace mission. And it's all a matter of face to them. If I were in their shoes, I'd feel just the same.*

"It's a shame that East Timor should have ever come between us," said Kevin. "But we are such close neighbours it must be settled, and I believe it has been. Indeed, I understand my government wants to resume joint military operations as soon as possible."

"Yes, I hear that also," said the other officer. "You take part?"

"No, I'm not operational. I am here purely as a diplomat. Perhaps this is not the time, but I would welcome the opportunity to set up a briefing by our ambassador if you wish me to arrange it?"

"Sound like good idea. I'll discuss with Budhi. I think he interested too."

For the rest of the afternoon, Kevin circulated among Bhudi's high-level guest-list and stuck to soft drink. Putting the delicate issue of East Timor aside, he was kept busy fending off similarly sensitive topics, including front and centre, the burning issue of Australia's recent policy on refugees.

"You push the problem back on us," claimed another guest he was discussing this with. "Our camps are full, and our villagers, poor. Who can blame fishermen when they offered much money by people smugglers? I know fishermen take people across to Christmas Island many times. They not mind getting caught. They find life easy in clean prison for one or two years. Worth prison for the money they get from the smugglers, much more than fishing."

"I've heard that too. But what efforts are being made by your police to round up the smugglers?"

"They too clever, too dangerous. Never deal directly. Impossible to prove because fishermen too frightened to say anything, and if they do talk…" The man drew a finger across his throat. Kevin laughed, because there was nothing he could think of to say, faced with the practicalities of such a fundamentally corrupt system.

As the sun was low on the horizon, Bhudi took Kevin aside quietly and offered him a fragrant

Indonesian clove tobacco cigarette, which Kevin politely declined. "You are Duntroon Officer, no?"

"That's correct. I've been very lucky to get my first assignment with the Embassy and experience life here."

Bhudi nodded and looked Kevin straight in the eye. "We know that military staff for the Australian Embassy often involved in, how you call it, 'information gathering', so I am in tricky position with you. I think you like my niece, no?"

Kevin nodded.

"She and me very close, see? Her daddy and mummy die when she young in car accident. I look after her since she baby. Maybe you good for her and can get her permanent visa to Australia. I think she better off in your country. But can I trust you? You take care of her, like me?" He put his hand up as Kevin started to say something. "Biggest question I have, what you here for? I know you cannot tell me, but if you find out things not good for Indonesia, I must report, you understand?"

Kevin nodded, feeling he was on a dangerous tightrope.

"We catch you, maybe we put you in prison, maybe you deported quick smart. Deal off! Understand?" Kevin nodded again.

"I like you Kevin. I think you being straight with me. But I want us have understanding. You come across anything bad for Indonesia, you clear with me first, okay?"

Kevin was astounded at this blatant proposition to compromise his position and undermine his agent status, but kept a straight face. "I can only promise to do that if there are questions which require clarification. I will run them past you, let's say as a journalist might. You can tell me the sensitivities."

Bhudi seemed satisfied with this answer and nodded his assent.

"I get you tickets for our National Day Parade. Big Honour. You must salute our troops! Sit next to me and Marayan."

Bhudi cast his cigarette stub aside and led Kevin by the arm to the drinks table, picked up a glass of wine handed it to him, and then took one for himself. "Come we drink to special understanding."

"Cheers!" Kevin responded.

Bhudi moved in closer and said in a low voice that no one else could hear: "Now Kevin, how we get Marayan permanent visa to your country?"

CHAPTER 22

A week later, Kevin had an unexpected call from Bhudi. "How are you my friend? I call to invite you join me in light exercise," he announced cryptically.

Kevin wasn't sure what he meant, wondering if he wanted him to watch his soldiers in the field.

"Do you play golf, Lieutenant Rowe?"

The light dawned on Kevin. "Yes a little. I used to play with my dad as a kid and help find his golf balls."

"I have friend play with me tomorrow morning at Jakarta Golf Club. You want come?"

"Why not? Yes I'd be delighted. But, I don't have any clubs," he said, fighting for an excuse.

"That okay. We hire set for you, no problem! We play nine holes, can do eighteen if you like?"

Kevin knew enough about golf to be mildly interested. There was also the invaluable opportunity to meet more of Bhudi's influential friends. His childhood experience had taught him the basics, and he had played the odd game with friends but nothing more than that. Concerned that he might disgrace himself, he rang the ambassador's PA, found out that there was a practice driving range where he could hire clubs and headed there that afternoon.

<< >>

Kevin was shown into the club by someone working in the reception area, who'd been warned to expect him. He discovered Bhudi wearing a khaki green tropical suit, sitting alone in the bar with a large glass of beer for company. There was nobody else. Bhudi got up and greeted Kevin warmly, immediately asking him what he'd like to drink.

"Same as you're having," Kevin said.

"Lieutenant Kevin, I'm sorry, but my friend who say they join us, not coming—too busy! We play alone, okay?"

At the professionals shop, Bhudi insisted that they take a golf cart and caddy along.

"The cart make easy in sun. Caddy know this course, much better than you or me. He help find balls and choose clubs. He very useful here, grass very long," he said with a laugh. He would not accept any money for the day, explaining, "only members allowed pay."

Kevin accepted it all graciously.

They set off along a path to the first fairway, a dog-leg corridor of untamed grass, with various mounds and bunkers, lined by tall palms and luxuriant undergrowth making an impenetrable 'rough' for the unwary. The sun was high in the sky and the all-enveloping quiet, interrupted only by a variety of unusual bird calls, created a relaxing respite from the normal background hubbub of Jakarta.

Bhudi insisted that Kevin have the first drive. The caddy handed Kevin a suitable club, "It short par four Boss. Swing ball around dogleg and aim for middle." Kevin laughed at this obvious briefing with the implicit assumption he wouldn't know what he was doing, or maybe wanting to test him out. *I'll show him!*

Rodney Jensen

Kevin carefully placed his ball on a tee, took a couple of practice swings and finally drove the ball high along the fairway landing close to the palms just beyond the dogleg. There was dead silence for a moment before both Bhudi and the caddy laughed. The caddy muttered something softly to Bhudi in Indonesian, which Kevin didn't quite catch. He looked inquiringly at Bhudi.

"He say you setting me up. He think me betting on you losing. Maybe you pro and keep quiet!"

"Beginners luck," said Kevin. "We've hardly started." Their unintentionally condescending attitude made him feel more determined than ever to show them a thing or two.

As it turned out, there was no contest. Bhudi was a hopeless player who succeeded in losing five balls against Kevin's one, on the first nine holes. Two of Bhudi's balls landed in water hazards, the others ended up in the rough and the caddy made only token efforts to retrieve them. On the eighth hole, Bhudi landed his ball deep in a bunker and took six shots to extricate it, finally lofting it far beyond the green. When he eventually made the small circle of closely mown grass, Kevin had lost count of his strokes, although the caddy seemed to be taking note.

By the time both men finally sank their putts on the ninth green, they were drenched in sweat and agreed to call it a day. The caddy produced beers from the back of the cart and Bhudi suggested they walk back along a shortcut, directly to the clubhouse, through a small belt of 'jungle'.

"He take our things in the cart, we walk, have privacy. Nobody listen," Bhudi added, conspiratorially.

Once they were out of earshot and walking along a shady path, Bhudi took Kevin by the arm. "I think you easier to talk with than Ambassador Marsden. He older than you. He not talk to me. Do not speak Bahasa, do not listen."

Kevin nodded.

"What in particular do you want to talk to our ambassador about, that he doesn't want to hear?" Kevin asked, demonstrating that he fully understood his boss's limitations.

Bhudi looked around him, as though he were making doubly sure that nobody could overhear what he was about to say. "What you know about Timor-Leste?" He asked. "How you think Indonesia like situation?"

"Difficult for you I suppose." Kevin paused before continuing with a more thoughtful response. "Anything I say is not the official line, understand? Making any commentary on your foreign policy is not what I'm here for. My job is simply to listen and report. But if you want to know what I think, the problem started with your previous president and the advice he was given. Maybe he called the referendum too soon and didn't make sure that the people fully understood what would become of their country if they decided to withdraw from Indonesia. He should have ensured that there had been more work explaining the economic benefits they stood to lose. That kind of thing."

Rodney Jensen

Bhudi nodded. "You right," he said. "Our new president bit smarter than those men before her. She want Timor back. It part of Indonesia. Now it make many problems for us. Other places in Indonesia want independence too. Aceh have freedom fighters. Aceh want independence and full Sharia Law. Many other places similar. Sulawesi have many Christians fighting Muslims. Neither side happy. West Papua, another where your country cause problem for us. We think Timor-Leste may, how you say, 'unzip' Indonesia. Indonesia become a thousand different islands again. Our government say 'No! Never go back!' We must not unzip. Have to stop unzip!"

Kevin was taken aback by Bhudi's sudden vehemence and chose his next words very carefully to avoid inflaming him further. "I'm not sure why you're telling me all this. Most Australians have supported Timor's Independence. They hope your relationship with Timor can become friendlier, soon."

"Fat chance, as you Aussies say!" Bhudi spat back. "I tell you for good reason, my friend. I know you not diplomat in embassy, but spy. It obvious. You not have to answer, just listen," he added as Kevin began to protest his innocence. "You tell your bosses we want deal with Australia over Timor-Leste. We want Timor-Leste back in Indonesia. No independence. Big mistake."

"What sort of deal? That's not my role. I'm no broker. I don't have the ear of politicians who make these decisions."

"We think maybe you do have friends who agree with us," Bhudi persisted. "So why you think Australia support Timor-Leste?"

"Again if you want my private opinion, Indonesia had no right to take over when Portugal deserted the place. It was only because America was terrified of communism that the Americans and Australia, following US Foreign Policy, turned a blind eye to what Indonesia was doing."

"You wrong and innocent, my friend. That what they want you think. You heard of 'Timor Gap'. That is what Australia really want. Australia want oil and gas that Indonesia own, now Timor-Leste taken and Australia grab. It nothing about history or communism, I tell you."

"An interesting take, and maybe there's some truth in what you say. But why do you think Australia might be willing to make a U-turn in its policy towards Indonesia and abandon Timor-Leste. And what preparations or plans does Indonesia have that could accomplish such a takeover in the face of world opinion?"

Bhudi stopped walking because they were nearing the end of the path and the clubhouse could be seen at the end of it, the voices of golfers chatting becoming clearly audible. He turned to Kevin and spoke softly. "That top secret. I not tell you details. Just say we have plan, but must have Australia's agreement not to interfere."

"Why would Australia agree to that?"

"Australia want strong Indonesia. Timor-Leste very small, very unimportant. Australia frightened of

Chinese. Big threat and get bigger. Indonesia big ally for Australia against China. But main thing, I tell you, Australia want more gas and oil in Timor Gap. If Australia help Indonesia, we give you all gas and oil in Timor Gap. Indonesia have plenty more. You need gas and oil."

"And what guarantees would there be?"

"Secret treaty. Both sides tell nobody else. Simple. Sign Treaty. We agree. You tell your bosses. Unless your boss speaks to our president we deny this conversation ever happen. You understand?"

"Okay, I'll agree to pass this on. Do I understand that you have any authority to be putting this to me?"

Bhudi nodded. "Yes that right. From very top," he said, tapping his forehead. "I am asked to ask you. But if leak, I deny. Nothing happen. Deal off!"

CHAPTER 23

"You must be on a better expense account than me," said Joseph Last, as he and Kevin stood waiting for their third guest. Last, the Embassy Press Secretary, was a foxy-faced middle-aged man, clean shaven and completely bald headed. He was wearing a crumpled linen suit, and scruffy shoes, well past their use-by-date. He looked under-dressed in the lobby of the Pumpkin Hotel, a modern five-star multi-storey edifice, built during the development boom of the 1980s, and nowadays increasingly popular with Jakarta's growing middle class.

"I can't complain," Kevin replied. "As you know I have to travel a lot and meet influential people…ah, here's Julie," he said, noticing his second guest coming towards them.

Julie Bristol was the Australian ambassador's PA and, while not Kevin's type, he had taken a shine to her and regarded her as one of his few friends in Jakarta, despite their age difference. She was an attractive blonde woman, in her mid-thirties Kevin guessed. She was elegantly clad in a long black skirt and matching lightweight jacket. She wore a simple silver pendant and high heels making her far taller than many others in the room. Heads turned as she received Kevin's kiss on both her cheeks, with casual panache, and Last's more awkward kiss on her extended hand.

Kevin beckoned the maître d', who hurried over and escorted them to a secluded table in one corner of the dimly lit room. A pianist was playing popular hits of the past and there was a low buzz of sophistication in the air.

"Jolly well done, I must say," remarked Last with approval, "you haven't taken long to find your feet here have you?"

Kevin didn't feel the need to respond, but Julie piped up: "It was my suggestion, as a matter of fact. The ambassador often dines here, and he recommended it as a safe option for entertaining visitors."

"You come here often then?" asked Last, staring at both of them inquisitively.

"Only when the ambassador needs a secretary along to listen and take note of what's being said. Usually it's his wife who accompanies him," she said more for Kevin's benefit.

Kevin had asked Last and Julie along to pick their brains so he could understand the ambassador better. He had something of a reputation for poking into other peoples' affairs, and that could be a problem if he got too close to Kevin's new contacts.

"So as Press Secretary, what do you get up to most of the time? I hardly ever see you in the office?"

"I've got my contacts of course," Last responded, "but at least half my day is spent catching up with various news sources, checking the internet, listening on shortwave sometimes, reading the local papers as best I can, and…"

"But," Julie chipped in, "I'd have imagined you'd be speaking to journalists, other Embassy staff, government people, wouldn't you?"

"That too, of course. It's mostly over the phone unless there's a big story breaking where I need to trace the story using sources of my own."

"What's your opinion," Kevin asked Last, not expecting to learn much, "of the way Howard's been handling the refugee situation in Australia and how Indonesia's been responding?"

"I never comment on our political master's policy stuff, old boy," he replied pompously. "I have my personal views of course, but from bitter experience I've learned to keep them to myself. Over time, I have worked out that whatever politicians may say in public is pretty much irrelevant to public affairs, or for that matter, to who's driving the real outcomes behind the scenes."

"Like who? I'd be interested to know who you think drives refugee decisions in this country," Julie said.

"I've heard rumours of course. There are one or two 'Mr Bigs' who run things, without revealing their identities. They're making fortunes at the refugees' expense, forcing them to pay extortionate amounts for seats on leaky boats. But it would be death to the boat owner who rats on them, I'm sure. That's why it's impossible to nail them. They're far too clever for that. If you're really interested in this, I suggest you have a word with Derek Seddon, who's currently liaison for Australian Federal Police."

There was a lull in their conversation as their attention was drawn to a small jazz ensemble that had taken over from the pianist. A few couples were dancing on a minuscule circle of hardwood boards in the centre of the room.

"How about a dance?" Julie asked Kevin boldly.

Kevin was only too eager to escape Last's know it all opinions on everything, and they left him to himself.

Rather than scout some other woman to dance with, Last beckoned a waiter and ordered another drink, staring morosely at his friends as they pirouetted happily around the floor.

Kevin wasn't a bad dancer, but Julie took the lead, obviously knowing a lot more than him. "What made you ask me to join you? Wasn't this intended to be a boys' night out?" Julie whispered in Kevin's ear as they started dancing a slower more intimate number.

"I know what you mean. I suppose I was hoping one of us might be able to draw him out a bit and tell us something of interest. Have you seen any of his reports?"

"Just scanned some of his stuff—they're supposed to be for the ambassador's eyes only, but they're always innocuous things which anyone could read in the paper."

"Waste of space in fact." Kevin paused before continuing with some hesitation. "Now here's the thing. I'm not sure that he is completely trustworthy. A couple of Embassy people have warned me to be careful what I say to him. So I've been planning to put him to the test."

"Is that a good idea? Mightn't it rebound on you?"

"I can't afford to have dealings with snoops and gossips in the Embassy. Quite simply, it could put my life at risk and I'm not having it. So, if you're amenable I want to tell him in confidence that we have decided to get engaged…" Julie raised her eyebrows but nodded.

"When we've finished this dance, make your excuses and head off to the powder room. Give me 10 minutes to sow a seed, and we'll see what he does with it. Should the ambassador hear that we've decided to get engaged, you'll be able to completely deny the rumour, and of course so will I."

"Oh that's very naughty of you. Poor man might lose his job."

"That's exactly what I have in mind."

"You're a ruthless bastard, you know that?"

"Yes, I've been told that before. Anyway, it's time to set the trap. Make it ten minutes, remember."

« »

Several days later, an inter-office memo came through Kevin's internal email system.

Ambassador Marsden requires your presence as a matter of urgency.

Kevin knocked on his office door and entered.

The ambassador was studying some documents on the table in front of him and took a full minute to look up at Kevin.

"Good of you to come so promptly. I've just been reading the background briefing on East Timor's Presidency. You may have already heard—Gusmao's become East Timor's first President."

"Yes, I had heard. It's no surprise given his popularity; it won't make the Indonesian Government very happy…Was there something you wanted to see me about?"

The ambassador shifted in his seat awkwardly. "Listen, Kevin, I find this extremely uncomfortable, but I have to check. I have heard that you have become engaged to my personal assistant Ms Bristol."

"Whoever told you that?" Kevin responded in mock astonishment.

"It's awkward—I can only tell you it was a confidential source."

"Have you asked Ms Bristol about this?"

"Not yet. I was hoping what I heard is wrong because such a relationship is against our regulations and one of you would have to leave if it were correct," he continued unhappily.

"Well I can reassure you on that score, and I know Ms Bristol will tell you the same—we are definitely not engaged. But I do happen to know who your source has been, because I set it up. I was warned that the man was not trustworthy, so I thought I would tell him something in strictest confidence and see what he did with it. The fact he's leaked it to you proves the warnings I've received were justified and that it is he who should be given his marching orders. I'll leave it to you to decide whether or not you feel comfortable having someone working around here who obviously can't be trusted."

With that Kevin got up and left the ambassador to ponder the situation, though lingered beside Julie's desk to see what happened next.

A few moments later, the ambassador spoke to his PA over the intercom. "Ms Bristol, could you come in please?"

Some days later Kevin received a curt note from the ambassador. It read:

Kevin, I am writing to let you know that Ms Bristol confirmed your version of events, and consequently I've been forced to ask for Mr Last's resignation. I have to say, however, that I am far from happy with your conduct in this matter and deplore the process of entrapment you have employed to capture a man who in my opinion has been a victim of his own gullibility more than malice towards either of you. So, take this as a warning. Should I discover any repetition of your high handedness in respect to any of my staff, you will suffer the same fate as Mr Last. Count yourself lucky on this occasion that I have decided only to give you this warning.

Yours etc.

Kevin smiled wryly as he read the note, squeezed it into a ball and threw it into his bin. He had it on good authority from Hadley that the Ambassador Marsden's days were numbered. "The man's main problem," Hadley had said, "is that he wants everyone to like him, and on many occasions has let things slide, particularly with regard to matters of security. It's not a post calling for a popularity award."

Kevin could only agree, and felt really relieved to have engineered the departure of someone who was far too nosey for his liking. But while the ambassador remained at his post, he vowed to keep his activities strictly secret, and for the eyes of his contact Hadley alone.

CHAPTER 24

Following operational protocols, Kevin wrote a brief report of his dealings with Bhudi, encrypted it, burnt the file onto a USB stick and put it into a small ziplock plastic bag. He left it at a previously arranged safe-drop for pick up by Hadley. Not long after that, Kevin discovered a rolled up copy of 'Indonesian News' in his apartment's letterbox. He made sure he was in the Frisco Bar later that evening.

Hadley finally showed up after 9.00pm, ordered a drink and stood in a corner for a while, before putting his glass down and leaving.

Kevin had consumed more beer than usual and was glad to make his excuses and head off after him.

Some minutes later they met in their usual spot further down the road and began to stroll casually together.

"I've passed on your Timor Gap report and it's been received with interest," Hadley said in a low voice. "However to quote you know who, 'there's not a bat in hells chance that any Australian Government would agree to such a deal!' "

"So what do I tell my contact?"

"Nothing. We don't want to inflame the situation more than necessary. If he asks, just say it's been received and is under consideration. Leave it at that. If it ever became public, it'd be dynamite. Australia's never going to be part of such a deal, much as we want their oil and gas." Hadley paused, waiting for Kevin to take stock.

"Anyway, this is not actually the reason I arranged to meet. Something else has come up." Hadley paused again to crouch down and tie up a shoelace, while covertly checking to make sure they weren't being followed. Then as he got to his feet, Kevin felt Hadley passing a document into his hand. "Keep that in your pocket and burn it when you've finished. Got to go— until next time then." Hadley turned up a side street and disappeared without saying another word.

Kevin followed instructions and caught a taxi back to his apartment. Once inside the privacy of his room he looked at what Hadley had given him. The envelope was plain with no writing on it. He slit it open and found a single sheet of paper inside, with a logo he'd not seen before: 'Aus Import/Export'. There was a short message without any further identification or signature, which read:

ADF's remote-sensing satellite has identified unusual troop and supply movements from the TNI base in western Java to 'Sumequat', a small town in central Sumatra. The town is located on the equator. Its main economy is based on tourists who want to cross between the northern and southern hemispheres for fun/curiosity. The roads are exceptionally bad which may partly explain why a new airstrip has been cut into a stretch of flat land close to the river that runs through this town. New tracks have also been bulldozed from there through to a nearby hill. A security fence is currently being erected around the entire perimeter of these works including the hill. Together, they represent a very large outlay of resources for such a remote area and we have set an urgent priority on learning the reason why.

Rodney Jensen

At this stage, media seem unaware of the sensitivity of what is going on and the only reports available suggest that this new base is being set up to deal with Acehnese separatists. That explanation is highly improbable however, given the distance from this location to Aceh Province. Our intelligence experts have suggested that the equatorial location might well be significant and possibly connected with space activities, such as a new rocket launch facility for geostationary satellites. While there is absolutely no evidence that Indonesia possesses such technology, if it proved to be correct, there would have major strategic and defence implications for Australia.

In order to help us clarify what is happening on this site and why, we need you to take a closer look from ground level. Please investigate on-ground activity and report ASAP.

Kevin read the text one last time before burning it in his ashtray.

« »

It was mid-afternoon and Kevin was still on the bus from Padang in south-western Sumatra, heading in the direction of Sumequat. It had already been an exhausting journey along winding roads, with several near misses with oncoming traffic. The driver and the passengers seemed completely oblivious to their near encounters with death.

Kevin had paid for two seats because he was much too big to fit comfortably into the minuscule seating the bus provided. He had parked his bags beside him to ward off inquisitive strangers and their questions.

But a man seated across the aisle still leant over and asked: "Where you heading, boss?"

"I'm here to explore some jungle areas," he said, using his prepared story. "I'm from Australia, and I am very interested in seeing animals such as Orangutan, which I'm hoping to photograph."

The man looked amused. "Many visitors want to see, but we not have Orangutan in this area. You need car? I get you one in Bonjol?" He said hopefully.

"Thanks. Maybe. I'm not sure." Kevin was puzzled and not sure why the man had mentioned Bonjol.

But when the bus came to a stop in that town and the driver beckoned him to the front of the bus, he learnt that they were not going all the way to Sumequat, but continuing instead along the main road towards northern Sumatra. He was told that he would have to find some other means of transport the rest of the way. "Ya Sumequat, two hours drive from here." the driver confirmed.

The passenger he'd been talking to across the aisle came running after Kevin as he alighted. "You want car now?" Kevin nodded and the man pulled out his mobile phone. "He my brother in law. I check." It dawned on Kevin that this man's main business was touting for customers like himself.

Before long, a battered Toyota Landcruiser dating from the 1970s rolled up beside them. A small Indonesian with a wide grin and several front teeth missing jumped out and grabbed Kevin's haversack. 'Dewi', as he was called, wanted to be paid far more than hiring a car in Jakarta would have cost. Kevin made a half-hearted attempt to negotiate but was hardly in a position to bargain with no other options available. He finally got in the front seat and the two set off leaving the tout to catch the next bus in the opposite direction.

"He live near Bukit Tinggi," remarked Dewi. "He my agent," he said with a hint of pride.

It quickly became painfully obvious that a 4WD was the only suitable vehicle to take on the badly degraded track. The combination of constant pounding over bumps and potholes, rock hard seats and even stiffer suspension made Kevin's body ache as though he'd gone sixteen rounds in a heavyweight contest.

Only halfway through the journey, Dewi exclaimed angrily and had to brake to a standstill as they came around a curve to find a long column of army trucks taking up the whole road. They had no choice but to remain trapped behind the convoy in an endless procession for the rest of the journey. Just when it was starting to get dark and sporadic lights at the edge of town had finally come into view, the driver of Kevin's car was flagged down at a checkpoint and pulled over.

"What he doing here?" the soldier demanded of Dewi in Bahasa, pointing at Kevin, who handed over a cover passport under the assumed name of 'Trevor James', turned to the page with the current visa stamp. "He working for media?" the soldier asked Dewi.

"He speak Bahasa, ask him yourself, I not know what he do. I drive him from Bonjol to Sumequat, that all"

"I come here to search for wildlife in jungle areas," Kevin said in Bahasa. "I am just a tourist. Do not work for media."

"No jungle near here!" the soldier said, clearly unconvinced with Kevin's story. "You wait here," he said to Dewi and walked off to discuss with another soldier who was standing at the kerb smoking. They talked for a few moments, before he returned still clasping Kevin's passport. Once again he addressed Dewi, ignoring Kevin. "Foreigners not come here. This prohibited area. Must take him back to Bonjol."

"But I have a booking to stay here tonight," Kevin lied.

The soldier pondered for a moment. "Okay. We keep passport. Come back tomorrow morning before 8.00 am. Then go back!"

With the help of Dewi, who actually lived in Sumequat, Kevin was introduced to a middle-aged lady and her husband who ran a small shop in the main street. They had five children and seemed to be scratching a living. The lady offered Kevin a bed for the night with dinner and breakfast. Dinner was served early and he sat down with the family to eat delicious local foods including a spicy curry and various fruits.

There was little conversation because Kevin found it difficult to understand the local dialect. He ate his food with relish, finding himself an object of fascination to the children who were unused to meeting white people, particularly ones who could speak Bahasa. The youngest of them, boy and girl twins, could not take their eyes off him the entire evening. They were very curious about his looks and giggled at the way he spoke to them, using very formal language compared to the kampung version they spoke.

Rodney Jensen

By the time it was late evening and the children had finally gone to bed, it was easy for Kevin to make his excuses and retire early, saying it had been a long day and he was feeling tired. His room was a very small outhouse behind the main building within an area that functioned as a farmyard, vegetables growing near the back fence, chickens in cages, a mongrel dog with a curly tail that snarled and sniffed at his legs and feet, and two competitive cats who brushed themselves against him and would have joined him in his room if he'd allowed them to.

Kevin set an alarm on his watch to rouse himself at two in the morning, before falling into a deep and dreamless sleep.

The vibrating alarm on his wrist took many seconds to penetrate. He fumbled to find his things in the darkness, not daring even to use his torch. He crept softly out into the yard hoping to avoid disturbing the animals, before leaving via the side entrance. He'd paid his dues in advance and taken everything with him, not expecting to be back.

It didn't take him long to work out where to go, having previously made a copy of an aerial photo from the Embassy library. It showed that there was only one road crossing over the river, and as he approached the junction with the main street, he was passed by more army trucks, heading in the same direction.

The constant troop movements kept him on his guard and he limited his advance to short stages, moving from one piece of shadowed cover to the next. The lack of street lights made it easier to conceal himself, but the bridge, an old Dutch structure with badly corroded metal trusses and a total span over the river flats of more than three hundred metres, was completely lacking in cover. To make things worse, there was no side path, and he had no choice but to jog quickly across via the road surface, hugging the balustrade, and hoping not to be spotted.

Not long after he'd started the crossing, the sound of a large truck approaching from behind set his heart beating faster and he sprinted the last fifty metres, throwing himself to the ground down an embankment once he reached the other side. The truck's headlights were already sweeping the bridge and he could only hope that the driver had missed seeing him in the gloom.

The truck thundered over the hardwood slats and didn't slow as it came abreast of his hiding place. Kevin breathed a heavy sigh of relief, and allowed his pumping heart to settle before continuing.

As he emerged onto the road beyond the bridge, he could see a floodlit area in which earthworks had been taking place: the new airstrip. It was far from complete, with an unfinished control tower and bare concrete slabs waiting for hangars or other buildings. It all seemed haphazard and uncoordinated. Several helicopters and a large troop carrier were parked to one side of the runway together with a large collection of trucks and 4WDs. The lights were confined to the working areas and there were none on the landing strip, nor any signs of soldiers. Kevin hoped that the lack of any obvious activity meant there would be no landings that night.

Rodney Jensen

He continued along the track circling around the end of the runway and slowly ascending. In the darkness, he could see a hill, looming above the skyline. Then, as he turned at a slight bend in the road, a boom gate barred his way, and behind that, a three-metre high fence, with a second gate on rollers, which he guessed would be locked.

Kevin chose not to try climbing over the gate but continued around the fence. Having gone about two hundred metres, he was beginning to regret his decision, his progress constantly impeded by mounds of loose rubble that had been excavated for the fence posts. But eventually he saw that the fence was still a work in progress with an unconnected coil of chain wire on the last of the posts. He looked carefully around to check there were no surveillance cameras, then walked directly towards the ridge line of the hill.

On his way, he had to beat his way through increasingly dense vegetation, while the slope became so steep he had to scramble and pull his way up with whatever handholds he could find. His watch was showing 3.30am. He gave himself half an hour to climb the last most difficult part, knowing that he had to get back well before dawn and hide up somewhere before retrieving his passport and returning to Padang.

It took him a full hour to reach the top of the ridge and rest in a secure observation point. It was a flattish expanse of rock leading to the edge of a cliff that defined the perimeter to a large enclosed basin. He crawled carefully to the edge of the cliff to take a closer look and could see that the basin stretched approximately two kilometres across to the opposite wall. The middle section of the basin was bathed in brilliant floodlight. He'd had some inkling of what to expect, having seen a loom of light as he'd approached the ridgeline. But now he was astounded to see the extensive lighting and evidence of troops on the ground.

"What on earth's going on here?" he muttered to himself.

He took up position on the flat rock surface, and watched through his field glasses, focusing on the central part of the basin. His Nikon was beside him. Below him he could now see a group of soldiers in the process of erecting a fence to form a circular enclosure around a deep excavation. At one side of the hole, a spiral track had been cut, wide enough to enable a front-end loader to descend to the bottom. But the focus of the soldiers' attention was a silver sphere centrally located in the excavated area. Kevin estimated that it was between 4 to 5 metres in diameter. It cast a harsh luminescence on the three men who were working around it. The spherical shape was somehow perched above them. Through the field glasses it appeared as though it was supported on a black plinth which rose to just above their heads. He picked up his camera and quickly took a series of wide angle shots and close ups.

The tractor's engine was idling, its bucket positioned high over the sphere, with a cable and hook dangling beneath. The soldiers were fixing some form of harness around the underside of the sphere, and then with the help of a makeshift ladder, hooking the webbing onto the cable.

Rodney Jensen

Apparently satisfied with their work, two of the men stood back and the third jumped onto the tractor, revved the motor and started slowly lifting the bucket using the tractor's hydraulics. Kevin watched fascinated: "What the hell is that? Do they know what they're doing?" he muttered.

The cable tightened as the webbing took the strain, but nothing happened, until the cable snapped without warning and the tractor lurched upwards throwing the driver out of his seat onto the ground.

Kevin could not help but chuckle at their cack-handed efforts, until the sphere abruptly changed from silver to red, and started emitting a powerful pulsating sound. It was as if some warning had been set off, with a deep frequency that vibrated in Kevin's chest. He picked up his camera again, and snapped more photographs while soldiers shouted from the ground outside the fence.

All three of the men who'd been working on the sphere had disappeared—winked out of existence. It wasn't that they had been injured in some way. They had simply vanished!

Christ, what's going on there? Kevin felt a deep sense of awe and fear. It was as if some primitive tribe had suddenly seen the effects of a twenty first century weapon.

The pulsating noise stopped abruptly while, above the sphere, the fence workers cried out in terror. One of them looking as though he was in charge, shouted and waved his arms towards a truck parked some way back from the excavation site.

They all began running to the truck, hauled themselves aboard, and set off towards the other side of the basin out of Kevin's line of vision. There must have been an access track to the site he'd missed, which might cross his escape route. He put his camera's memory chip into a hidden compartment inside his boot sole, then buried the camera and his field glasses close to the rock ledge, thinking that any of these items would be a complication if he was caught. He then began retreating in the same general direction from where he'd approached the rim.

He found the descent even harder than his climb. The darkness didn't help, and because he now had what he wanted, he was tempted to move too quickly over the obstacle course of loose rock and tangled undergrowth.

As he crashed through some hidden creepers, one pulled him back, twisting his ankle and throwing him flat on his face. He lay still for few seconds regaining his breath, then gingerly tried to get to his feet, grimacing with an agonizing pain that shot up his leg. To make matters worse, the sound of a truck engine slowly approached in low gear—he had tripped right above the access track and was in clear view of its headlights. *Hope I can bluff my way out of this,* he thought resignedly and crawled to the edge of the track, flagging the vehicle down.

The truck stopped abruptly and there were shouts. Two soldiers jumped out of the back of the truck with guns drawn, screaming at Kevin to remain on the ground. They searched and dragged him into the back of the truck, throwing him roughly to its metal floor.

Rodney Jensen

One of the men rested a boot on his back, and warned him not to move.

The truck returned to the military base, where Kevin was locked in a cell with nothing but a bed with a thin cotton covering, a flask of water and a bucket in one corner.

It was many hours before an officer came in with another soldier. They dragged Kevin to a separate room, put the camera and field glasses he'd buried in front of him, and began asking questions.

"What you doing here?" the officer asked him in English.

"I was searching for Orangutan and Sumatran Tiger," he said using his prepared story.

"If true, why you hide these?" they asked pointing at the damning evidence on the table.

"I was intending to come back for them later," he said, hearing how thin this sounded and realising he'd made a big mistake in attempting to conceal them.

Then the interrogators showed him the passport he'd been ordered to leave at the checkpoint. "You arrive yesterday. Guard tell you, must leave this morning. Why you not leave?"

"I was intending to leave as soon as I got back to the town. I twisted my ankle and had to get a lift otherwise I might have died out there."

Another officer came in who spoke reasonable English. "We very certain you lying, my friend. We photograph you and see what we find. You know penalty for spy in this country is death. So you think very carefully why you come here before next time we talk. If you tell truth, maybe we help, but if you go on lying, you know what will happen…" The man clenched his fist with his index finger pointing at his head like a gun. The meaning was clear.

Kevin was briefly taken to another cell where a camera was set up and photographs taken. He was thrown back into his cell, and allowed only water for the next twenty four hours.

It was cold at night despite being in the tropics, and his mind wandered. He had dug himself in a hole from which it would be difficult to escape without confessing. But if he told them the real reason it would only open up another can of worms. He had reached his lowest ebb. He had been trained in the art of interrogation methods and how to overcome standard tactics to break him at spy school. Now the reality of being held in isolation for hour after hour without much sense of time was very different from the theory.

He was lying on his bed staring at the ceiling, when steps approached in the corridor and a voice he recognised said to the guard in Indonesian, "Wait outside, I'll call if I need you."

The door was thrown open and General Bhudi Wistranto walked in.

"Ah my friend what have you got yourself into?" he asked, staring quizzically at Kevin. "We know what you doing here—that obvious. What I want know is how you find out about this?"

Kevin thought for a moment. *Should I continue trying to brazen my way out or should I level with Bhudi.* He decided that there was only one option—to venture an edited version of the truth. "We have a source who got wind of this. I cannot tell you who or how he came by this. I don't have a clue myself. But having seen what I saw the night before last, maybe it's time for cooperation or assistance from Australia?"

Bhudi laughed loudly. "My friend for someone in such bad position, I admire your courage. You know, one word from me, and firing squad!"

Kevin could only nod.

"But we think this not, how do I say this…"

"Originate from Indonesia?"

"No we think it not originate from Indonesia, not anywhere in this region."

"How did you come across it?" Kevin asked, growing bolder.

"Geologist looking for gold use metal detector. It register very high field and he search for centre of field where he start digging. It take him long time and he find something. You see it, yes?"

"Yes I saw it," admitted Kevin, "and I also saw what it did when your men tried moving it. It's not something I'm expert in, but there is no weapon I know of that could do what it did. It's a real mystery, unlikely to be solved easily. Could it really be that there's only one conclusion?"

Bhudi nodded solemnly in agreement. "Our scientists say it must be put there a long time ago but not by our people."

"And that worries you?"

"That worries us much. We not know its purpose, and that worries us. Maybe your scientists advise us, but keep secret?"

"I'm sure that can be arranged," said Kevin. "First you'll have to get me out of here."

Bhudi laughed again. "Maybe you live, you more use to us alive. Maybe my niece angry with me if she find I send you to firing squad! You be nice to her, okay!"

"Yes, just get me out of here first."

« »

Kevin and Hadley met in Jakarta some days later. This time Kevin handed over the camera's memory chip and a separate USB stick containing his encrypted report. "I've no idea what's going on there, and I don't suppose the military has much of a clue either. I'm not really the right person for this. They need scientists to inspect it properly and maybe that's what Indonesia is hoping we can provide. From what I understand from my contact, I think the Indonesians have no choice but to seek outside help and I reckon they'd prefer it to be us rather than the Yanks. It's quite obvious now why they're keeping this discovery so much under wraps."

"I'll pass it on," said Hadley. "There'll probably be repercussions with this one. One thing I can tell you, which I probably shouldn't, but I'm going to anyway, is that we have a source within TNI High Command. He was the one who first put us onto Sumequat. The rest you pretty much know?"

Kevin nodded.

"Anyway, our source advises us that the powerful field which resulted in the disappearance of the men, has not manifested since. All military have been withdrawn to a safe distance. Their own scientists who have been brought in to detect and measure the radiation have drawn a complete blank."

"It seemed to me that it wasn't man made and I wouldn't be surprised if there's alien involvement."

"You're not alone. The interesting bit is that AuSecurity hinted that they know of other spheres like the one you've seen."

"Where?"

"I can't tell you. I don't know myself. The information's classified. Our government, in common with others, is not exactly keen to admit there are more powerful forces than ours in the universe."

Kevin nodded, unsure what else to say.

CHAPTER 25

Kevin was in a bind with both Marayan and Bhudi. He felt strongly attracted to Marayan, though saw no obvious signs of her wanting to take the relationship to another stage. At the same time, perversely, she seemed willing to accompany him to various functions, mostly in neutral territory and to which she would also bring along Annisa as chaperone.

Bhudi's opportunistic wish list, including a special visa for his niece, was an even bigger problem for him. It bordered on blackmail in exchange for his ongoing protection from Indonesian security. He realised that it was a path fraught with danger. If he capitulated, it threatened his ongoing position in Indonesia. Bhudi simply had too big an interest and virtual control over him now, since his involvement in the Sumequat episode.

In any event, the situation was partially resolved when Kevin received an unexpected call in his Embassy office from Marayan herself. It was the first time she had ever called him other than to confirm something he had arranged or initiated.

"I go to Bali on Friday," she said. "It for work. I meet government officers in Denpasar, talk about many foreign tourists damaging important temples and places. It take all day. Then I fly home. But I think, maybe you want come too? We stay in Bali on Saturday and Sunday and I show you many places. You like?"

Kevin paused to think of a suitable response, one that wouldn't sound as enthusiastic as he felt. He wasn't sure what to think, this seemed so out of keeping with her normally demure behaviour.

"I'd love to come. But what would your uncle or your office think about it?" he finally offered, carefully. "They wouldn't approve, I think?"

Marayan giggled. "Maybe not. But I not tell them. I have my life. I grown up. This my idea."

"Well you can certainly trust me not to let anyone else know." He paused as a thought occurred to him. "Maybe it would be best if I arrange the place for us to stay. That way, you won't have to explain to your paymaster, if he or she starts asking embarrassing questions?"

Marayan laughed again. "It not like that in my office. I do what I like, when I like. It up to me. Everyone know my uncle very powerful man. No one want to make him angry. No interfere with my office arrangements."

Kevin shivered inwardly at her casual remark, confirming his worst fears. "That's very reassuring," he lied. "Look on this as a token of goodwill between our countries. For me it's just the same as you. Nobody in the Embassy ever checks my movements or expenses, it's up to me. In any case, I'd much prefer to arrange it myself and make sure that whatever we do is kept under the radar."

"What you mean 'radar'?"

It took Kevin a while to explain.

"Thank you," said Marayan. "I need you teach me proper English."

"It's actually slang. But yes, it is a common expression. There are plenty of other things I can teach you, if you like," he added, with a sly grin she could not see.

Marayan giggled again. "I not simple, I know what you think. You keep your thoughts on Bali history, not me, not what you want!"

Kevin sighed and promised to let her know what he'd arranged. The prospect of a weekend to himself with such a desirable young woman, her elegant clothes and heady perfume—it was making him go hard at the thought, simply too tempting to refuse.

Nothing ventured, he reflected.

« »

Kevin made tentative enquiries from hospitality staff at the Embassy, and found there was an old-style Dutch hotel in Bali's capital Denpasar, noted for its quiet atmosphere and excellent service. He arranged bookings under his pseudonym, just to be on the safe side, and they travelled in separate rows on the early morning flight.

After unpacking in their adjoining hotel rooms, Marayan went off to her work meetings which ended up only taking a couple of hours. Upon her return she insisted they did some typical tourist things, such as looking through shops and markets, visiting Hindu Temples.

The next day they hired a driver to take them to the northern coastline, via the impressive volcano 'Gunung Agung'. They discovered the northern beaches had magnificent surf and much fewer crowds than around

Kuta. Kevin also noticed a deeply suntanned and elderly white male sitting on the beach with a sign advertising surfing lessons and surfboards for hire. He claimed to have been instrumental in starting the surfing craze single-handed in Bali's early 1970s. Kevin had enjoyed surfing when growing up, so negotiated with him to teach Marayan the rudiments. Realising that Kevin was a fellow Australian, he gladly agreed. She proved to be a quick learner and by the end of the afternoon was able to stand up and catch small waves up to the beach.

As the sun set, their driver took them back to Denpasar, landing up in a bar close to the hotel late in the evening. Kevin was exhilarated and happy to have found something in common they could enjoy together and suggested they surf some more the next day. They had ordered a typical Balinese meal of fried rice noodles and special spices, while a rock band played popular favourites for Westerners. He persuaded Marayan to join him on the dance floor and they ended up doing crazy steps, attracting some attention from others in the bar.

Despite being completely unaccustomed to alcohol, Marayan took to all the cocktails they ordered, like a duck to water. After three 'Cock Sucking Cowboys', the quantity of vodka entering her bloodstream made her tipsy and dangerously beguiling. She stroked Kevin's face softly murmuring, "Naughty man, I know what you want!" in a slurred voice. Kevin could hardly keep his hands off her and chose to ignore the fact she was getting drunk. "I like you very much, you have the most beautiful eyes, I could eat you up. Let's go back to the hotel," he urged.

Marayan nodded. "Naughty man. I need to sleep. Take me to hotel and please excuse me. I feel, how you say, very tipsy."

Kevin guided Marayan up the stairs and put her to bed. He opened the adjoining door to their rooms and left her to sleep it off. He showered in his own room and clambered into bed in a state of turmoil. He knew very well that the line he'd be crossing with Marayan would be a one-way journey, even a threat to his career if he was sprung. But his lust for her exotic looks and the heady perfume he could still smell on his own hair gradually overcame any warning voices, and with new resolve he re-entered her room.

She lay there on the bed face down, her long dark hair draped over the pillows. Her mouth was slightly ajar, a small dribble of saliva sliding down her chin. She looked so fragile it was too much for Kevin, who slid in beside her and began caressing her body.

She regained consciousness drowsily as he pressed his hardness against her side. Suddenly she realised what was happening. "Kevin! No!" she cried loudly.

He couldn't have her causing unwelcome attention when they weren't supposed to be there in the first place, so before she had time to cry any louder, he put his hand over her mouth, muffling her screams. He whispered "It's OK darling, just relax, I know you want this as much as I do", and moved on top of her.

This is what they had come to Bali for, wasn't it? They had spoken about it and, with his head reeling from the vodka too, it made all the sense in the world to ignore her resistance which he was sure was coyness.

Rodney Jensen

He forced himself into her unable to control himself, so pent up that it was over in a few short seconds.

He waited until her shaking and sobbing subsided to remove his hand. She recoiled from him immediately, radiating her sense of violation and fear, and began to lash out, scratching and pummelling his face in shock and disgust. He tried to fend her off, pushing her against the bed where she banged her cheek on the bedside table and sobbed even louder.

What have I done?

He left the room quickly, leaving her lying on the bed crying. As soon as he left the room she rushed forward, slammed the door, and locked it.

A few minutes later, she turned on her shower—Kevin could hear it through the door.

Once she was done, she made a phone call, mumbling into the receiver, then moved around her room. Drawers opened and shut. The door from her bedroom into the hallway opened and shut. Then silence

« »

On Kevin's return to the office the following day, there was an ominous message waiting for him:

GENERAL BHUDI WISTRANTO WANTS YOUR ATTENDANCE AT MEETING ASAP TNI HQ.

Bhudi did not waste time launching his attack. "My informants say you and my niece make visit to Denpasar on weekend and stay in rooms at Netherlands Hotel. But what make me very angry, I find that on Monday morning she go to Bali Airport and catch first plane back to Jakarta alone. She look very unhappy. She say nothing, but it obvious what happen. You want explain?"

"How long have you been following us?" Kevin made a feeble attempt to divert the question.

"Since day one. You go with Marayan to lunch, she bring friend Annisa."

"Why would you do that?"

"It obvious. I am not stupid. We know you spy. We know that maybe you like my niece, but we think you want our information more. Now I tell you, you not welcome here in my country and I give you two choices."

"First choice, you resign from Embassy. You tell ambassador now and leave when you can. I give you two weeks. You think of good reason to tell ambassador. I not care what is."

"The alternative?" Kevin asked.

"I make one phone call and you get deportation order. Must leave in twenty four hours. I prefer not use this choice because it bad for Indonesia and Australia. We not want it in newspaper. If you sensible, find reason to leave so we not deport you. But one more thing—no one else know about this."

"And that is?"

"Some time, we want intelligence report from you. Our agent in Australia give you questions. If you not help us we tell your government why you leave Jakarta."

"Why should I believe this?"

"Because our pictures will make you listen very careful to what we ask," Bhudi replied. "We photograph you at first meeting with Marayan and all other time you meet her." Bhudi slid a file of colourful photographs, annotated with dates and times across the table. The last image was taken of Marayan, leaving the Bali airport, indeed looking unkempt and terrified quite unlike her normally happy appearance.

Kevin hung his head in shame. He didn't deserve any choices. Still, there was a decision to be made. If he were deported, his intelligence career would be at an end after only twelve months in Indonesia. Alternatively, he could leave of his own volition. He stared at Bhudi. "I'll be out of here in two weeks."

"Good choice. You never come back here. I make sure of that," said Bhudi.

Part Three

Rodney Jensen

CHAPTER 26

There was a muted atmosphere in the Parramatta Regional Office for NSWPol as Kaz returned to her desk after her interview with AuSecurity. It wasn't long before Stewart invited her outside for coffee, in the conveniently located café, in the square below their office.

"I thought you'd given up on us," he said, as he sipped his cappuccino absently. They were sitting inside in a corner of the café well out of view. Stewart was looking at Kaz with a regret that seemed to have nothing to do with police business.

"AuSecurity has notified you of the new agreement, haven't they?" she sighed.

"They have indeed. It puts me and the others in a funny position though, doesn't it?" he replied with some heat.

"No I don't think so. I've had to agree that anything I intend to pursue has to be vetted in case it touches on areas that are classified. I don't think that's unreasonable given the delicate nature of our relationship with Indonesia."

"But it makes the situation between us even more difficult now than it did before, doesn't it?"

"You mean that you can no longer treat me as an underling?" she replied, waiting for him to react, or not.

"No, that's not it at all. I've never treated you as an underling. I just think it's a recipe for more conflict between us. In any relationship there's bound to be conflict, but usually more personal in nature. Now I see endless scope for disagreement about these work-related matters and how you do things."

"That sounds like you're already regretting 'us'?"

"I didn't imagine this would happen. It makes matters awkward. In future, we must agree to disagree if we start getting into an argument, and particularly if it's in front of my staff."

Kaz took a deep breath, calling on herself to stay calm. "I really think you underestimate me, Stewart. Do you think I would be so insensitive to do such a thing? If that's your perception, it's pretty unflattering. I've been playing by your rules, and if you're honest about it, neither you nor the SAPol team would have got where we are without my efforts."

"I'm not suggesting you haven't made a contribution but I'll stick to my description of your role. You came to us with no police experience and now you've got pretty much carte blanche to do what you like. Is it surprising I'm not exactly enthusiastic about your new status and where it leaves us? I'm pretty certain your SAPol contacts will feel much the same."

"Well, you'll all just have to get used to it. That is, if you want this inquiry to proceed. The one thing I will undertake to do is to keep you in the loop. The first step, for your information, is that I'm heading to Jakarta tomorrow morning to try to get a handle on what Kevin got up to there."

"Whether he sired a string of illegitimate children in the short time he was in Indonesia, you mean?"

Kaz ignored his weak attempt at humour. "They'd all be adults by now. And if such people exist they're probably not even aware of him. To be honest, given the way in which I suspect Kevin operated, I am not overly hopeful of finding what I'm looking for. But I've got to start somewhere. Indonesia seems the best place to track down his history. The information I've gleaned from AuSecurity and Julie Bristol hasn't shone much light on his private life. The only chance I have is to find others who had personal dealings with him while he was there."

"Okay Ms Ingham. Have it your way. We both know there's not much I can do to stop you. But yes, do please keep me in the loop. I might even be able to help you if you ever run out of ideas."

Kaz could not help feeling sorry for Stewart. "Of course. I meant what I said, and I'm sure I'll need ongoing help. This isn't my choice," she smiled disarmingly at Stewart.

"Now if you'll excuse me I've got to get my head around what I need to take with me, and pack."

"Perhaps I can help you with that?" he said with a wry smile.

"Sorry, now's not the time," she returned his smile, "but thank you for the kind offer. I will definitely let you know when I'm back."

"Then can I help you unpack, give you a massage or something?"

"I am sure we will think of something," she murmured.

CHAPTER 27

After the seven-hour flight to Jakarta, Kaz spent an evening in a hotel in the northern sector of Jakarta known as 'Kota'. She was up at dawn, because of the time difference between Sydney and Jakarta, and spent some hours before venturing out, going over what she'd gleaned so far about Kevin. Then she realised with a start that it was already 9.00am local time and hurried to catch a taxi, only to find that traffic was in gridlock and what should have taken less than half an hour took three times longer. She contacted the Embassy via holo to apologise. "No worries, it's an everyday occurrence here. We'll see you when we see you," the ambassador's PA told her.

On finally arriving, she was taken straight up to the ambassador's offices located on the top level of the building. There was complete privacy, all natural lighting coming through overhead skylights. The floor was cushioned by thick carpet and the room temperature was set to very cool. It was also quiet, even the sound of the chaotic traffic outside had become muted to a low hum.

"Brigitte Cumani," the Ambassador said, introducing herself. A middle-aged woman, she was wearing loose clothing, her dark hair was cropped short, and she was without head covering. The only apparent concession to her part-Indonesian ancestry was a small gold lotus blossom pendant. She offered Kaz her hand and smiled warmly as she welcomed her into the office.

"Thank you for agreeing to meet me on such short notice," Kaz said. "I must apologise for being much later than expected. I hadn't bargained for the traffic here. My taxi has been standing behind stalled cars for over an hour, while I choked in the fumes. I seriously need a gas mask!"

Cumani smiled sympathetically. "Get used to it! It's becoming worse each year. You wonder why we still allow driven cars on the main streets, and even worse, parked ones! The reality is that Indonesia is such an anarchic place the authorities wouldn't dare change things. They're still turning a blind eye to pick-up parking, two or three abreast on some of the busiest roads. Then try introducing driverless cars. They've made matters much worse if anything. But I'm sure you're not here to talk about our traffic. What can I do for you?"

"I think you're abreast of our inquiry into the recent discovery of Kevin Rowe's body?"

Cumani nodded. "Sure, I've read your memo. Actually, before reading it, I knew nothing about this man, let alone his Embassy connection here before becoming prominent in politics back in Australia, and then his disappearance and rediscovery—amazing after all this time!"

Kaz nodded. She could see that Cumani had taken an interest in the case and seemed to want to contribute.

"I'm curious about some obvious gaps, and what it doesn't say," Cumani continued. "For example, do you have any real evidence for this supposed 'Indonesian connection' with his murder? It sounds highly speculative to me."

It's all we've got so far and, to be frank with you, we have to start somewhere."

"Correct me if I'm wrong, it's all based on the premise that Kevin might have had an illegitimate child, from a chance sighting by a stranger who was visiting Adelaide at the time?"

"Yes, when you put it like that, I agree it sounds very tenuous, but there's more to it as our inquiries have progressed. I need to learn more about Kevin's time in Jakarta, and it would be much better to do that here rather than from Sydney."

"So how can we help?"

"The first person I *would* have liked to meet was a former general in the TNI, Bhudi Wistranto, who according to my sources was someone Kevin met on many occasions."

"Yes, a very well-known name. But he's dead, are you aware of that?"

"Unfortunately, yes. According to my research, he passed away in 2026. Still I'm hoping to take a look at any files you may have on Bhudi, particularly anything which might throw light on Kevin's relationship with him, and reveal any other contacts that we *could* follow up."

"If he was a senior general in the TNI, we'll doubtless have a file on him—but, as you've no doubt discovered, any connection with Kevin dating back to the early 2000s would have been archived long ago."

"In the Australian Commonwealth Archive?"

"Correct. And as you probably have already learned, many of those have been sealed."

Kaz nodded, momentarily stumped. "Then perhaps anything you currently have on Bhudi, could still be helpful?"

Cumani shook her head and dodged the question with one of her own: "Is this your first time in Jakarta?"

Kaz was not about to be put off. "It is, and quite a shock to the system. Which is why I have one more special request."

"Yes?"

"Would you be able to lend me somebody to help me find my way around for the next couple of days? A guide who really knows Jakarta would be of great assistance to me."

"No problem. In many ways I'm just as interested in this matter as you and would like to help you as much as we can. Let's go back to my PA who can introduce you to one of my staff who can act as your driver. He knows this place extremely well and speaks Indonesian fluently. I'll also ask our archivist Gloria to dig out whatever we have currently on General Wistranto."

"Thank you," Kaz stood and followed her out

CHAPTER 28

Gloria Jones, was a seemingly ordinary looking woman, but obviously endowed with a very good memory and a pride in her ability to track down items in the Embassy's vast information library, however long ago it had been collated and computerised. She was already prepared for Kaz's inquiry and explained: "We have a bio on General Bhudi Wistranto and his principal achievements which I can give you a copy of. He was seventy-eight when he died in 2026. Under next of kin and relatives," she continued, "our files show that his wife died some years before that. But he has a sister by the name of 'Nadia', who as far as I know, is still alive. Unfortunately, we do not have an address or any indication of whether she is older or younger than Bhudi."

"Do you have any suggestions on who might know more about the sister?" Kaz asked.

"Why not visit the TNI Base? Surely there'd be someone there who can help you track her down," Gloria suggested.

Kaz's driver took her to TNI headquarters at Cilangkap, located to the south of the city and close to the main road to Bogor. The super wide entrance to the complex resembled a toll plaza, with enough sentry boxes to service a freeway. Within the base, the sight of trucks loaded with reinforcing mesh, the sound of hammering from a forest of scaffolding surrounding a massive new building, all provided clear evidence that the TNI was entering a new growth phase.

The uniformed serviceman in charge of public relations, Lieutenant Jimmy Hardono, welcomed Kaz to a small reception area and offered her a drink of water, which she declined politely. He wasted no time, before asking her, "Why you investigating Bhudi?"

Kaz had almost got used to the directness and intense curiosity of Indonesian encounters and replied without evasion. "We are trying to follow up some of the history of his friends in our Embassy staff many years ago. We know that Bhudi passed away nearly ten years ago and is recorded as having a sister, Nadia, but we don't know how to contact her."

Hardono took a moment to interpret what she was asking, before smiling unexpectedly. "You come at right time! We invite guests to Bhudi Funeral. It was long time ago, but still have all addresses. We invite many people. Many, many people," he repeated. "Bhudi, he Christian religion, lot of friends come. He popular, people love him. His sister is guest of honour. Please wait. I find address for you."

Hardono disappeared into another room for a few minutes, before returning and handing a slip of paper to Kaz. "I give you Ibu Wistranto's address. Show this to driver. He take you there. She live in Glodok—here address, easy to find."

"Could you please call Nadia and explain that I'd like to meet her as soon as possible and perhaps later this morning if that's convenient? I think it would come better if my request was from someone in this office, rather than a foreigner from out of the blue," Kaz said.

"Yes of course, I do that. I am sure Ibu Wistranto happy to meet you."

Ibu Nadia Wistranto lived in a small house, accessed by a narrow laneway close to the Chinese quarter of Glodok. There was a heavy steel-barred security gate and an intercom which Kaz used. She didn't have to wait long. The woman, who came to the door, had a lively expression and Kaz judged her to be in her late 70s. She was wearing a cotton smock, smudged with a multitude of paint smears and a head-scarf. She had spectacles dangling from her neck on a cord.

"Excuse my appearance," she said in very good English, "but I am just finishing the last of a series of paintings I've been doing of this locality. That's before it's all pulled down, of course!" she laughed.

"Oh may I see?" asked Kaz.

"Sure, why not? But please do not expect too much. I am just amateur."

Nadia led her into a studio with a side balcony and a large window. Nearly all surfaces in the room were cluttered with paint jars, brushes, rolls of paper and other bric a brac, including some unusual items such as a Buddha bust which she might have used for still life studies. The pungent smell of turpentine and thinners pervaded the room. Her half-finished painting was mounted on a large easel in the middle of the clutter. It was a bold impressionistic streetscape, using bright colours, laid down in broad palette knife planes.

It certainly makes a statement, thought Kaz.

"Wow, that's fantastic I'd really love to go and see the place you've been painting," she said sincerely.

"I'd be happy to show you around if you like. It's unusual for me to get foreigners visiting, particularly since my husband died and especially someone from Australia!"

She turned to Kaz with an intense and curious expression. "Now to business! The PR person who spoke to me from TNI mentioned you're inquiring into my brother's involvement with another of your fellow Australians, is that right?"

"Could we sit down?" asked Kaz, "Because I have quite a lot to explain. While my questions are important for our investigation, they may dredge up unwelcome memories for you."

"I see," said Nadia. Without saying anything further, she led Kaz out onto a veranda at the back of the house, down some steps into a space that resembled a clearing in a beautiful pocket jungle. A thick grove of bamboo shielded the seating area from neighbouring houses. Seats were positioned around a low outdoor table on a paved area next to a large pool. Gorgeous white lotus flowers floated on the water. Nadia motioned Kaz to sit down.

"So," continued Kaz, "the person of interest, who we believe Bhudi had some dealings with, was the Embassy's military attaché. His name was Kevin Rowe. He apparently knew your brother but, more importantly from our point of view, he is also thought to have met Bhudi's niece. Could that have been your daughter?"

"No, you must mean Marayan. She was the daughter of my elder sister and brother in law. They were killed in a car accident when Marayan was only five years old. Bhudi and his wife could not have children, they badly wanted to have one, so they took care of Marayan until she was old enough to look after herself."

"Did you know Marayan well?"

"Well of course I did! She was a beautiful child, although there was always a lingering sadness about her, I thought. Once she grew up I saw a lot less of her, and then she died young herself."

Kaz's interest quickened, but she struggled to remain impassive. "Oh that's very sad, whatever happened to her?"

Nadia pondered for a moment and then shrugged. Her voice had become emotional. "Well I suppose I can talk about it, Bhudi would never talk about it himself, but it's a long time ago now. Marayan's story was hard to hide from someone like me. I finally discovered she had been expecting a child and died giving birth. It was terrible news, and it was an embarrassment and tragedy for Bhudi, who loved her like she was his own daughter. I only found out sometime later. You see, she was unattached to the father. Bhudi kept her pretty much in seclusion from the moment her pregnancy was obvious."

"Do you know who the father was?"

"No, not for certain. He would never say. The one thing that became more and more obvious from the moment I first set eyes on the baby was that he must've had a white father."

"I suppose you didn't get to see the birth certificate?"

"No. As I said, Bhudi never wanted to talk about it. To avoid confusion I suppose, the boy was known as James Wistranto and his real parentage was left for people to guess."

"So then what happened?"

"There's not a lot more I can tell you. Once he finished at his primary school here in Jakarta, James was sent to a school, in Australia somewhere. I never saw much of him after that, except on one or two occasions when he came here for the long vacations in summer. By the time he was about eighteen, he announced that he wanted to stay in Australia, most of his friends lived there and I think that he had come to see Indonesia as something of an embarrassment. It hurt Bhudi terribly, but he allowed James to have his way."

"Did this young man attend Bhudi's funeral?"

"I don't think so. I didn't see him there. He might not have been asked. I remember Bhudi saying, some time ago, that he had no idea what had become of James."

"You don't know what school he went to in Australia?

"No, but I'm remembering now, it was in Adelaide."

CHAPTER 29

Once back in Sydney, Kaz lost no time in heading to the Parramatta Office to catch-up with Stewart and Len.

She found the men deep in discussion, their body language indicating that they were not seeing eye to eye. They looked up in surprise as she walked through the door. Kaz got the distinct impression they might have been talking about her.

"Kaz. We weren't expecting you back so soon, let's go to my office," said Stewart. He turned to Len. "We're going to need the latest information we've had from SA. Look it up and make sure my system's in sync? Immediately!"

Stewart held the door to his office open for Kaz, shutting it behind her as soon as she was inside. "How are you?" he asked standing very close to her. "You look well."

Kaz raised her eyebrows. She'd given her reflection a mere cursory glance in the mirror that morning, buoyed by renewed enthusiasm for the case. She was on a mission: firstly she needed to get back to Adelaide, then research all the schools there, and hopefully find a record of Rowe's son. "Thank you," she managed, realising Stewart was waiting for an answer. "You do too." In all honesty, he did—he smelt good too, wearing the same aftershave he used on their last date. She smiled thinking about them together in bed, even more so when he smiled back. "I wish we had more time to catch up, but we also have so much work to discuss."

"And this is work-time, as we agreed, so we should stick to work. Still, it's lovely to see you." Another smile. "I just wanted you to myself for a moment, and to say that before Len gets back."

"Thank you. So there isn't anything particularly new from SA?"

He shook his head. "No, but it'll keep him busy checking."

Len knocked on the door.

"Come in."

"What have I missed?" Len asked, taking a seat next to Kaz and directing his question to her.

"Only pleasantries so far. Did you find anything new from SAPol?" she asked.

"No, there's nothing new today, or since you left for that matter."

"But now you're both here," Kaz straightened in her seat, focusing, "I can tell you that I have a lead on Rowe's potential killer."

"Don't say you got the 'illegitimate son' in Jakarta?" remarked Len, sarcastically.

Kaz ignored his attempt to mock her efforts. "Not quite. But we had a breakthrough via a relative of one of Rowe's main contacts in Jakarta, General Bhudi Wistranto. He died some time ago, but I met his younger sister, Nadia, who's still living there."

"Good work. Sounds interesting," said Stewart. The two men had glanced at each other, surprised. Kaz couldn't quite work out what they'd been expecting, but apparently not this result.

"It turns out that Bhudi was the uncle and guardian of a woman known as Marayan. Nadia said that Marayan died, a long time ago, in childbirth. And the interesting bit is all this happened around the same time that Rowe was working in Jakarta. The pregnancy was hushed up by Bhudi because Marayan decided to go it alone, probably against his wishes."

"So what's the connection with Rowe?" Stewart asked.

"According to the PA to the ambassador of the time—that was the Julie Bristol I met in Adelaide, remember—Rowe originally came across General Bhudi Wistranto and his niece at an official party she organised for the Embassy. Another of our sources, James Last, the Press Secretary, also mentioned hearing some gossip about Rowe having an affair with an Indonesian woman, though had no evidence to prove it."

Kaz could see mounting scepticism on the two men's faces. "The clincher is I was finally able to track down the birth certificate of Marayan's baby. It was a boy, born in an out-of-town hospital—I'm guessing Bhudi chose it deliberately to help safeguard his reputation. The baby was named James Wistranto and, according to Nadia, the facts of his actual parentage were never discussed with anyone. Nadia said it was obvious from the moment he was born that he had a white father. So most people who met the boy would probably have assumed he was adopted."

"Sounds like you might have something, but where's this heading?" Stewart sounded eager.

"Well the curious thing is that it appears Bhudi himself signed the birth certificate, remember Marayan herself had died by this time and could not do it herself. He put down the father's name as Rowe."

"Hmm…and why do you suppose he would have done that?"

"Well apart from anything else, it tells us who the father was. There can be little doubt that James Rowe aka Wistranto is the illegitimate son we've been looking for," Kaz concluded.

Stewart and Len both seemed taken aback for several moments. Stewart was the first to speak. "Why do you suppose Bhudi Wistranto actually put Rowe's name on the Certificate, knowing that his niece had taken great care to conceal her pregnancy from everyone, no doubt including the father?" he asked. "Could it simply have been mischievousness, or was there something more to it than that?"

"Definitely more to it. I agree it seems strange at first sight. The reason, I'm guessing, was that Bhudi may have wanted James to be able to claim Australian citizenship at some point. Maybe James was an embarrassment to him. Maybe he could foresee sending James to an Australian school, providing him with an opportunity not just for a good foreign education, but to keep him out of the limelight? Who knows?"

"Maybe he wanted documentary evidence to pin Rowe?" said Len.

"Yes that's quite plausible. I'd imagine there was no love lost between the two of them when Bhudi discovered what he'd done to his niece."

"So what has become of this 'James Wistranto'?" Stewart asked.

"That's the question, isn't it? I'd say it should be our main line of inquiry, I'm sure you'd agree?" said Kaz. "According to Nadia, he was sent to a secondary school in Adelaide, we're not sure which one. But here's something else, at least as significant for us. She said that James chose to remain in Australia once he completed his school and university education. She was vague about the dates. We need SAPol to help us with this now. We know from the birth certificate that James was born in 2004. Assuming he went to high school in Adelaide, I think we should start searching foreign pupils in the various schools there from 2015 onwards. If we can get a lead with the school he attended, then there's a chance we can work out where he is living now from some of his old school contacts."

"Looks like you already decided this James is the main suspect in our inquiry now?" Len said.

"Yes I'd say so. He may or may not be the killer but he probably knows something. And he's very high on the list given that we've come up with no other suspects so far. This is still speculation on my part, but I'd say the person who met Rowe at Adelaide Airport and looked like his son, was his son. At this stage we can only guess why they met, but maybe James wanted to get something out of Rowe. Maybe Rowe wouldn't have any of that and James killed him."

"And what made him do that, you think?" Len persisted.

"I've thought about James a lot since Nadia told me about him. The picture is very unclear, but the experience of being brought up by his uncle, a powerful man with a strong disciplinary background, with pride in his position, cannot have been easy." Kaz stated.

"I'd guess he was kept secluded; he had no mother. Nadia said that she saw very little of him. Maybe Bhudi had mixed feelings about this child who had become his responsibility almost without warning. Maybe he lacked the empathy and love that a growing child needs in such circumstances. Perhaps he saw James as a nuisance, left him with the maids or housekeepers as much as possible," theorised Kaz without drawing breath.

"Then as James grew up, he would always have felt he was different from other kids around him, particularly when he went to a boarding school in South Australia, and I'm betting it was a snobby upper-class college in Adelaide, where many of the other children would have tried to bully or tease him because he was different. As we all know, kids can be very cruel to each other at times." Kaz finally stopped talking, deep in thought.

"I'm beginning to hear the faint sound of a choir," Len remarked.

Kaz ignored him and continued. "And then he lacked the support that his real father might have given him. From what Nadia said, I think it's most unlikely Bhudi would have told him who his real father was, but at some point, he would have got his hands on the birth certificate and worked out his paternity. Perhaps he discovered the document when Bhudi died? Our records show that Bhudi's death was in late 2026, not long before Rowe went missing. Maybe that's no coincidence."

"I'm also thinking," Kaz continued, "that James has the same brains and drive as his biological father," she went on. "That, coupled with a burning resentment, might have driven him to find out more about his father. Maybe he engaged a private detective to do some investigations. Once he learned who Rowe really was, the high-profile he'd achieved in politics and all that, the drive for him to want to meet Rowe and possibly make demands would have been stronger. As he'd see it, Rowe should agree to take some responsibility for him, to share some of his wealth. Maybe they had a falling out. The last thing Rowe probably wanted was to discover he had this illegitimate son, and one who wanted something that Rowe couldn't or wouldn't provide. It would have deepened the resentment and anger. Maybe deep enough to kill?"

"So I think it all adds up to a clear line for our inquiry. This man had the motive, means and opportunity to kill Rowe."

"I think you've been watching too many crime fiction vids," said Len dryly.

"It is a lot of assumptions built on one supposition after another," conceded Stewart. We need a lot more evidence to get to the point you've reached."

"Well Len asked me the question, but you're right of course, so I'm heading for Adelaide tomorrow," said Kaz, standing.

"My Indonesian report will be with you tonight."

Stewart made eye contact with Kaz and nodded. "Very well and thank you Kaz."

Len said nothing.

CHAPTER 30

Instead of staying in the Parramatta office, Kaz headed back to her small terrace house in Surry Hills, close to the centre of Sydney. She spent the afternoon going through notes she had made in Indonesia, typing up her report, and trying to work out how she would structure her search procedures for the man known as James Wistranto.

By nine o'clock, her stomach reminded her she hadn't had a proper meal for many hours. Thinking she needed not only food, but some light exercise, she pulled on a coat and set off to the nearest pizza house, conveniently located beside her local pub. When she arrived, the pub looked crowded, and she didn't feel like waiting for a meal from the bar. Instead, she ordered a pepperoni pizza next door. By the time it arrived, finding the smell of hot cheese and spicy sausage irresistible, she teased out one segment and wolfed it down... then another. It wasn't long before she'd devoured the entire pizza as she slowly wandered home, tossing the empty carton into a bin.

The night was dark as she walked up Devonshire Street in the direction of her house, with few others around, on a normal weeknight. But she had a sensation that she was being followed. As she reached a cross street, she stopped and seized the opportunity to look back, while making a show of checking for cars. She could see nothing but shadows, only a single pedestrian on the opposite side of the road some distance behind her. It looked like a woman who'd had too much to drink, swaying as she walked.

My imagination at work, Kaz told herself. Too much murder on my mind.

She continued walking resolutely back to her house, checking behind her at the gate, and making sure the front door was locked from inside.

Then she poured herself a glass of water, and had a shower to help relax.

The shower was in a small cubicle next to her bedroom on the upper floor, and its window looked out onto a narrow laneway at the back of the house, which in former times had given access to the 'dunny men' on collection days. She gazed out through a chink in the window's blinds as she wrapped her hair in a towel and dried herself with another. She pulled her bathrobe off its hook, then switched off the bathroom light and walked into her bedroom, illuminated only by the soft light of a bed lamp. She stooped to pull back her bedclothes and reach for her nightdress, when there was a pressure pulse that she could feel rather than hear, and a sizzling burning smell from the wall opposite the window.

Kaz dropped to the floor in shock, then crawled across the rug under the line of the sill to switch off the bed lamp at the wall plug. The room was now in darkness and she paused to think. Had someone tried to shoot her? She needed her holo, but it was in her purse, which she had left downstairs in the kitchen. It took all her courage to venture into the darkness and the suddenly forbidding lower storey of her house. Keeping low beneath the line of the window in the front room, she scrabbled for her purse on the table and finally found her holo. She had Stewart's contact on her list and pressed 'Call'.

His voice answered the call sleepily. "Hello?"

"I'm at home. Someone's outside my house. Whoever it is has managed to get hold of a blaster. They just tried to fry me through my bedroom window. I can tell it wasn't a conventional firearm. The sound, smell and form of impact were quite different. I've no idea how whoever it was got their hands on such a weapon. Please help me! Can you get someone here?" She was panting and had trouble getting the words out.

"Remind me of your address," he sounded calm.

"20 Osborne Street, Surry Hills."

"Okay Kaz, stay out of sight. I'm on it and will be back to you in two minutes. Keep this line open and stay close to the floor if you aren't already. Draw all your curtains if you can. Is your front door locked?"

"Yes."

"Good, I'll get back to you in a minute."

In less than five minutes she heard the footsteps of several people outside. Then someone thumped on the door. "Police open up," a man shouted.

"Would you mind sliding your warrant card under the door?"

A familiar card appeared immediately. She unlocked the door allowing three armed men wearing protective vests to enter. One of them stood guard with Kaz, while the other two searched the house before returning outside and inspecting the rear lane.

"We'll stand by until your boss arrives," one of them said.

"Stewart Richardson, you mean?"

"That's the one."

There was a squeal of rubber on the street outside.

Kaz's heart beat faster. No matter what else had happened between them, he clearly cared for her.

He strode towards the door, wearing an overcoat over stripy pyjamas, his hair tousled and unbrushed. "You okay?" he said looking her over, then guiding her into the lounge out of earshot of the others.

"Just a bit shaken."

"Would you like me to stay here with you tonight, on guard?"

"I…" Her lips quivered.

"It's okay. I don't mind. But I'd like it if it's okay with you," said Stewart.

"Okay."

« »

Very early the next morning Kaz woke up to the sound of snoring. Stewart was dead to the world with his mouth half open, breathing deeply. *Some watchdog,* she thought with a combination of amusement and tenderness.

She decided not to wake him up, but went into the kitchen to put on the kettle and make some toast. Moments later, she heard fumbling movements in her bedroom followed by flushing water in the toilet. She could not help smiling at the sense of intimacy.

Rodney Jensen

"Good morning," he said as he stumbled into the kitchen, rubbing his eyes.

She gestured for him to join her at the breakfast bar. "Good morning. I hope you slept well?"

"I always sleep well. How about you?"

"Only because your men did such a good job of helping board up my window last night."

She passed him the toast.

"Leave me a key," he took a bite, "and I'll have it fixed before you get home. Might I suggest that you have a permanent louvre put up? You'd still have some light but it would prevent anyone seeing in?"

"Yes that's a good idea. I'm not going to feel comfortable in my bedroom from now on otherwise."

"Consider it done then," said Stewart. "When do you leave?"

"My flight's booked for eleven o'clock this morning."

"Are you sure you should go? You know, considering?"

"Yes, it would be best for my peace of mind to keep to schedule," she announced as Stewart chewed thoughtfully on his toast.

"Okay, before you go, though, I'd like to accompany you to headquarters, because this has become an entirely new ballgame. Whoever took that pot-shot at you is almost certainly connected with Rowe's killing, and has also managed to get their hands on an unauthorised weapon. The Rapid Response Team confirmed the damage to your window and bedroom wall were not caused by a rifle."

"I think it could be connected too." She poured him some coffee. "I don't have any enemies I'm aware of, let alone anyone who'd have done that. I don't move in criminal circles either. Like you, it seems no coincidence that I've just come back from Indonesia and am getting close to the person I think may have murdered Rowe. I've assumed that he would be located in South Australia, but there's no reason of course to assume any such thing. If he's actually living here in New South Wales, is it simply a coincidence that he's worked out that we are onto him, or has he been following us all along?"

"It certainly puts a new perspective on things doesn't it," said Stewart, pausing to drink his coffee. "You do realise you're going to need 24-hour protection from now on, until we've nailed the bastard? That goes for while you're in Adelaide as well. In fact, now that I come to think of it, I'm uncomfortable about your going there at all. I'd have thought the South Australian police were perfectly capable of following up the schools without you, and have other ways of tracking down this James Wistranto character. It doesn't have to be you, does it?"

"I think it does. Call me egotistical, but if it hadn't been for me, we wouldn't have reached this point in our inquiries. They were getting nowhere. Now I have the uneasy feeling that's exactly what this is all about."

"That's all well and good, but you'll be going into unknown territory and facing someone who might easily get you the next time. Let's get you over to police HQ, take your statement and then decide what to do— but first I need to change. There are some spare clothes in my car. Whether you go this morning or tomorrow to South Australia, it doesn't much matter. I am really concerned about your safety now," he said earnestly.

"Okay, makes sense," Kaz mumbled. He'd never spoken to her this ardently before. "In fact, it's nice of you to think of my safety so much. I appreciate your sentiments Stewart." She leaned over and kissed him softly on his cheek. "Let me get dressed and sort myself out, you too, then we'll go to HQ and arrange some protection."

"Someone has given me a warning. That person is probably deranged, but not stupid. He's probably hoping that I'll do precisely what you're asking me to do and not go to Adelaide. By showing his hand like this, it proves he's feeling the heat. You and I have got to do a lot of thinking and not allow our emotions to get in the way. Actually…" Kaz paused, gathering her thoughts. "Something else has just occurred to me. This completely changes the profile of our killer, the one I have theorised as a young man who's had a difficult childhood and needed to discover the father he never knew. Until now, I imagined he might have killed Rowe accidentally and simply wanted to cover it up. But this is now looking much more like the work of a psychopath." Stewart nodded.

"So, let's get this statement over with, and then you can take responsibility for the search in New South Wales, while I do the same in Adelaide." She put up her hand to stop him, immediately reacting against this. "I know you don't want me to go at all, but I do. I'll go with protection if I must, but I'm still going. This is my fight now. It's become personal. In any case, AuSecurity has made it clear I'm to take the lead in this inquiry."

Kaz could tell Stewart was seriously unhappy, and all prepared to try some ultimatum to prevent her going ahead with her plans. Forestalling him, she suddenly hit her head, as a compromise occurred to her.

"I've just remembered I booked myself into training on the Henning at the gun range but had to postpone. How about I commence training immediately? You can arrange that given the importance of my self-defence. Would that make you any happier?"

Stewart sighed, and looked undecided for a full twenty seconds before finally relaxing his frown and nodding at her. "Okay, I'll agree to that on one condition. If you go to Adelaide, you will be protected by a professional at all times. Otherwise it still represents an unacceptable risk and there's no guarantee you can remain safe from this maniac."

"I understand, I really do—but I won't be bullied either.'

« »

Stewart was good to his word and arranged for the instructor to show Kaz how to use the Henning blaster the next day. She met him in the special training and practice facility located in an underground bunker close to the Parramatta office. There were two target corridors about 40 metres in length, painted white over bare concrete. The way into the corridors was blocked by a low counter. At the end of each corridor lay an illuminated display. The target graphic showed was a single black figure in silhouette.

Her instructor was the head armourer, a man in his 50s, who looked like he was ex-military with his close cropped grey hair and manner of speaking in clipped sentences. He held out a dry palm when she introduced herself and stared intently into her eyes. "Scott Nicholls. You done much weapons training?"

"Virtually none," she admitted. "My dad took me rabbit shooting with my brother once. He'd already been out a few times and was two years older than me. But I was a way better shot, and it really pissed him off. Anyway I left him to it, and told my dad I never wanted to go out again. I hated killing any animals, even if they were a pest."

Scott laughed. "At least you've had some weapons experience. But now you must forget all that— this is the new tech!" He was holding out a blaster like the one she'd seen at Pittwater Glades, with the moulded black case the size of a cling-wrap dispenser and snub-nosed barrel. Looking more closely at it, she now noticed that it had an illuminated panel on one side with a set of icons. The projecting finger guard, trigger and two sighting cylinders mounted along the top of the case made its actual purpose more obvious.

"This blaster is completely different from a rifle," said Scott. "There is no kick and very little sound apart from a slight sizzling. It's totally deadly for any living thing within a thirty-metre range. It projects a tightly focused packet of nanoparticles, which travel at close to the speed of light. The particles act more like a light beam than the bullets of a conventional weapon. The beam can be spread slightly so that the effect on the target is more like a shot gun than a rifle." He paused a moment to make sure Kaz was following him.

She was, but also wasn't happy. "Scott, just looking at that weapon, it's simply not practical for me. I can't lug a thing like that around, particularly when I'm in civvies. I need something that I can use at all times, small enough to conceal ideally."

"I see what you mean," said Scott, staring thoughtfully at her. "Funnily enough you've come at just the right time. Just give me a moment." He disappeared for a moment into a tiny office beside the firing range. Kaz could see him through the door squatting beside a safe and keying in a code.

He returned carrying a large plastic case with a red "classified" sticker on the lid. He opened the case and pulled out a bubble-wrapped object, then removed the wrapping. It appeared to be a small hand weapon, unlike anything Kaz had seen. The casing was of similar moulded black plastic to the Henning Blaster, but no larger than a man's wallet. It had a simple flared opening on one side where a barrel might have been expected. Scott demonstrated its single press button on the top with a sliding hood, and a touch pad on one side of the casing.

"I am not supposed to be showing this to anyone," he said, "because it is still in the research/ development stage and was sent to me for my professional opinion and evaluation. But I think it addresses your problem. Basically it's a micro blaster. It doesn't quite pack the punch of the assault model but it's slim enough to be carried in the small of your back in this special holster." He showed Kaz a webbing pocket with a belt to secure it around the waist.

"The pocket's lined with form-fitting plastic, which enables you to pull your weapon out simply and quickly."

"Can I try it on?" Kaz asked.

"Of course, see how you go."

Kaz put it on and experimented with inserting and removing the micro. "I like it," she said finally.

Scott seemed pleased. "I think you're right about its practicality," he said. "So instead of training you as I'd intended, we'll concentrate on this weapon. If you are happy to do that, it will not only afford you pretty much full-time protection, but also help me with my evaluation. Would that suit you?"

Kaz nodded her head. "Definitely, it will make me feel a lot less exposed than I have been feeling since the attempt on my life."

"Okay, let's make a start then," Scott continued. "Now, rule number one is always have the safety slide on, unless you are ready with the weapon aimed on target." He showed Kaz how the slide worked. "Rule number two is safety slide back on the moment you have completed firing."

With the slide open, the indicator light glowed a red colour. "That light's indicating your weapon is active. If it's flashing in half second intervals, the power pack needs re-charging and it cannot be used until it's fully charged. You can change the beam settings with the touch display, including a narrow beam and a spread beam. There's another setting that allows you to alter the duration of firing. It goes from 0.1 to 3 seconds. The shorter the pulse, the longer your battery pack lasts, and in my experience, you're hardly ever going to go beyond 0.1 or 0.2 seconds. That's sufficiently deadly, and more energy efficient."

He paused again and handed the blaster to her. "So now it's your turn. I want you to take aim at the figure," he said, pointing at the target at the end of the corridor. We can set the image to a single person target or groups of up to four. Now we're just going with the single target today. Groups require a different approach. We'll come to that later."

It took Kaz a moment or two to position her elbows on the counter, press the slide to safety-off mode and then take aim.

"Okay, now I want you to gently squeeze the firing button, then put the weapon back on the counter and press the safety back on."

Kaz did as she was instructed. There was a slight sizzling sound, then a red dot appeared on the target close to the centre ring.

"Not bad for a newbie," the man remarked. "Now try again…"

The lesson went on in similar fashion for the next twenty minutes. Scott instructed Kaz to try varying both the duration of the beam and its spread. By now the red indicator light was flashing and Scott took the weapon back. "I think we can call it a day," he said. "From now on, I want you to do a training session every morning with me for the next week, before your work shift. The operation of this weapon must become second nature."

Rodney Jensen

Kaz sighed inwardly at Scott's rigorous safety standards and seriousness. He looked at her intently again without a smile. "I can tell you're getting bored but let me remind you that I care about your safety and learning how to defend yourself."

"I'd have thought a week's training is a bit over the top. I need to get to Adelaide ASAP and can't really afford that much time."

"Trust me. I know what I'm doing and you're going to do it my way if you want to gain the special certification for the use of this blaster. I need that to be able to equip you with it for your visit to South Australia. The training schedule I've set is the absolute minimum I consider necessary to pass your final tests on safety, speed and accuracy. You might live to thank me one day, with that killer on the loose," he concluded.

Kaz could see he was immovable and decided not to press the point any further.

As she left the range, she was glad to be out of the airless and gloomy atmosphere and to feel the pleasure of normal daylight and air again. Her sense of relaxation was interrupted by a call from Stewart on her holo. "I've just read the report you filed, briefing us on your interviews in Indonesia. I want you to arrange a meeting to discuss your conclusions and I also want SAPol involved. Let's make sure that Gotto from SAPol will be in on the conference call so we're all kept in the loop and SAPol can bring us up to speed as well with what they've been doing."

CHAPTER 31

Kaz and Briony Caravaggio (nicknamed by her colleagues in SAPol 'The Car') were headed towards 'Free Bodies School', near Mount Barker in the Adelaide Hills. Both Stewart and Adelaide's DCI Tania Bilson had insisted that Kaz be accompanied at all times by Briony, a highly respected armed response constable. She was a small woman with blonde hair tied in a ponytail and looked super fit. She moved with the agility and concentration of a predator.

When they'd first met a week earlier, Kaz had noticed the weapon she was carrying. "I see you're using a Henning," she said. Briony nodded. Kaz reached behind her back and withdrew the Henning Micro.

Briony jolted when she saw what Kaz was holding. "What's that for God's sake?"

"It's the latest our Weapons Research Division has come up with. I'm the first person certified to carry it, because it's still under wraps and evaluation. The intention is that it will cater for clandestine use, particularly by female operatives."

"That so," remarked Briony irritably. "Can't imagine how a non-professional like you would get first dibs on it, let alone be considered qualified to judge its effectiveness. How did you swing that?"

"Basically, because my life's under threat, and it's not practical to have a minder around every waking hour."

"Ever had to use it in action?"

"Fortunately, no. Have you with yours?"

Briony stared back at her seriously for a few seconds. "Let's not go there," she remarked finally.

Kaz had quickly taken to Briony. They had gained mutual respect and learned they shared a debunking sense of humour. For the trip to Free Bodies, they were using an AutoCab, enabling Briony to concentrate on Kaz's protection, and throughout most of the journey she had remained serious, uncommunicative and focused on surveillance of their surroundings.

The AutoCab was slowing down. Briony took a look at the Nav Panel and then the approaching intersection. "Not far to go now," she broke the silence at last, as they turned off the freeway. "It's only a couple of clicks from here."

Kaz breathed a sigh of relief. Once they'd left the freeway, it had been a long winding journey, much of it along a narrow lane, and she was keen to get out and stretch her legs. The preceding week had been exhausting, during which she had patiently checked every possible high school that James might have attended twenty years ago. It turned out there were more than a dozen schools that catered for boarders in South Australia, including some 'agricultural high schools' that catered for students who wanted to pursue careers in sectors such as agriculture, horticulture, viticulture and forestry.

Kaz had visited nearly every one of the schools in person and spoken to the principal, the librarian or anybody else who was responsible for records. So far she'd drawn a blank. There were only three schools left on her primary list.

"Have you been at this job long?" she had asked Briony.

"Yes except that being a bodyguard is not my normal thing. We work mostly in armed response groups."

"Oh!" said Kaz, feeling a little put out. "Well, I suppose it puts you in the firing line even more then, doesn't it?"

"That's true. You may think I'm not very chatty, but I have to concentrate the whole time on what I'm seeing around us for any possible threat to your safety. The drive here's been a breeze, but now I've got to start concentrating again. Here's the school, and if anybody, by some extraordinary chance, is following your movements, you're going to be out in the open and a sitting duck for at least some of the time."

"If anybody was following me, they would have had another crack at me by now, I'd have thought," remarked Kaz.

"Let's hope you're right."

Their AutoCab had already turned off the lane onto an even narrower driveway, leaving a cloud of white dust in its wake. They made several sharp dog-legs, before climbing a hill and landing up in a generous car park below the school buildings. The school lay close to the prominent escarpment of Mount Barker. To one side of the parking area was a large playing field with Australian Rules goal-posts. Boys and girls were kicking and marking balls with each other. Beyond that lay tennis and basketball courts, where trainers blew their whistles and shouted orders to children in sports clothes as though they were on a parade ground.

"They do love their whistles don't they?" Kaz remarked.

"It goes with the territory," said Briony.

She continued to cover Kaz as they walked up the gentle slope to the front entrance. Children stopped their games and stared in fascination at them both. "I'll come inside and wait at reception for you. Please don't go outside the building by any other exit without me," she said.

They found a small reception area beside the front entrance. Briony stayed on watch, keeping an eye on the area outside via the slit window next to the door. Kaz made herself known to the receptionist, explaining that her bodyguard would be waiting for her there while she met the school's principal.

The principal's office had a panoramic glass window overlooking the playing fields below and down into a valley. With the escarpment beyond, it resembled a Hans Heysen landscape painting.

"Brian Thorpe," he said, extending his hand.

"It must be hard for you to concentrate with such a beautiful view there," she gestured at the window.

"In all honesty, it simply becomes part of the background, but I must admit it's terrific to be able to work in such a peaceful place without too much distraction."

Thorpe was middle-aged, with a full head of hair and dressed in a well-tailored grey suit. He had the intensity of an academic and his room was lined with bookshelves. Apart from a large uncluttered table and chairs there was not much else in the room.

He invited her to sit opposite him at his desk.

"Before we get into the reason I am here, can you tell me a little bit about the school for my own interest?" asked Kaz.

"Yes. As you can probably see, this place is relatively new, as schools go. It was designed to service the need for a private college catering for all genders with no particular religious bias. I might say I'm agnostic myself and while the school does provide religious instruction for some, the focus is more on humanism, philosophy and ethics. The pupils can choose to study any of those things. In line with our agricultural focus our curriculum is strong on science, technology and knowledge programs."

"Do you have many boarders or overseas students?"

"Yes, we've always tried to board about seventy-five percent of our students, because of our country location. Of course there are a few locals who are day students."

"And that's always been the situation?"

"Yes, I've been Principal here since the school was founded in 2010."

"You must have been very young then?"

"I was. I guess the good people who chose me were looking for somebody slightly unconventional in the private school stakes. I also think there was a good deal of luck involved in me getting the job. It's why I've lasted so long here. I really wouldn't want to leave."

Kaz edged forward in the seat. "You might recall when we spoke on the holo a few days ago, I mentioned we're trying to track down a boy who would have come here around the time of 2015 to 2017. We're not certain which of those years he would have commenced studies. He was born in Indonesia with an Indonesian mother and Australian father; his name was James Wistranto."

"Yes I recall the conversation, but I must confess I haven't been able to check it out. The problem from my point of view is that we have close to twelve hundred students attending this place each year. While it's quite possible that James was one of our students, I can't immediately remember anyone by that name. In a minute, I'm going to introduce you to our librarian who has photo images and lists on file from those periods, but they are incomplete, as she'll explain. Unfortunately, the records which would have been most assistance to you, namely the academic records of each year, were archived some time ago. Following our enquiries with the repository, we've learned that they've been unable to find any records dating from that period."

Thorpe pressed an icon on his intercom. "Millie, it's Brian here. I've just been talking to Kaz Ingham who is heading the inquiry into one of our alumni. Could you come meet us in reception and show her around?"

« »

Brian showed Kaz back into reception, where Millie was already waiting. She was a short woman, wearing glasses perched on a longish nose, secured by a loop around her neck. She welcomed Kaz warmly. "Let's go to my office, I've already pulled out the documents I think you're going to need."

She led Kaz down a corridor into a small office and appeared to have set up a table with its own workstation for her to use.

"OK what are we looking for: Eurasian, boarder, around 2015 to 2017?"

"That's right," said Kaz. "All we've got to go on is his date of birth and some information we've been given that suggests he was sent to a boarding school in South Australia. Yours is one of the few, out of the many SA high schools, that do provide boarding places. We sort of left you until last, we thought we'd eliminate the easy ones in the metro area first. Your principal mentioned some academic records have been mislaid?"

"Yes that's right. They might turn up, but I somehow doubt it. Doesn't make our job any easier. What I do have, are annual photographs for each of the houses that this pupil might have stayed in."

"That sounds like a good start. We think his name was James Wistranto. And that's about the only information we have. We don't even know what he looked like. It would be terrific if we can track him down, because if we do, there's much more chance we can find who his friends were and maybe find our 'Holy Grail': a more recent image of him."

"Well that all makes sense so let's make a start. We have twelve boarding houses. Each of them has about seventy five students and the photographs I've put together for you are in separate folders by year. There are also separate lists which give the names of the pupils in the photos, but they don't include anyone who was an absentee. That means there could have been as many as say six students who weren't in the photo for whatever reason and wouldn't have been listed."

Kaz's heart sank. "Oh! Well I suppose looking on the bright side, six out of seventy is long odds that we'd miss our target, and we've had no luck with the other schools so far. Surely he couldn't have been absent from every year's photo?"

"No, I suppose not," said Millie, "but we might have to enlarge the range of the years we check, if he doesn't turn up in the three years you've nominated."

Kaz paused for a moment. "And I suppose I should have asked you the obvious question: you don't remember a student by that name by any chance do you? The principal had no recollection of him, even though he was in charge at the time himself."

"No," said Millie. "It was long before my time."

Kaz began her search with the year 2015, carefully going through the photographic name lists, house by house. Millie sat next to her and did a cross-check. "No luck with these ones is there?"

"No let's try the others." Again they both drew a blank going through the lists of close to a thousand names for the next year, 2016. Kaz was beginning to lose hope that they would find James. Surely he wouldn't have started high school at too much of a later age.

As they were nearly finished with 2017, Kaz noticed a name jumping out of a list: James Rowe. "My God! I think I've found him. Here he is!" she said, jabbing a finger at the entry.

"I thought you said the surname was Wistranto?"

"Yes I did, but his biological father's name was Rowe. We've been thinking all along that James was unaware of his father's name until much later in his life. Now it looks like his guardian must've told him before he started high school here. I'd really like to see the photograph now. Can you help me find it please?"

"Let's see, Gordon House, for the year 2017," Millie muttered to herself. It took several moments of agonising suspense for her to find the file. "Here's the Vis-File," she said at last.

"The list indicates Rowe to be on the second row down, fourth student from the left," Millie noted. They both stared at a black and white image on the screen. It was of only moderate resolution. Kaz enlarged the section containing the second row and slid the image across the screen. A grainy image came into view of a boy with curly dark hair and probably Eurasian. She had a portrait of Rowe that she had prepared to help with comparison.

"This shows how the father looked at the age of twenty, when he'd just started his officer training at Duntroon," she said. "What do you think? Could this boy be his son?"

The two women studied the two photographs. "I'm not sure," said Kaz, "it's difficult to make out his features. I suppose there are some similarities but it could be anybody's son."

"I agree," said Millie, "it doesn't jump out does it?"

"We're only going on what one of our sources tell us. The person claimed he'd seen Rowe meeting someone who could have been his son, much later on than this photograph was taken."

"Wait a minute," said Millie. "Let me check the lists for this house when this boy would have been around eighteen." She went back to her files and found there was someone called James Rowe, this time sitting in the front seats. "He must have been a prefect by that time," she remarked.

Kaz was growing more excited by the minute. "Can we take a look at the Vis?"

"Here it is!" Millie slid her screen across so Kaz could see better. "He's seventh from the left in this list."

This James Rowe, a young man, was still a grainy image, but his facial features were strangely different with a harder chin and a more defined nose.

"My God! I think that's him. They're almost the same age and there's an eerie resemblance, don't you think?" Kaz breathed.

"Yes there definitely is. I can see it now," said Millie.

"We can't prove this yet but if you can give me copies of this Vis-file and the list, I'll get our people back at the office to see whether they agree with this conclusion. The other thing is we now have the name of the boys and girls who were James Rowe's peers. We've now got a much better starting point to find out more about him. What a pity your records have gone!"

"Well at least you're not leaving us empty-handed!" exclaimed Millie.

CHAPTER 32

Kaz returned straight to the SAPol headquarters and tapped on DCI Tania Bilson's door.

Bilson was concentrating hard on something displayed on her desk monitor and looked up with a start. She waved her hand for Kaz to enter. "How did you go at Free Bodies?" she asked finally, tearing her attention away from the screen.

"With their help, I'm pleased to say we've finally made a breakthrough on James Wistranto."

"Really?"

"When we looked into their lists we found someone whose name was James Rowe and the image of the boy was definitely Eurasian. By his eighteenth birthday there's a striking resemblance to his father at a similar age. Look, I'm certain that he's the person we're after."

Kaz pulled the images out of her briefcase and placed them on Bilson's desk. A man in one of the photos could be seen carrying a trainee officer's cap under one arm and was accompanied by other trainees. "That's Kevin Rowe's at Duntroon," she pointed at the first image, "and that's James in his house photograph at the school aged eighteen. See what I mean?"

Bilson took her time, finally pulling a magnifying glass from a drawer under her table and examining the two images minutely. "It's a 'could be'," she finally pronounced. "But I'm not quite as certain as you are about this Kaz. I think the best thing to do would be to get the image experts to check them before we rush to conclusions. As we all know, sons are not always sufficiently like their fathers to be recognisable as such.

In a case like this, where the mother is believed to be Indonesian, I'd say the chances of recognisable similarities are even less. Let's get that done first. Then I want you to arrange a conference call with your colleagues in NSWPol. I think it's time for them to help us coordinate our searches from here on in."

Kaz felt deflated, annoyed with Bilson and to some extent herself that she could be accused of cutting corners. But thought *if I'm honest about this, I've been so excited to get a result, I'm not following procedure. I must have something more than the librarian and my guesswork to confirm this lead.* "Okay, I agree with you. But please can you emphasise that we must have their cooperation in getting this done urgently."

Bilson gazed at her sympathetically. "Yes it's become important for your peace of mind hasn't it?"

Kaz nodded.

"Okay, no question, there is some urgency. Let's schedule that meeting late pm tomorrow and I'll try to ensure you get a report from forensics before that."

« »

The South Australian team was assembled in the SAPol conference room late the following afternoon with a holo-net to the New South Wales offices so that Len and Stewart could take part.

Bilson opened the meeting. "Ms Ingham has some important news to share with us all. She now has the floor."

Kaz, assuming that Bilson would have more to say, now found herself unprepared and in the spotlight. She took a moment to centre herself and remain calm and objective rather than spruiking her latest findings. "Thank you Tania. There has been some progress at this end and the purpose of this conference call is to coordinate our searches better from now on. The good news is: we are pretty sure we've identified the person we've known as James Wistranto. The bad news is: so far there's no trace of him in any of the directories and standard data files. I should explain that the real breakthrough was discovering a boy by the name of James Rowe, who attended Free Bodies School—near Mount Barker, from the age of thirteen to eighteen."

"With the help of the school's information and library specialist," she continued, "we've been able to find an image of James in his final year. The really important thing for everybody to realise is that he's been calling himself James Rowe from the time that he started at the school. To be more certain that this man is related to Kevin Rowe, we have had our face recognition experts compare his image with that of his assumed father Kevin. Both shots were taken when they were close to the same age as young men. We obviously would not have expected a hundred percent match, but the analysis shows an eighty per cent certainty they are closely related. I have already sent you copies of the comparison images for you to see for yourselves. I'm sure you can see the similarity?"

"Yes, it's indeed striking," said Stewart. "But I have a couple of thoughts for you. Firstly, I suggest that we now need your face people to prepare simulations of how this man James would have looked at the time Rowe was murdered, and secondly how James might look now. We need to show the first one to the engineer who made the sighting of Rowe meeting the young man at Adelaide Airport. It's important for him to corroborate his story and confirm he recognises the young man as James Rowe. The contemporary simulation will also be useful for our ongoing search including giving it to the media, that is, assuming you've decided to go public with this?"

"Thanks Stewart, we have been thinking along those lines," said Bilson, "but we're jumping the gun a bit. I believe Kaz has some other ideas as well."

"That's correct," said Kaz. "I think we definitely should make a media call, but I'm also intending to focus our searches on to the period after James' school days, including checking university lists in SA. It's obviously vital that we keep the heat up, particularly if, as it appears, he's found some way of tracking my movements."

There was a collective pause as everyone digested the risks she was now confronted by.

Tania Bilson was the first to break the silence. "Stewart, have you got any further with identifying the gunman? Surveillance cameras, people noticing him in the neighbourhood, that sort of thing?" she asked.

Stewart appeared on screen "No, we've drawn a complete blank. Whoever it was seems to have been a professional. Likely to have had training in this sort of operation and knew how to cover his tracks."

"In any case, we've only just got this latest news about James Rowe, if indeed he's the killer. What we now need to know is where he went after he left school. He could be in South Australia, he could be in New South Wales, he could be anywhere for that matter. That being the case, your own security must be in everyone's minds right now, Kaz. I think we must assume that James Rowe is armed and dangerous."

"Forensics has now confirmed that the sniper used a blaster in the attack on you. How he could have got his hands on such a weapon raises another concern, namely whether he might have military or government security or indeed police connections. It was clearly not accidental, and would definitely have killed you if the beam had not been deflected slightly by the glass. You suggested to me that it was a warning, however I'm afraid it was much more than that. He wants you eliminated from this investigation."

The meeting rooms on both sides of the continent went silent as everyone absorbed this, but Stewart had not finished. "Tania, might I suggest that it *would* be timely to put out a call to the media sooner rather than later to assist us with our enquiries. I have a feeling that he will not turn out to be discoverable from the usual sources. He seems clever and will almost certainly have found ways of covering his tracks, assuming he was responsible for Kevin Rowe's killing and Kaz's attempted murder. Based on the shooting at Kaz's house, he has now turned feral and will have done what he can to hide his identity and location. This being the case, conventional searches will produce nothing. With a media release there's more chance we might find a lead."

"Not a problem," said Bilson. "My feelings anyway, the searches proposed are going back such a long way, I consider they are likely to have limited value. I'm happy to cooperate with your office, and yes we will prepare a public announcement along the suggested lines. At the very least, if he gets to see it, and I'm sure he will, the sight of his image on the screen will rattle the cage and again I strongly agree that we have to keep a close guard on Ms Ingham, until we've found him."

Bilson paused for a minute to look around the room, "Kaz, anything else you'd like to add or does anybody else have anything to say?"

Kaz shook her head. *What have I got myself into?*

CHAPTER 33

Maureen Swanson was a short busty woman with curly dark hair and an engaging smile. As she introduced herself to Kaz, it sounded as though she had not long emerged from an immigration lounge after leaving Ireland.

Kaz was working from the SAPol offices and welcomed Maureen into the interview room. Belinda Gotto had agreed to sit in. Kaz said to her in an aside, "Please let me do the talking. Just listen and watch her body language. I've got a feeling she's got something personal to tell us. She hinted as much when we first spoke to each other."

They sat down and Kaz activated the recorder, formally announcing the time, date and the names of those present for the purposes of the record. Then glancing at some notes she had scribbled down, she began her questions.

"Thank you very much for responding to our call Maureen. Can I start by showing you a photograph of our person of interest? I just need you to confirm that the image you saw on our broadcast is definitely the person you see in this photograph and you have known as 'James Rowe'?"

Maureen took a quick look at the photograph and nodded solemnly. "That's the man. No doubt of that. I'll carry his image to me grave!"

"He must have made some impression on you then?"

"He did. Bastard he was. Absolute bastard!"

"Can we start from the beginning? When did you first meet James?"

"Well it was a windy day at the sailing club. There's a marina at Outer Harbour, and it's windy there at the best of times. Probably why they have a club there. That's the University of Adelaide Yacht Club I'm talking about."

"Can you remember exactly *when* this was?"

"Let me see…it was me second year at Uni, which would make it, em… 2027, yes 2027. It was the middle of winter."

"The man we're trying to locate was born in 2004. That would have made him twenty three or twenty four when you met him?"

"That's the man. A little bit older than me but not much, I'd say."

"And you met James at this sailing club?"

"As I said, the University of Adelaide Yacht Club. I'd just joined, see, because I used to love sailing as a child with me dad in Ireland. The waters are much colder and rougher there, but I was missing the spray on me face, the wind in me hair, you know that sort of thing."

"And James was keen on sailing as well?"

"Yes he told me he'd learned to sail in the tropics himself and was beginning to wonder whether sailing in Adelaide would ever be the same. Anyway I met him after one of the Saturday races. It was a very windy day and me own boat capsized because the stupid girl on the tiller didn't have a clue and jibed when she shouldn't have! I had a change of clothes at the club but was still freezing cold. This man showed up at the bar, saw that I was shivering and offered me his thick jumper for a lend."

"Was that it?"

"No that wasn't it! He plied me with drinks saying that would help me warm up a bit. And you know how it is. Maybe I was feeling a little amorous and this gentleman cottoned on quick smart!"

"Then what happened?"

"A friend of mine had given me a lift from Adelaide to Outer Harbour and wanted to get back early for some reason I can't remember. I thought I was having too good a time with this feller and so I decided to stay. He was quite attentive, and you know the jumper it sort of bonded us a little. I could smell him on it. There was a faint hint of tobacco. It was a smell that reminded me of me Dad. Anyway, there I was, me lift had gone and it was quite an expensive taxi ride home. He asked me where I lived, I told him I had a room in North Adelaide and he offered me a lift there. Of course I accepted, why wouldn't I?"

"I've got a feeling I can see where this is going," said Kaz.

"You're not wrong! He drove me to North Adelaide and we parked down the road from where my room was. We both got out of the car and by now I was a little tipsy. I'd had a lot to drink and he had his arm around me tight and sort of hauled me along the footpath towards the building. When we got to the door, he asked if he could come inside as he needed a pee. I felt I couldn't refuse him as he'd been kind to me and let him into my room. He seemed to have forgotten all about the toilet, wanted his jumper back and when he helped me pull it over me head, continued undressing me. By now I'd sobered up a bit and I quite clearly said to him 'No, That's enough now, Stop!'."

"And he didn't stop?"

"No, he didn't stop, he carried right on. Fortunately for me I was living in a place where every tiny sound could be heard in the corridor, they were paper thin walls. When he kept on ripping off me clothes, I started screaming and slapping his face. That didn't stop him either. But there was a loud rapping on me door and somebody calling out, 'You okay?' That stopped him in his tracks and he looked at me all crestfallen like, hoping that I wouldn't make anything of it."

"I got up, put me clothes back on and showed him the door. One of me neighbours was standing there in the passage all curious like, and Rowe was looking like butter wouldn't melt in his mouth. Me neighbour, who I was just on nodding terms with, said, 'You sure you're okay?' I decided to pretend everything was okay and get the scumbag out of my sight. If she hadn't been around, he would have raped me for sure. Anyway, he got out of there and hightailed it off in his car. I never went back to that sailing club. I never saw him again and I hope I never will."

"You were lucky, I'd say."

"The Saints be praised! I was that. That whole afternoon's carved into me brain as though it were yesterday. Ever since, I've regretted not reporting him to the police. And I feel guilty for the many other girls he's probably had his hands on. So when I saw the photo of him on your HoloCast it was like: *here's a chance to do what you should have done all along Maureen. So here I am.*"

"Well you've done the right thing Maureen and you've helped me a lot. Do you have anything else you'd like to add?"

"Not really, but I can tell you Kaz, this man has a very mean streak. When I met him first at the yacht club, to be honest I thought he was charming and quite good-looking. But the moment he got his hands on me, he changed. It was like a switch. He turned real nasty, quite rough and I felt frightened for me life if I didn't give into him."

"Do you mean like a split personality?"

Maureen pondered the question for a moment. "I wouldn't rightly know what that means, but he became a different person that's for sure. You wouldn't want to live with someone like that."

"No. I know what you mean. Now is there anything else you can tell me about James? What was he doing at University, where did he live?"

"I got the impression he was doing an arts degree because he seemed to know a lot about history, that sort of thing. But he didn't seem to like talking about himself much. I don't know where he lived, he didn't say as far as I can recall."

"Did he mention anything about Indonesia?"

"Not that I can remember...although he did mention sailing in the tropics..." Her voice tailed off, but then her expression brightened. "Now that I come to think of it, I thought that he might have some Asian blood in him. His hair was quite black, for one thing."

"You've never seen him since, or know anybody else who might know of him?"

Maureen shrugged the shoulders. "No, but perhaps you could try the yacht club. I don't know how long he'd been a member there but there may have been other people who knew him then."

"I can't thank you enough. You're really helping us fill in the missing pieces of the puzzle. The fact that you've told me you think he had a violent side is of great interest to me, although I'm afraid I can't explain why. If by any chance you see him again, would you please contact me immediately? If you let me have your holo, I'll flash my contact details onto it."

Maureen passed her holo to Kaz and, once it had connected, continued to stare thoughtfully at her as she put it back in her purse. "Has this chap got a record then?" Maureen asked.

"If he does, we're not aware of it. But from what you've told me he probably should have. Thanks once again."

"We'll have to be very careful, when we do find him," Belinda said once Maureen had left "given his apparent inclination for violence."

"I agree," said Kaz, remembering the pressure pulse assault in her bedroom, and the sizzling burning smell as the nano-particle beam had struck the wall opposite.

CHAPTER 34

Kaz closed her eyes and felt the low sun radiate through Stewart's kitchen windows and over her face. It was a warm winter's morning, two weeks after her return from South Australia. Stewart had arranged for her bedroom window to be fixed, as promised, but then suggested she stay for a while at his apartment, on the twentieth level of a King's Cross high rise, with agents patrolling in the warm hallway outside the apartment. Apart from the added security, she had the benefit of a smart place to live with distant views across Sydney Harbour.

Stewart had made her stay easy, even fetched her fresh croissants from a local bakery that Sunday morning. As they finished them, along with coffee, he'd told her she could stay as long as she needed to, "or more permanently if you like," he'd added casually. To Kaz it sounded like a throwaway line rather than a definite invitation, and now that she looked at Stewart, she noticed that he was wearing hiking boots.

"You going somewhere this morning?" asked Kaz.

"Don't you remember, I've arranged to go on a bushwalk with my walking group."

"Oh yes. Where are you going?"

"Georges Heights, Middle Head, I think, but I'm not leaving until lunchtime."

Kaz sipped her coffee and steeled herself to say what had been building up inside for the last few days. She was still sifting through the various sources of data in the unsolved hunt for James Rowe, but she didn't want to outstay her welcome. "It's been very nice staying here, Stewart," she finally managed, "but I've got to pick up the pieces and get back to my own place."

"Aren't you happy here? I thought you wanted to stay with me. I'd miss having you around."

"It's much more complicated than that though isn't it Stewart? The way I see it is we both need a bit of space if this relationship is going to survive. Yet at the same time if we're to stay like this, living together, we should be more committed than we are. It's bad enough that we're working in such close proximity every day out at Parramatta. Then when we come back here, we somehow have to switch that off and turn into different people. Then on top of it all, everything is so casual. I don't like the secrecy and I also don't like the feeling that we're being talked about behind our backs."

Stewart was looking more and more perplexed, unprepared at her disquiet. He wanted to respond, but she cut him off before he could get a word in. "Let's be honest Stewart, if I'm reading you correctly, you're not quite ready for a commitment. I might not be either, yet here we are."

"Geez! That's a lot to take in on what was supposed to be a relaxing Sunday morning. Sounds like you've already made up your mind about what I'm supposed to be thinking about us."

Kaz was half expecting Stewart not to be listening, or not hearing what he didn't want to hear, as most men she'd encountered in the past.

"Yes I suppose I have. But here's my headline for the morning: I am looking for the long haul. I'm not after a fling, particularly given our work situation. I've been down that road before and it doesn't lead anywhere. I don't want that sort of relationship. I'm being straight with you Stewart, because I love you and you deserve my honesty."

"So, here it is: we should be more committed than we are if I'm to continue staying here with you, but because I don't think you or I are ready for that—I think I should move out."

"That sounds so…terminal." Stewart sounded genuinely dismayed at the way the conversation was heading.

"It's not meant that way at all. You've been very kind to me, making sure that I'm safe, and I really appreciate that. But I want more, and I have my own independence to think about. I'm really feeling at the moment that this search for James Rowe has put an axe through my life. Can you imagine what it's like having to look over your shoulder every time you walk along the street, wondering where the next blast's going to come from?"

"I'm not quite sure what to say, Kaz. I love you too, and I don't want you to move out of here. I've really loved having you around and have realised how lonely and somehow un-functional I've become over the years since Margie died. Maybe my grieving process is still not totally resolved, and that's what you're picking up on. It's ridiculous, I know, but I still feel a sense of guilt that I'm not being true to her memory."

He paused for a moment to sort out what he wanted to say, then continued, taking Kaz by her hand.

"But that's the way I feel, I'm ashamed to admit it. Maybe I need to see a shrink to sort myself out."

"There's no shame in doing that, Stewart. I think it would be good for both of us if you get some help and I'm happy to give you all the time you need. But from my own place, for now."

Stewart nodded. He seemed uncharacteristically indecisive, like he'd not been expecting Kaz to bring their relationship to a head so soon. "I can't stop you from going back to your place if that's what you want to do, but I'm going to absolutely insist that you take further precautions. If the killer is keeping our movements under observation, he'll seize the opportunity to have another go. I'm certain of that."

"Just let me know, remember I still have my Henning Micro" Kaz said with a smile she didn't feel.

She waited until Stewart had left for his bushwalk to pack her things and head back to her place in Surry Hills.

She left a short note on the breakfast table. It read:

I know this is for the best Stewart. A little separation can't hurt us if our feelings are based on something more than convenience. When we see each other in the office, we must try and keep the professional relationship going and not allow emotions to get in the way, otherwise it will be impossible for me to bear. Just know, Stewart, I meant what I said this morning. I really do love you and will always be your friend, whatever happens. Much love Kaz.

« »

Rodney Jensen

Kaz was sitting by herself in her Surry Hills terrace, watching a broadcast on her holo projected into her living space. The news bulletin was about the latest stand-off between India, Pakistan, China and Tibet. China was proposing to build a new high-speed MAG connection under the Himalayas into northern Burma.

There was a knock on the door. "Who is it?" Kaz called out.

The voice of a youth answered, "flower delivery."

Kaz peered through the spy hole on her entrance door and saw a boy, approximately fifteen years old, clutching a large bouquet of flowers. She opened the door and allowed him in. He handed her the flowers and she permitted him to scan her universal identity chip implant.

She made a cursory inspection of the bouquet but there didn't seem to be any card. "Who's this from?" she asked.

The boy tapped his holo to bring up the details and finally came across the right one.

"Stewart Richardson," he said.

"Ooh, they're lovely thank you very much."

Kaz let him out and went back into the apartment, put the bouquet on the table, then went to the drinks cabinet, loaded a glass with ice from the dispenser and poured herself a stiff whiskey. It had been a week since she had decided to return to her own place. Flowers coming out of the blue were disconcerting, yet welcome. Stewart had not been romantic like this with her before.

Practical, determined, clear thinking. But romantic? What's this about?

On impulse she pulled out her holo and keyed in Stewart's contact. His face appeared on the screen with a welcoming yet curious expression. "Anything wrong?"

"I'm just ringing you to thank you for the beautiful flowers!"

"What flowers?"

"The bouquet you've sent me, of course."

A shadow of fear narrowed his gaze. "I've not sent you any flowers. Don't touch them. In fact get out of there immediately, I'm sending a bomb squad over!"

Kaz reacted quickly. Without thinking, she opened her door and ran out into the street, hoping that the courier might still be there. The street was empty. But she didn't have long to wait before an unmarked car screamed up to her house only minutes later.

Two men jumped out with duffel bags full of gear over their shoulders. Kaz ran over to them and showed her ID. "That's my terrace," she said pointing at her door. "The flowers are on the table in the living room I haven't touched them."

"Okay, we had DCI Richardson's call. Please wait here."

The men ran inside and nothing happened for several minutes. Then one of them came out again. "It's safe for you to come back inside now miss." A man who had been walking his dog stopped to see what the excitement was about. Kaz ignored him and followed the bomb squad operative into her terrace, shutting the door carefully behind her.

The other operative was trying to sweep up the mess on the dining room table. "Sorry about this," he said sheepishly. "I'm afraid we had to ruin your bouquet."

"Better than it ruin me!" said Kaz.

"Yes whoever did this knew exactly what they were up to. Check this out!" He showed Kaz a folded note.

"Oh I didn't see that before," she said.

"Lucky for you," he said. "It was hidden behind the tissue paper." He carefully and slowly opened the note as Kaz looked on horrified, realising immediately what he was talking about. A small silver v-shaped spring was glued to the paper, so that the other leaf would break an electrical contact when the folded paper was opened.

"That's a pressure switch glued to one side," the man continued. "Some cards like this activate a music chip. But this one's been carefully reconfigured so if you'd looked at the card, it would have triggered the bomb. There's enough plastic explosive wrapped around those flower stems to have wrecked this apartment. No doubt it would have killed you. No doubt at all," he repeated, as if he was talking about the weather. "Whoever did this, had access to military grade plastic explosive. We're going to bag the whole thing now and check it for fingerprints, but I doubt we'll find anything. Whoever did this is much too clever to have overlooked something that obvious."

"What about the boy who delivered it?"

"I expect we'll find that it was a private arrangement. Maybe the perpetrator found a florist who was willing to do a side delivery for a special fee, not realising the risk they were taking. Did the boy mention the name of any company he was delivering for?"

Kaz shook her head. "No, I'm afraid not. I only asked who had sent them."

"That's a pity. But try to remember as much as you can about this delivery boy. We might be able to pick him up by checking video cameras in this area. We've a fairly accurate idea of the time he'd be showing up on camera. If we find someone fitting the description we'll get you to come in and confirm his identity."

"Yes I will certainly do that, otherwise I can identikit him for you."

Just as the two men were packing up their things and leaving, Stewart arrived. He thanked the men, flashed his ID, and waited until they'd left to give Kaz a hug. "You okay?"

"Yes, I've been incredibly lucky this time."

"Thank God for that! Kaz, pack your things, come back with me, lock this place up. Until this killer has been tracked down, I won't be able to sleep thinking about you alone in this place. Please just do it for me. If you love me, you'll come. "

"Well," said Kaz, feeling her body shake, "I do love you…"

CHAPTER 35

Kaz and Stewart were in the Parramatta office when a call came through to Kaz. Stewart watched her as she listened with an expression of surprise. "Who was that?" he asked.

"It was my contact at AuSecurity, Marcus Searle. He's never called me before like this, but he would like to meet to talk about our investigation asap. He has a lead that may be helpful."

"I thought you were keeping him pretty much in the loop?"

"Yes I have been. Maybe he's got some fresh intel for us," Kaz thought aloud.

Stewart frowned. "I've never been very happy about the way AuSecurity has interfered in our work, as you know. Can I just say be very careful what you say to him, particularly as we still don't really have any further leads on James."

"I will."

Kaz found Marcus sitting in an AutoCab outside his office. "Jump in," he called out to her.

"Where are we going?"

"I want to show you where I think Rowe may have been hiding."

"Why don't you just give us the address?"

"Because it's not quite that simple. It's taken us quite a time to track him down, we think he might be holed up near a decommissioned army base in south-west Sydney."

« »

Shortly after Kaz had left the office, a holo-call came through to Stewart from DCI Bilson in South Australia.

"I was hoping to talk to Kaz Ingham," she said. "I'm sorry to say there's been a bit of a stuff-up up this end."

"Oh?"

"Yes, I'm afraid Kaz left a long to-do-list for Belinda Gotto, including a search for James Rowe on our births deaths and marriage registry. Gotto put in the request and it came back incorrect, because someone had entered 'Rose' instead of Rowe. That was corrected and resubmitted. The result came back while she was on leave, and it somehow got forgotten. Kaz sent a reminder a day or two ago and we've only just discovered something that is possibly very important."

"And what's that?" asked Stewart, impatiently, wishing the woman would get to the point.

"Well it turns out that James Rowe, and we're pretty certain he's the one we're after given the birth certificate he submitted—it originated in Indonesia and the date of birth tallies—anyway he made an application to change his name in 2027. It was registered that same year."

"What was the name he changed it to, for Christ's sake?"

"He registered his new name as 'Marcus Searle'.

"Marcus Searle?"

"Yes. We've only just found this out and we've been running checks in South Australia, but haven't come across this character so far."

"But that's who she's with right now!" Stewart snapped angrily. "Kaz's life could be in danger."

He cut the connection, and immediately tried contacting Kaz, making sure his image was suppressed from anyone who might be with her.

"Kaz Ingham speaking?" she answered finally. The image was muted.

"Kaz this is Stewart, do not say anything for a moment. Can you just reply 'yes' or 'no' Are you with Marcus Searle?"

"Yes."

"Kaz, you've got to make an excuse and come back here immediately. Can you do that?"

"No, not possible." She paused for a second, before turning to Marcus and saying, "are we going to be long getting to Moorebank?"

"No, not long," Marcus replied.

"Okay, understood," said Stewart. "We're almost positive that the man you're with is actually James Rowe. He changed his name using the SA Registry. It was the same year that Kevin Rowe went missing."

"If you haven't recognised him as such, it means he may have undergone face surgery to change his features. Don't stare at him! It will only make him suspicious that we've blown his cover. If and when he stops, jump out of the car and run for your life wherever you are. Do you think you can do that? Just answer 'yes' and then hang up."

"Yes, understood." Kaz hung up as ordered.

Stewart immediately contacted the Rapid Response Division. A man wearing a headset came into view almost immediately. Stewart gave him Kaz's communication code. "Can you track this person? It's extremely urgent."

"See what we can do." There was a pause of several minutes before he came back on the screen. "Okay, we have her under surveillance now. We can identify the AutoCab she's in. We'll also send a couple drones up to keep her in our frame. They'll be pursuing the vehicle at least 300 metres above the road. The driver won't see them."

"Yes please do that. And can you tell me which way they're heading?"

"They've just entered an old military installation at Moorebank."

"Land a team via chopper far enough away from them not to be observed and approach with extreme caution. Also, send a separate chopper for me. It can land on the roof of this building. There's an emergency pad up there. I can't stress the urgency enough. This woman's life is at stake. I'll be on the roof in five minutes."

The chopper's blades were already slowing as it waited for Stewart to emerge. He'd decided to bring Len along to handle the comms, while he concentrated on observation.

"According to RRD, the AutoCab's now parked out the front of the base. Two people got out about ten minutes ago and headed into the complex. The drone's been watching them constantly and they're about halfway out towards the airstrip. The place looks deserted," Len reported.

"It's been decommissioned some time ago. Bit of a mystery how he got in." Stewart studied an aerial view of the complex on the Holo-Scan. "Can you put us down close to the airstrip but out of sight? Also tell Flight Control to relay the drone's aerial feed to me."

« »

When the AutoCab stopped at the entrance gate to the Base, Marcus got out and touched the sensor. Kaz's heart pounded as she tried to decide whether or not to attempt to escape. *If I tried running, it would signal my suspicions. Searle looks like he's in good shape and would have no difficulty outrunning me. The place is devoid of cover and there's nowhere to hide. I'll keep up the pretence for now*, she thought.

"Why would James Rowe be hiding here?" she asked innocently. "How would he have gained access to this military installation?"

"You'll have to be patient, Kaz. Both James and his father have had some involvement in a top-secret project. It's in the part of the files that remain classified."

"But this base looks abandoned. There's no sign of life. The buildings are boarded up. Potholes everywhere. You must be having me on!"

"No, it's all cover. There's an installation near the airstrip, which is where we're heading now."

"If it's all so secret, why are you showing me?"

"I've got clearance to show you inside the research lab. I persuaded the powers that be that you needed to know." Kaz nodded, deciding to let Marcus show his hand and stay with him, wherever he was headed.

The AutoCab finally drew up alongside a large building sited some distance behind the airstrip, and screened by a narrow belt of trees and native shrubbery. The site and building looked like they had been completed at least a decade earlier and seemed neglected, judging by the weeds, broken branches and leaves covering the approach driveway.

The building was about twenty metres high, cylindrical in shape and built of un-rendered and un-painted blockwork. It presented a blank and uncompromising appearance, without any windows, the only unusual feature being the roof, which was in the shape of a cone, with a fully glazed roof surface. Steps led from where they were parked to a simple entrance portal.

Marcus pressed his finger to a touchpad located next to the door. It slid open and he showed Kaz inside. The door closed behind them with a soft thunk and an undecorated blockwork corridor led them to another security entrance.

Marcus, once again, opened the door with his finger on a scanner and led Kaz into a huge space that seemed to occupy almost the entire interior of the building, similar to a high volume industrial plant. Centred within it was a transparent sphere, about four metres in diameter. The wall above her contained a narrow catwalk encircling the sphere and gave access to what appeared to be laboratories or workshops leading off to the sides of the building. The glazed roof above included a sliding segment on rollers resembling the roof to an astronomical observatory.

Within the sphere itself was a riveting display of intensely bright pins of light and streaks of diffused light. Kaz guessed that it was a representation of a galactic cluster of stars and interstellar 'dust'. Then, as she looked more closely, the pin points of light moved slightly. Her feet were registering a slight vibration and a soft low pitched humming sound surrounded her in every direction.

"What on earth is that?" asked Kaz, pointing at the sphere.

"I think it's time we stopped playing games, Kaz. Because I know that you've worked out who I really am, haven't you?"

"I don't know what you mean."

"Yes, you do. I saw your expression when you took that call, and artfully asked me where I was heading. That was your boss telling you who I am, wasn't it?"

Kaz remained silent.

"Well I'll take that as a 'yes'." He scratched his chin, and looked at Kaz intently. "I've brought you here for a reason, so please don't do anything stupid, because I'm armed and won't hesitate to stop you if you do." He patted the holdall he'd been carrying. "I also suppose you think I was responsible for my father's death in Adelaide?"

"Your father?"

"Nice try. Yes my father, Kevin Rowe. Let's stop playing around, shall we?"

"So, you admit to killing your father?"

Marcus stared at her for a moment before continuing. "It was an accident. He fell on the sharp corner of a table and died instantly. There was nothing I could do to save him."

"We've only got your word for that, and if you try and do anything to me, you'll be digging your own grave."

"Just trust me for a moment." Marcus had become solemn, as though he were a different person, calculating what to say next. "My father was a behind-the-scenes agent for AuSecurity. He was offered the post because of his experience in Indonesia, working for the Australian Embassy as an agent. His most important discovery was this object you're standing in front of now."

"It came from Indonesia?"

"I'll get to that in a moment. My father was asked to investigate some unexplained troop movements and construction work in central Sumatra. He managed to get to the remote location with some difficulty, and worked out something was going on in the range of mountains lying behind the town where he'd landed up."

"In a later report, which he presented to AuSecurity, he described seeing the military at work on this sphere. It had been discovered buried in the base of an ancient volcanic crater. While he was watching a working party attempting to move it, they somehow activated one of its mechanisms, and all the men in the party completely vanished and were never seen again."

"As you can imagine," he continued, "the shit hit the fan. The Indonesian Military were totally ill-equipped to explain what had happened or decide what to do. They were confronting something suddenly very dangerous, possibly part of an alien system, completely beyond any human technology."

"Despite being captured while attempting to leave the site, my father brokered a deal whereby Australian scientists could bring this sphere back to Australia and place it in this research establishment. All that you see here was purpose-built and located within an existing military base, where it is well hidden from prying eyes."

"I'm beginning to understand why this part of Kevin's file was given a 'red seal'. What did our scientists make of it?"

"Good question. We only have part of the answer, in that this sphere is actually a transporter. What you're seeing inside it presently is a three-dimensional representation of our part of this galaxy. But others can be selected with the right key." He pointed at a low console with a screen and keyboard. "Our scientists got to the point where they could highlight particular destinations and zoom in, but they were only just beginning to understand how to activate the device in the way that occurred in Sumatra when everything was put on hold."

"So they're no longer experimenting with it?"

"No. It was decided that further experimentation was simply too dangerous. The scientists themselves were divided in coming to that conclusion. Many felt there was considerable risk this sphere could act like a Trojan horse, create a link from some distant point in the universe for an invasion by an intelligence we cannot as yet conceive."

Kaz nodded as everything fell into place, everything apart from what Marcus had in mind for her. "If all this information is top-secret, though, why have you brought me here now? You know the role I'm playing in tracking you down and that I am honour-bound to turn you in, if I ever get out of here."

"You're quite right of course. But things have changed. Your request for security clearance, and your recent forays into Indonesia and South Australia to track me down, have raised the stakes in a way nobody was expecting."

"What do you mean by that?"

"Some of my senior executives have been very concerned you would discover my real identity, and of course they were right. We knew that this, in turn, could also lead to your finding out more about the transporter, something which AuSecurity was determined should remain a closely guarded secret. You've shown a remarkable ability to uncover information that you should not be privy to. So it was decided we should stop you before you learnt anything more."

"So it *was* you behind the two attempts on my life in Surry Hills?"

"I was never keen on the idea of your being assassinated, but the problem now is it's difficult to keep you alive. You have the power to put me away, because it's only my word that says my father had an accidental death. So I'm in quite a dilemma."

"I see." Kaz took a breath, trying not to be unnerved by the casual way he kept referring to her existence as a problem that needed to be solved. He sounded more like a psychopath than a quietly spoken government servant.

"Thank you for your consideration. I'm assuming that you have a plan?" she said trying to humour him.

Marcus cleared his throat. "Well, this trip was to convince you I'm not making this all up, and to offer you two choices."

"Heads you win, tails I lose?" Kaz remarked sarcastically.

"I don't think you are taking me as seriously as you should!" barked Marcus. "Although I have to admit that actually is the case, and you may not like either option. But for one of them, you do at least remain alive."

"I'm listening."

"The first choice is you help me to escape from Australia to Indonesia. And by 'help', I mean that you won't make any attempt to stop me doing what I'm hoping to do, or try to escape before I've dropped you off in Indonesia. Once I'm there you're welcome to return to Australia."

"And the second choice?"

"That should be obvious, shouldn't it? I thought I'd made it clear that you really only have one choice." He grabbed her by the neck and pushed her across a threshold into a low glazed pen surrounding the sphere. He then pressed a button and the gate shut behind her.

"One thing I omitted to tell you was that the scientists did find a way of transporting objects and animals to unknown destinations. The troops who disappeared from Sumatra have never returned, and so nobody can say where those animals are or where you might end up."

"I happen to know the code that will send you to 'who knows where', and can do it if you don't agree with the first choice. Alternatively if you prefer, I can simply terminate you right now. It might be simpler and possibly more humane." He pulled a nano-blaster out of his holdall, flicked off the safety button and pointed it at her.

"So," he continued, "will you give me your word that you will come with me and not try to escape while we make the trip up to Port Macquarie airport? There's a light model scram jet four-seater that can travel at Mach 2, fuelling as we speak. It will get me or us to West Timor in a couple of hours. You'll have to come with me, and then I'll let you return. I really don't want to kill you, but I don't want to spend my life in prison either. It's your choice, and I haven't got much more time to waste, so what is it to be?"

Suddenly, two figures wearing safety vests and helmets sprang into the cavernous space surrounding the sphere via the door behind them. "Hands on your heads and freeze!" one of them shouted, pointing a Henning blaster at them both. Kaz's heart skipped a beat. She knew the voice, and now had Stewart to worry about as well as herself.

Rodney Jensen

Marcus reacted fast, aiming his blaster over the glazed screen directly at her head. "Put your weapons down, or Kaz will be the first to die," he shouted.

Kaz prayed that she'd undergone the same training in weapons defence as Stewart. She dropped to her knees before Marcus had time to react, while Stewart's nano-particle beam sizzled so close to his head that a small tongue of flame set light to his hair. Marcus dropped to the ground and aimed carefully as another beam missed him again.

This time Stewart was thrown backwards as though he'd been rammed by a truck and lay still on the ground. The other man, who Kaz could now see was Len, kept Marcus pinned down with a series of nano pulses, so Kaz could crawl to one side of the pen, out of the firing line. She carefully felt for her micro blaster. Marcus was concentrating on Len as Kaz quickly rose to her feet, aimed at Marcus through the transparent screen, and pressed the firing button three times in rapid succession. Marcus turned his head with a startled expression on his face and collapsed in a heap.

Then silence.

Len blasted the lock on the pen's gate, allowing Kaz out. She went over to Marcus' prone body and raised him by his shoulder. He seemed clearly dead.

"Kaz, are you all right?" asked Len.

"Yes, I'm fine… What about Stewart?"

Stewart was still prone on the ground but groaning loudly. Len pulled back his overall. It showed a circular burn mark. Underneath Kaz could now see he had been wearing an undervest of high tech carbon-based material. "Come and help me get his body armour off. I think it's saved his life."

"How did you find us?"

"You can thank the drones," Len remarked casually. "You've been under constant surveillance, until you entered this building.

CHAPTER 36

The next morning Kaz visited Parramatta Central Hospital, well before visiting hours. She knew that Stewart had been air-ambulanced to the roof level helipad, much to his annoyance, as he claimed to be fine. But he wasn't fine—he was severely bruised, required scans to check whether there were any serious internal injuries or fractures, and his doctor had demanded he stay at least that night and the following day for observation.

There was another person in the room with Stewart, a middle aged woman she didn't recognise.

"Sheila Armstrong, Exec. Officer with AuSecurity, NSW," she brusquely introduced herself.

"AuSecurity has a lot of explaining to do, but I'm wondering if this is the best time?" Kaz remarked angrily.

"We have to talk now," said Sheila almost shouting.

"I agree it's not a very good look for AuSecurity. Marcus Searle has not just led you up the garden path, but us as well. It appears that he has been run by a cell within our ranks. It's the only explanation for his erratic and completely unauthorised behaviour. It's now become clear that he could not have been acting alone. He would have needed help in keeping his high level Indonesian connections from us and facilitating his role as a double agent for the TNI."

"There will be an inquiry into his role and how as a rogue operative working within this cell he was given the job of terminating you to prevent blowing his cover."

"Still, I'm quite amazed that you are fronting up here now, while Stewart is still recuperating. Surely it can wait?" Kaz said.

"We've read your report, and it raises issues that simply *can't* wait."

Kaz was about to launch into an angry rebuke, but Stewart tried to raise his arm painfully. "Let's hear what she's got to say."

Sheila sat up in her chair more purposefully and placed the handbag she'd been carrying over her shoulder on her lap. "The first thing you should know is that Marcus obviously had no intention of having you around while he tried to leave Australia. The pen next to the sphere where he locked you up was there for a purpose. Scientists who've been investigating the sphere used it to contain experimental animals."

"You mean, ones they transported somewhere?"

"That's right. Marcus was planning to do the same with you, because his twisted mind had worked out that the transporter offered the perfect solution of disposing of you without trace. It was far more effective than a burial site in the Mount Lofty Ranges."

"So how come Marcus knew the codes required?"

"That information was contained in the documents that have been sealed indefinitely. We're not sure yet how Marcus managed to get his hands on them, or how he had his fingerprints set up for security clearance into the complex. It also raises the far bigger issue of how our overall security has been compromised by other double agents. We don't think Marcus played an isolated role. He must've had help and our biggest worry is that there's a cell acting within us, working on Indonesia's behalf rather than ours."

"Have there been other leaks?" Stewart asked.

"Yes, but I can't go into details. In fact, there has been something of a history going back several decades in connection with issues such as terrorism, the Timor Gap and the boat people. And that brings me to the reason I'm here," she said.

"Oh, I thought it was simply a goodwill visit and an apology for the fact that one or more of your agents has done their best to kill me and Stewart, and the others remain at large and out of control!"

Sheila shuffled the large handbag she'd been clutching. "Please be assured Kaz, that we do have someone in our sights apart from Marcus. He'll be brought to justice shortly, but the proceeding will have to be held *in camera*. I promise to let you know once he's been properly dealt with and is resting in a high security correctional facility."

"So what was the real purpose of this visit, then?" Kaz asked.

"The fact that you, Stewart, Len and others have been witness to the installation and the alien sphere it contains. This information *cannot* and *must not* be divulged to anyone else. Every single person who has been party to your rescue operation will be required to sign confidentiality agreements. I would like you to sign yours straight away," she fumbled in her handbag and withdrew some printed forms. "And Kaz, it will be your responsibility to provide me with a comprehensive list of all the people who may have gained access to this classified information. I…"

"Please leave the forms on the table and we'll deal with them later." Stewart interrupted furiously. "I think you've got a bloody nerve coming in here and laying down the law like this. Don't you hold yourself at all accountable for what's gone wrong? Once I've recovered from this episode, I'll be making a formal complaint to your minister. Now, would you please leave us in peace?"

Sheila's face went white. She carefully placed the papers and a data stick on the table, then flounced out of the room without another word.

Stewart and Kaz waited until she had gone, Kaz closed the door behind her, they stared at each other for a few seconds, and started laughing. "Well done, Stewart! I would have liked to have put that floozy in the pen myself and push the transport button."

"I thought you were used to self-important government people?" Stewart winced in pain. "It hurts to laugh."

"Yes, but she's one of a kind. You come across them all the time. Their main concerns are staying in the job at all costs. Not an ounce of humanity!"

Stewart stared at Kaz long and hard, his eyes glistening.

"Christ, Kaz I thought it was over for us yesterday. You're all right aren't you?"

"Yes, my darling, nothing happened in the AutoCab, if that's what you're wondering. And I've been feeling the same about you, when I saw you go down, you know…" she faltered.

"We've got to put it behind us haven't we?" Stewart said, once he had his own emotions more under control.

"That's not exactly what I meant. When something like this happens, it puts a new meaning on things doesn't it?"

"Yes I suppose it does. I've been lying here, feeling pretty helpless, thinking what life might have been like without you around."

"Without an unpaid carer, you mean?" she joked.

"No, much more than that, a permanent arrangement."

"Is that a very roundabout way of saying what I think you're trying to say?"

Stewart became very serious, trying to arrange himself better on the pillow. "Yes it is Kaz, but would you have me, knowing what a grumpy bastard I can be at times?"

Kaz leant forward, tried to kiss and embrace him for her answer. Stewart groaned in agony. "I'll take that for a 'yes' then. But please no more bear hugs. It kills!" He caressed her face. "Seriously, though, there is one condition that we have to agree to."

"And what is that?"

"Well, actually, there are two. First, we'll have to agree which of our two places we live in."

"And?"

"We'll also have to toss a coin for my job. You and me in the same office is not a workable arrangement is it?"

"No, I suppose it's not." Kaz noticed Stewart staring at her with a new and serious expression. He seemed to be thinking about something else.

"It's difficult for me to bring this up before we've really got going, but one reservation I have about us is children."

"What do you mean—you want them or not want them?"

"Margie and I never had children and I feel very sad about that. If I knew you were dead against having children yourself it would be OK but better to know now, rather than later."

"Gosh you have a great sense of timing. I'm not sure what to say."

"Is it not something you ever think about?"

"To be honest, no. I've been happy with my job up to now and, before you, I've never found a man I would contemplate having a child with. If I were to start a family, I wouldn't do such a thing if it meant sacrificing my career. We'd have to share the responsibility, because I'm not going to be the one who'd always be changing the nappies, losing sleep night after night, and having to drop off and pick up baby from day-care…"

"Okay—I get the picture. But at least it's not an outright *no* then, is it?" Stewart asked.

"Too early to say. But, I suppose," she reconsidered, "no, it's not an outright *no*. It's a 'maybe'. We'll see. How about we get over the next hurdle first?"

Rodney Jensen

"You mean who gets the job of running Major Crimes?"

"No, don't worry. I don't really want your job. I think you do it very well and it's a bit late in my management career to take up police work, let alone deal with the conservative police culture that defies change. I'm more than happy to go back to State, where I think Jock Tarding and I will be having a similar discussion."

"Why, he's not thinking of leaving is he?"

"No, but if there's a change in government, he will probably leave or be shafted. That might open up better prospects for me." She paused for a moment, weighing up whether to say what was on her mind, *but what the hell!*

"Actually, the real truth is I'm more interested in you than all these other questions. Can we stop being serious and start taking some risks with each other?"

"Hmm…why not. I am thanking my stars that I'm getting this chance to start again when I'd all but given up meeting someone like you." He reached up to wrap his arms around her, then groaned in pain as he felt his ribs grinding into each other. "Be gentle with me. I need another hug."

But no sooner were his arms around her than his holo vibrated on the side table.

Much to Kaz's annoyance, he took the call, and listened intently. Finally he put it back on the table and stared at Kaz.

"There's been a report from AuSecurity that the sphere has changed its internal display. It's now showing what appears to be some form of binary countdown. They want you to get over there immediately, monitor what's going on. While we might have assumed James Rowe's passing would close the investigation, it looks like we're now faced with something worse. I'm sorry, Kaz, but you've got to go."

"Now."

EPILOGUE

2026 June

The young man Kevin Rowe saw waiting outside the carousel area was in his early twenties, with dark brown eyes and a full head of black hair. Facially he bore some resemblance to his father, including a longish nose and high cheekbones. He stood with his arms crossed agitated, but when he saw Kevin coming out of the airport, his face lit up and he walked over to greet him.

"Well, here I am. James isn't it?" said Kevin as the two met. They shook hands awkwardly. James looked like he wanted to hug him, but Kevin moved back slightly as if to discourage it. Father he might have been by name, but not by choice.

"Thanks for coming, there's an AutoCab waiting to take us into Adelaide," said James.

Kevin was only half listening. The passenger he'd sat next to on the plane was standing twenty metres away, staring at them intently, looking like he hoped to cadge a lift. Kevin preferred to avoid him.

"Okay let's go then," said James, and the two walked over to the waiting AutoCab. But Kevin paused for a moment wanting to know more before getting into the Cab with someone he'd just met. He stood still and faced James. "So what have you got in mind?"

"You're booked in at the Montenegro Hotel in North Adelaide," his son replied. "Then I thought we could take a drive to Eden Valley in the Adelaide Hills where I'm living at the moment." He took his father by the arm and helped him to take a seat in the passenger bubble.

The two sped off, leaving Kevin's fellow passenger behind with pursed lips and a sour expression.

« »

James' home was an old bluestone cottage buried in a large unruly garden containing several dilapidated sheds and a battered ute parked in the driveway. "I'm renting this place from a farmer in exchange for doing some repairs and basically keeping the house watertight," said James. He led Kevin into the building and invited him to sit down at a table that was already laid with a tablecloth, various foodstuffs and two bottles of wine. "I hope you like Clare Valley wines? There's a cab sav and a riesling," he said.

"Clare Valley sounds good. I've always preferred South Australian reds to New South Wales ones. You've obviously gone to an awful lot of trouble for my benefit. Thank you."

Kevin left his small travel bag beside the door, then plonked himself down on a settee that had frayed upholstery and lumpy springs. After a few moments of silence, he pulled up his knees and stared at his host. "Okay James, I've come all this way, with some reluctance as you know. It was a big shock when you tracked me down. And then I heard nothing more from you. I assumed perhaps it was enough for you to have discovered who your biological father actually was. But now you've connected with me again after all these years."

"Back then was too soon after my guardian died…," James interrupted.

"Well I'm not sure what it is you want, other than to meet me in the flesh? Is it as simple as that? Or is there something else? Time is an issue for me I'm afraid, I do have a lot of parliamentary business to attend to back in Sydney."

James's expression fell. "You're in a rush. Is that what you're trying to tell me?" He tutted and looked away. "I suppose you just can't understand what it's been like for me, brought up with no idea who my real father is. Even if you didn't know about me, or want to know for that matter, it's the same result for me. So yes, I've wanted to meet you for a while now, perhaps to discover you might have some spark of interest in me, rather than the total rejection I got the first time I called you."

"But beyond simply meeting you? Well, it's not about money, if that's what you're thinking. I don't need your money. My guardian was a very wealthy man and left most of his considerable estate to me. No, it's about you and my mother—I have many questions I want answers to."

"You must understand how difficult this is for me, James." Kevin told him, "to recall things that happened more than twenty years ago. When you called me out of the blue, that first time, you were still at high school, I'm afraid I was a bit abrupt because it came as such a complete shock. So you'll have to forgive me for that. But I'll do my best to answer your questions now."

"Can you tell me more about my mother Marayan then? How did you meet her?"

"Well, I first met her at a party organised by the Australian Embassy. She came along with your guardian, Bhudi, who I'd just learned was a senior general in the TNI. I was immediately attracted to her and thought she was beautiful. She *was* beautiful. We struck up a friendship and on one occasion it became more than that. I guess you could call it a fling. But it was a mistake—we were a mismatch and we both knew it. Marayan knew her guardian would never accept me into their family. So we parted company and that was really the last I heard of her." Kevin paused in his carefully prepared version of events to allow it to sink in.

James stared at him intently, not moving a muscle.

Kevin finally continued. "I had no idea that she'd given birth to you. It also came as a complete surprise for me to find my name on your birth certificate which you sent me a copy of. I see it was signed by Bhudi, because I'm presuming that Marayan was unable to do it herself?"

"That part of your story at least is correct," said James. "But your version of the events leading up to my being born to Marayan, is strikingly different from Bhudi's."

"Well he was hardly in a position to be objective, was he?"

"Right until I was a teenager, I learned very little about the circumstances of my birth, other than the obvious thing—that I had a white father. Then shortly before his death I made a special trip to Jakarta to see him, as it turned out, for the last time. It was then he told me more about you and handed over some papers, including my birth certificate. What he had to say about your conduct was clearly still causing him anguish."

"For a long time, I have thought about whether I should do anything, and not try to meet you. On the other hand, the picture he had painted of Marayan was of an innocent and lovely woman whose concern about my future was always at the forefront of her thinking. It was for that reason she gave up her job and relocated during her pregnancy to make sure none of her contacts would know about me, and once I had been born, Bhudi could pretend he had adopted me. But as things turned out, there was no need for her to protect her reputation as she died within twenty-four hours of giving birth."

"I never knew that. How terrible. She did such a good job of concealing her pregnancy. You may not realise, but I had left Indonesia more than eight months before your birth certificate was signed."

"I haven't quite finished," said James. "I had a very close relationship with my guardian and always trusted whatever he told me. He was no liar, I can assure you, and he had no reason to lie about the accusations he made against you. He said that he had clear documentary evidence prepared by his security agents that you'd abused Marayan and probably raped her."

"That's not how it happened. How could he know that? He wasn't in the bedroom, nor were his agents!"

"Marayan told him what you did to her, eventually. But he had to dig it out of her, because guess what, she felt ashamed. What a joke!"

"Well I can tell you it's not exactly uncommon for women who get themselves into trouble to invent stories like that. It finished my career in Indonesia and I was sentenced by judge and jury Bhudi with no recourse whatsoever to defend myself against his or her allegations."

"It's also not uncommon for men like you who have abused women and have been caught out to claim they were engaged in consensual sex. As I said I have no reason to believe that my late mother's account of what happened, supported by the evidence of my guardian, was anything but the truth."

"You're pulling a very long bow to assume we had any more than a lover's spat while we were in that hotel…" Kevin's voice was rising so he paused to ground himself. This meeting was getting out of hand. He took a sip of wine and resumed in a gentler voice. "Turning to the question of paternity, apart from Bhudi and Marayan's word on this, do you have any other definitive proof that I'm your father?"

"No I was anticipating you would be asking me this, so the main purpose of my request to meet was to ask you to have a DNA test. That would settle the matter once and for all. Would you be willing to have a test?"

Kevin took another sip of his wine. "Supposing I agree, and it proves negative, then I assume that will put an end to this?"

"Not entirely. The fact remains that whatever the tests show, I shall always believe that you had an abusive relationship with my mother. In any case, I am confident that the test won't be negative," said James quietly.

Rodney Jensen

"Now look, James, I think you're a decent enough young chap, so now I've answered your questions, I would like to leave now, if you don't mind, and think things through. There's nothing much else we can do anyway, until we've undergone the tests and then we can decide where to go from there."

James anger seemed to evaporate as he switched on a beaming smile. "Okay, agreed! Why not finish your drink and relax. You've come such a long way and it would be a shame to waste the journey. I was hoping we could somehow meet more often, providing the tests are positive, and I could show you something of the beautiful countryside around here."

Kevin took a long swig from the glass nearly finishing it, and put it down, not knowing quite what to think. "I can't really understand, if you believe all that stuff about my relationship with your mother, why you should want to have anything more to do with me?"

"It's simple. You are my father and..." James's voice trailed off, Kevin's vision of him becoming blurred as though he was at the end of a long tunnel.

Kevin's eyelids drooped and he swayed precariously. "That drink must be very strong..."

James's voice came through to him again, more loudly. "Are you feeling all right, Kevin? You don't look well."

The room rolled like a ship in a swell. He lost his balance and fell awkwardly as his knees crumpled under him. His head cracked like a pistol shot on the sharp corner of the low table in front of him.

James knelt down. Kevin was on his back, his eyes wide open. He put a shaking hand to his father's pulse, and tried to feel whether he could sense any slight breath coming out of his mouth and nostrils. *That wasn't the plan, shit! I must have got the dose wrong. But I suppose it saves me from the interrogation I had lined up. Let's just assume uncle's version of events is true and this disgusting man has got his just deserts.*

« »

Later that evening under a moonless sky James manhandled his father's body into the back of his ute. He threw a pick, shovel, rake and an old wheelbarrow in beside the body, and set off on a thirty kilometre journey to an area of the state forest he'd identified on an online mapping program.

The darkness made it difficult for him to find the entrance track, but he finally found it and drove five hundred metres into the forest where he stopped and searched around for a suitable place to bury Kevin. It was almost dawn by the time he'd finished, covered up the traces as best he could and returned to his ute. He got in, slammed the door, and headed back to his home, closing a chapter in his life forever—or so he thought.

THE END

Please review this novel

I hope that you enjoyed 'Covert State'. I would appreciate it if you could spare a few moments to write a sentence or two in review.

This helps other readers to decide if it is something they might also enjoy, and also it very much helps me as an author.

https://www.amazon.com/author/rodney-jensen-books

《 》

Rodney Jensen

Acknowledgments

I wish to acknowledge the contribution made by my editor, Zena Shapter, whom I first met through the Northern Beaches Writers' Group (NBWG) which she founded and manages. She provided me with both broad review of early weaknesses and meticulous editing.

Other members of NBWG have provided great help and encouragement in reviewing previous drafts. I also owe a huge debt of thanks to my partner Liz McCarthy who has helped with critical appraisal and multiple improvements in the final draft, as well as strongly encouraging me in my new writing projects. Thanks also David Gaughgran, Pem and Penny Gerner, Guy Hallowes, Peter Jensen, Chris Lake, Andy McGee, Canary and Simon Tang, Debbie Terranova, Leonie Henchske, Gillian Noble and John McCarthy.

« »

About the author

Dr Rodney Jensen PhD, an urban designer, has during the past 20 years focused on journalism before gravitating to creative writing, and self-publishing for speculative fiction novels.

He has written for the Australian, the Sydney Morning Herald newspapers and Australian Property Investor and many other magazines. He received merit awards from the Planning Institute of Australia for Cityscape (a collaborative newsletter produced in partnership with Dr Pem Gerner) and a commissioned documentary film on the heritage of the inland town of Wentworth in NSW, Australia.

In addition to the **Covert Trilogy** he has written **'Tales for the Time Traveller'**, an anthology of re-imagined traditional tales.

He has contributed to a variety of Northern Beaches Writers' Group publications including:

'Message in a Bottle', a ballad (original melody and lyrics) contained in Rhapsody, anthology of short pieces based on songs, 2021.

'The Nursery Attendant and the Duct Maintenance Droid', a short story in 'Of Beasts and Butterflies', anthology, 2019.

'The Salty', a short story in 'Saltwater', anthology, 2019.

'Countdown at Quarry Lake',a short story in 'Noise on an Island', anthology, 2018.

'The Guitar Wizard', a co-authored novella and winner of 'Best Book WABIAD Award 2017'.

'The Final Journey', a short story in 'A Fearsome Engine', anthology2016

Rodney Jensen

Reviewers' comments on Rodney Jensen's books

Covert Messages - *"If you enjoy futuristic science fiction and extra-terrestrial experiences, this is the book for you. The references to the past COVID-19 pandemic are chilling and force you to consider our own current situation, as the more serious pandemic of 2035 unfolds in the book. Rodney Jensen utilises his knowledge of Australian geography as he weaves a sombre tale, but includes the more positive romance or two as well."* **Elizabeth Saadeh**

« »

Tales for the Time Traveller - *"…a number of common themes emerge, which tie the collection together nicely. The role of technology, especially ongoing debates regarding its exploitation, and the rise of AI, feature prominently. A sense of exploration is also at the heart of the collection, both in terms of physical space (deserted island, new planets, outer space) and big ideas (such as tradition vs. progress, and what is 'real' vs. what is 'fake'—and how can we tell the difference, anyway?)"* **Chloe Barber-Hancock**

« »

Rodney Jensen

Other books by Rodney Jensen

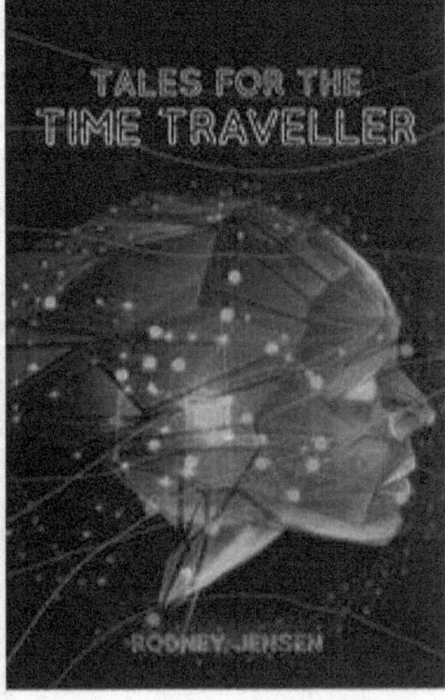

www.ingramcontent.com/pod-product-compliance
Lightning Source LLC
Chambersburg PA
CBHW031937110726
47902CB00001B/211